"Eve Masterson is missing."

Eve Masterson. Locating the beautiful television star was a job Matt Ross would once have jumped at, but now he had more important issues to handle—like a young daughter, a new partnership, a difficult ex-wife...and the upcoming Christmas holiday.

As if reading Matt's mind, his cousin—and partner—added, "Eve's parents are freaking out because nobody's heard from her or been able to reach her for months—ever since she left for Atlanta."

"Listen, Eve Masterson is a TV personality," Matt told Bo. Lowering his voice, he added, "Doesn't this sound like something a television personality would do for publicity?"

"I don't think so. The Eve I used to know wouldn't let her family and friends worry—if she could help it."

Matt glanced at his calendar—December. The only notation was "Dec. 25: Ashley with me." Which meant he'd pick up his daughter around twelve and drive to his parents' home, where they'd have delayed their celebration to include him and Ashley. God, he hated the holidays!

"Okay, I'll go. But I have to be back by Christmas Eve."

"Cool. Shouldn't take you more than a couple of hours. Fly in. Find her place. See what the hell's up. Read her the riot act if needed, then fly home."

Matt rolled his eyes. Something told him nothing concerning Eve Masterson would be that easy.

Dear Reader,

I knew very little about Matt and Eve, the main characters of this book, when I stared writing the first story in this trilogy, His *Daddy's Eyes*. Eve was a beautiful but aloof ex-girlfriend. Matt didn't come into focus until Bo, my hero of the second book, *Back in Kansas*, needed his cousin's help. All I knew going into this story was that Eve was missing and Matt was the only one who could rescue her.

In writing this book, I discovered that Matt was lost, too. An accident had changed everything in his life: career, marriage, his sense of identity. Locating Eve—a woman he knew only by her glamorous image—is Matt's first step on the road to reclaiming his life.

My thanks to Jim Brisco and Lorry Allen for sharing with me their beautiful, romantic Yucatan home called Casa Rosa. I couldn't think of a more appropriate spot for Eve and Matt to fall in love. It's where my husband and I spent our twenty-fifth wedding anniversary.

To my friend and future sister-in-law, Karryn, I thank you for sharing your medical knowledge with me and for helping me understand the subtle nuances of adoption—I will always remember Dottie with a smile. I thank my friends and fellow writers, Susan Floyd and Melinda Wooten, for helping me tie up all the loose "endings." And my sister, Jan O'Brien, for liking all the "beginnings"—no matter how many times they change.

I love hearing from readers. Please write me at P.O. Box 322, Cathey's Valley, CA, 95306. Or e-mail me at either www.superauthors.com or through the authors' alcove at eHarlequin.com. Happy reading!

Debra

Something About Eve
Debra Salonen

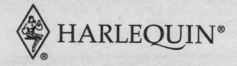

TORONTO • NEW YORK • LONDON
AMSTERDAM • PARIS • SYDNEY • HAMBURG
STOCKHOLM • ATHENS • TOKYO • MILAN • MADRID
PRAGUE • WARSAW • BUDAPEST • AUCKLAND

ISBN 0-373-71003-8

SOMETHING ABOUT EVE

Copyright © 2001 by Debra K. Salonen.

All rights reserved. Except for use in any review, the reproduction or
utilization of this work in whole or in part in any form by any electronic,
mechanical or other means, now known or hereafter invented, including
xerography, photocopying and recording, or in any information storage
or retrieval system, is forbidden without the written permission of the
publisher, Harlequin Enterprises Limited, 225 Duncan Mill Road,
Don Mills, Ontario, Canada M3B 3K9.

All characters in this book have no existence outside the imagination of
the author and have no relation whatsoever to anyone bearing the same
name or names. They are not even distantly inspired by any individual
known or unknown to the author, and all incidents are pure invention.

This edition published by arrangement with Harlequin Books S.A.

® and TM are trademarks of the publisher. Trademarks indicated with
® are registered in the United States Patent and Trademark Office, the
Canadian Trade Marks Office and in other countries.

Visit us at www.eHarlequin.com

Printed in U.S.A.

To Zilla—
your insight and patience help me shine.

And, of course, Paul—
I couldn't do this without you.

CHAPTER ONE

MATT ROSS PRETENDED to dribble the basketball-shaped tangle of twinkle lights in his hands as he walked to his couch. He sat down with a sigh. He'd turned down tickets to the Knicks game to spend time with Ashley. He didn't regret missing the game, but he had hoped to avoid the Christmas issue altogether.

"You *have* to decorate for Christmas, Daddy," she'd insisted, dragging him to the storage room for two battered and dusty boxes marked Xmas. "Christmas is next week. You *can't* pretend it isn't happening."

Can if I want, he'd almost blurted out, remembering at the last second that he was thirty-six, not twelve.

"Where do you want the reindeer candles, Dad?" Ashley asked.

Reindeer candles? I have reindeer candles?

He looked up from the rat's nest of wires in his lap to watch his slim daughter parade from window to window. She moved with a leggy grace that made him start humming a Dan Fogelberg song about running for the roses. In her outstretched hands were a pair of molded brass candleholders, which seemed vaguely familiar. No doubt a hand-me-down from his mother. For some reason, it hadn't occurred to him to lobby for holiday decor when he and Sonya split up three years ago.

"You pick," he said with a shrug. "You have a better eye for that kind of thing than me."

"Ha!" she cried triumphantly. She spun around to face him, a reindeer at each hip. "That's right. I do. Which means you should trust *me* to hang the Picasso. Right?"

Matt rolled his eyes. She'd been bugging him for a week to hang the lithograph. He'd put it off—reluctant to get too comfortable in his new digs. "Okay. But only if I don't have to buy a tree," he bargained.

Ashley's narrow, auburn eyebrows scrunched together the way his did when he was frustrated. "Fine," she said, her bottom lip pouting. She dumped the wobbly reindeer on the closest window ledge then dashed away. Matt could hear her rummaging in the kitchen for a hammer. Matt was sure he heard her mutter something about a grinch.

Smiling, he concentrated on separating another couple of inches of green plastic-coated strands. He couldn't believe he'd put them in the box that way. What did they do all summer? Mate? "Oh, hell," he muttered a minute later. "Maybe she won't notice if there aren't any lights." *Fat chance, buster.*

Ashley materialized at his side. "I found the perfect spot. Come see."

Matt set his task aside and followed her to the foyer. While not huge, the three-bedroom/two-bath loft occupied a choice corner of a majestic old building. Creatively arranged, the rooms on the main floor were angled as if making up the tip of an arrow. A short wall directly opposite the entrance diverted traffic to either the guest-bedroom wing or the living-room and kitchen area.

"Perfect," Matt said, seeing her choice. "Where were you when I was decorating my old place?"

She gave him a droll look. "I was nine when you and Mom split up. Nobody thinks a nine-year-old can do anything."

Together, they collaborated on the proper height and center point, then Matt handed Ashley the hammer and a nail. Concentrating, she sucked in her bottom lip as she carefully pounded the nail into the ivory plaster. For all her professed worldliness, Ashley's occasional childlike gestures made Matt all the more aware of how fast time was passing and how much he'd missed of his little girl's formative years.

As she stretched to place the hammer on the floor, Matt could see that she was growing up…and fast.

"This is going to look so cool here, Dad. Way better than where you had it hanging before."

She reached for the painting, but Matt beat her to it. As he hoisted the print to eye level, he said, "You seem pretty excited about this apartment, Ash. How come?"

She gave him an arched look—so adult it made him gulp. "Dad, this place is practically uptown. It's awesome. I'll be able to go shopping without you hovering like some mother hen. Right?"

No comment. Matt pretended to concentrate on snagging the wire at the back of the painting. She went on, "It's safe in this neighborhood—if you play it smart. I know the risks, Dad. It comes from having a cop for a dad."

He bit down on a smile. He'd taught her well, but

he also knew you were never one hundred percent safe no matter how smart you were. Even a cop with nearly twenty years under his belt could wind up in the hospital without any warning.

"I can't wait to explore all the cool places around here." She rubbed her hands together as if preparing to dig in to a meal. "That bookstore down the street looks awesome. And the antiques store next door has the coolest jewelry in the window. And I'm dying to go back to that Thai restaurant we went to when Uncle Bo was here from California last week."

She ducked under his arm to stick her hand behind the painting to help guide the wire over the small hook. "There," she said triumphantly.

Matt stepped back so he could level the colorful abstract. His gaze fell to the name penciled in the bottom corner—Marina Picasso, the artist's grand-daughter. The print was Matt's single windfall while employed by the New York Police Department. He'd helped recover the shipment of lithographs that had been hijacked and held for ransom. As a thank-you, he'd been offered the opportunity to buy a print at a very discounted price. The piece had become a major source of contention during the divorce.

"You know this place is only temporary, honey," Matt said, walking back to his spot on the sofa—a butter-soft leather number that his cousin hadn't wanted to risk in storage. "I can't afford to buy it." The loft belonged to Matt's uncle, Robert B. Lester, who was in a rehabilitation center recovering from a severe concussion. His wife, Matt's aunt Ruth, and son, Bo, had suggested Matt rent it so that he could set up a home office there.

Ashley shook her head. "That's not what I heard Aunt Ruth tell Grandma." The twinkle in her eyes was too appealing to make him scold her for eavesdropping. "Aunt Ruth said she was through with Uncle Robert's philandering and if he got back the use of his you-know-what, she was going to make sure he kept it at home. He wouldn't be needing the loft."

A strangled hoot escaped his lips. His daughter was his one source of joy; he just wished their time together wasn't so sporadic. *I've got to talk to Sonya about keeping a regular schedule—no more last-minute cancellations.*

"Anything else you want help with, Daddy?" Ashley asked, poking through his box of decorations. "I still think you need a Christmas tree."

He'd considered buying a tree for Ashley's sake but couldn't see spending sixty bucks for one day of Christmas spirit. Splitting holidays was the worst part of being a part-time dad.

"I'll think about it. I've got a whole week to decide, don't I?" Matt picked up the ball of lights and gave it an overhand toss. It swished cleanly into the box.

Ashley shook her head. "Does the word *bah-humbug* mean anything to you?"

Matt chuckled. "So should I take back those gifts I've already bought?"

She made a face and held up her hands. "Only kidding."

Matt rose and walked into the kitchen to put away the hammer. Ashley followed but kept walking to the bank of windows in the living room and peered out. "I can't believe the snow is all gone already,"

Ashley said. "The arena's going to be a real mud pit."

The equestrian arena. Matt frowned. He'd have to drive Ashley home soon. Sonya insisted Ashley sleep in her own bed the night before riding lessons—unless, of course, she was invited to a sleepover with friends, Matt thought caustically.

"Do you want to cancel?" he asked, cringing at his hopeful tone. "We could get some Thai food and watch another movie." How pathetic that his big event of the week was staying home with his daughter! His old friends on the force would get a big kick out of that. Not that he saw much of them anymore. Something had changed after his accident, and Matt felt it every time he walked through the precinct door.

She shook her head. Her light brown hair danced across her slim shoulders. At twelve she seemed more poised than a girl her age should be. Did the divorce do that? he wondered.

"I can't. Miss Wheaten said she'd cut our privileges if any of us missed again. She said people always get busy during the holidays and the horses suffer." Ashley smiled—her lips curling awkwardly over the new metal wires in her mouth. Just the uppers so far but more braces were coming he'd been told.

"You'd better hope that cousin of yours can keep you busy," Sonya had admonished last week, referring to the job Bo had offered him. A partnership in RBL Investigations. "Braces don't come cheap, you know."

Matt flinched from the spurt of acid that hit his stomach. Lately, Sonya had seemed increasingly contentious, and Matt didn't understand why.

Or maybe it's that she's moved on with her life and I'm still in limbo.

"Do you like Miss Wheaten?" he asked, refocusing his thoughts.

"She's okay most of the time, but sometimes she gets really bossy and put out over trivial things. I mean, we treat our horses good—it's all the other stuff she makes us do that's a drag—cleaning stalls, moving feed, grooming other people's horses besides our own."

"Oughta be a law against making kids work for their fun," he teased.

She rolled her eyes. "You're such a grown-up."

Matt, who was on his way back to the couch, pretended to be wounded and flopped theatrically into the soft cushions. His gasping sounds made her laugh. "Daddy," she said in mock outrage.

The phone on the wall above the kitchen counter rang. Ashley dived for it, but hesitated, waiting for a second ring to confirm which line was ringing. "It's your personal line, should I get it?" she asked.

"Of course. It's probably for you."

"Ross residence. Ashley speaking," she said formally.

Something about the simple phrase caught him off guard. He turned away to keep his emotional reaction private, but when he put his weight on his right knee, it suddenly gave out. He grabbed the arm of the sofa for support.

"Daddy's right here, Uncle Bo. Hang on a sec."

Matt could tell by her little-girl tone that she'd seen his near tumble. He waggled his knee to get proper alignment and walked gingerly across the room. The doctor had predicted a full recovery with this rebuilt knee, but in the twenty months since his accident, Matt still couldn't count on it one hundred percent. Which was one reason he'd let his cousin talk him into joining him in the private-eye business instead of returning to a desk job with the city.

Matt took the phone from his daughter, pausing to pull her into a quick hug—even though Sonya had told him young girls didn't like open displays of affection.

Matt put one hand over the receiver and said, "You left your CDs upstairs, hon. Better gather up your stuff."

She sprinted away, gangly legs in clunky shoes that made a loud clanging sound on the metal rungs of the spiral staircase. Matt had considered making his bedroom on the first floor instead of the loft, but Bo had insisted he use one room for an office, the other for Ashley. "Sadist," Matt had grumbled, eyeing the corkscrew steps.

Bo had shrugged. "Better you than a client."

Matt couldn't argue with that logic, so his bedroom now occupied the upper level of the two-story loft. His king-size bed was positioned like a tongue in an open mouth, facing the ninety-degree wall of windows. It had taken him a week to dislodge the image of his uncle and some young beauty making love in this ideal bachelor pad. Somehow, Matt couldn't picture himself playing the part, even though he was what his mother termed in the prime of his life. At thirty-six he was single, not bad-looking and healthy—except for the knee. The rest of him worked fine—just not very often.

"Hey, cuz, what's up?"

A muffled sound preceded Bo's somewhat strangled "Funny you should ask." There was another sound—a sultry female laugh. "Claudie, stop it. I have to talk to Matt."

Matt couldn't help grinning, picturing Bo's fiancée, Claudine St. James. Matt had been privy to his cousin's rather unusual courtship—in fact, he'd used his computer skills to track Claudie to Kansas when she'd disappeared on a self-imposed mission to rescue her younger sister.

"Tell my future cousin-in-law hi for me," Matt said.

Bo's sigh was a mixture of laughter and frustration. "She's going to be the death of me, but what a way to go."

Envy gnawed at him. Matt had known the same kind of happiness when he'd first fallen in love with Sonya, but he no longer trusted those emotions. Which was why he'd ended his relationship with Karen, the physiotherapist he'd dated six months ago. She'd wanted more than he could give. He told himself he wouldn't mind a sexual relationship with the right woman, but he'd had it with love. Period. "What's going on? This is a little after hours, you know."

"That's what Claudie said. She thought you might have a hot date. I told her she'd confused you with someone who had a life."

Matt held his sigh. This theme had come up more than once since Bo's return to Sacramento. For some reason his cousin seemed to think that since he was in love, everyone ought to be—starting with Matt.

"Listen, I'm glad you're happy, but leave my sex life out of it. I've got a full plate right now, thank you." A new partnership. A daughter. An ex-wife. The blanking holidays.

"Okay," Bo said. "If that's the way you want it." He paused, then said, "The reason I'm calling is I just got off the phone with Ren. He and Sara are really worried about Eve."

Eve Masterson. Matt knew Eve had once been engaged to Bo's friend, Judge Lawrence Bishop. Her name had come up a dozen times in the past two weeks. Locating the missing beauty was a job Matt would once have jumped at, but now he had more important issues to handle.

As if reading his mind, Bo added, "I know you decided to put it off until after the holidays, but Sara just talked to Eve's parents and they're freaking out because they haven't been able to contact her. It's *Christmas,* Matt."

Although Matt had yet to meet Ren's wife, Sara, he thought she was the most determined person he'd ever run up against. He pulled out one of his uncle's Z-shaped chrome bar stools and sat down. As was his habit, he picked up a pen and started doodling on the back of an envelope. "I thought Eve's parents were in Australia."

"They are. But Mrs. Masterson's ready to hop the next flight home and start tracking Eve down herself. She said she's called Eve's number a dozen times and has left messages at the station where Eve's supposed to be working, but nobody will tell her anything. One receptionist said Eve was out on medical leave. Naturally, that upset her mother even more."

Matt's doodles took on a fanciful nature. A large-breasted woman reclining in a small box topped with a pair of rabbit ears. "Eve Masterson is a television personality," he said for what surely must be the twentieth time. Lowering his voice, he added, "Doesn't this *disappearance* sound like something a television personality would do for publicity?"

Bo sighed. "If you remember, I was the one who suggested that a couple of weeks ago, but now I'm not so sure. I mean, think about it. Eve dumps her network job in New York for something in Atlanta. We don't even know what since she hasn't been seen on the air in Atlanta—and she doesn't bother to contact her friends or family in over a month. That really doesn't sound like the Eve I used to know."

Matt added floating question marks to his picture. The Eve Masterson in his memory was a sexy, exotic, poised news anchor who'd made a big splash in television when she was interviewing the outgoing president and he made a pass at her, unaware her microphone was live. Her beauty had garnered a huge following, which had included Matt. He'd drooled over her while eating his cereal.

"Sara called me yesterday," Matt said conversationally. He'd been on his way out the door to pick up Ashley, so he'd tossed out a few lame promises to get away. He still felt guilty about it. "She's quite persistent, isn't she?"

Bo chuckled. "You could say that. I told you what she and Ren did, right? They bought a round-trip vacation to Niagara Falls and put it up for auction knowing I'd bid like hell to get it for Claudie. Our dream honeymoon."

Matt grinned. He'd heard the story of Bo's extravagant gesture several times from several sources. The romantic story seemed destined to become an urban legend. "Have you set the date yet?"

"The first weekend in June."

"Will your dad be well by then?"

"He promised Claudie he'd walk her down the aisle if she wanted him to," Bo said.

"I talked to your mother this morning," Matt said. "She was at Mom's when Ashley called to get some genealogy information for a school project. Aunt Ruth says Uncle Robert is dazzling his speech therapist, but his motor skills are returning a lot slower."

Bo's chuckle sounded wry. "And why should that surprise anyone? You never could shut him up for long." After a pause, he added, "But, back to Eve. Bottom line—can you fly down and check things out next week? I know it's a lousy time of year to travel and you're still settling in, but I kinda promised Sara you'd do it. An early Christmas gift, you know?"

Matt glanced at his calendar—December, the last month of a difficult year. He'd be glad to have it behind him. The only notation was Dec. 25: Ashley with me. What that really meant was Matt would pick her up around noon and drive to his parents' home where they'd have delayed their celebration to include him and Ashley. He hated the holidays.

"Fine. I'll go, but I have to be back by Christmas Eve."

"Cool. It shouldn't take you more than a couple of hours, actually. Fly in. Find her place. See what the hell's up. Kick her butt if needed, then fly home."

Matt rolled his eyes. For some reason he doubted

it would be that easy. For one thing, he didn't know where Eve lived or the name of her new employer. His computer program was designed for cases just like this, but his PC had been giving him fits since the move. "I could shoot for Wednesday or Thursday," Matt said, frowning at the calendar. "The computer tech is coming Monday. Without a modem, I can't run a complete background check."

"So?"

"I like to know what kind of skeletons I'm gonna bump into when I start opening closet doors."

Bo snorted. "I guarantee you she's neither deranged nor dangerous. All we want is a visual confirmation that she's alive."

While Bo reviewed his original notes on the case for Matt's benefit, Matt studied his doodles. The curvy body in the television set didn't look anything like the Eve Masterson he'd seen on billboards all over town, but the question marks that surrounded her were apropos. Why had she left? Where was she now?

As Matt hung up, he heard Ashley ask, "Are you going out of town, Dad?"

Matt looked up. Ashley trotted down the steps, dressed in a navy pea jacket, baggy tan cords and several layers of soft cotton sweaters and shirts. "Bo didn't give you fashion lessons while he was here, did he?"

She gave him a droll look and ignored his question. "Did I hear you say you're going somewhere?"

"You shouldn't eavesdrop. But the answer is yes. I have to go to Atlanta on business."

Hopping down the final three steps with a loud

clank, she asked, "Are you really looking for Eve Masterson?"

"When I put you on the payroll, I'll be free to discuss my jobs. Until then, you're on a *need-to-know* basis."

She pouted prettily. "I *need* to know, Daddy. My friends would be totally impressed if I told them you were going to meet Eve Masterson. She's like the coolest person on television. I nearly died when she told the president she'd rather have sex with a lizard."

Matt laughed. "That's not what she said."

"She might just as well have. She put him down."

"Well, yes, but with a bit more class."

She rolled her eyes. "A put-down is a put-down, and as far as I'm concerned she shot him clean out of the water. No survivors." She grinned. "I plan on using the same technique on Billy Lebreonski...if he ever gets the gonads to ask me out."

Matt blanched. "Ashley, don't ever use that term in the same sentence with a boy's name again. Please. That can be my Christmas gift. I'm just not ready for it."

She dropped her backpack and dashed to him, hugging him but laughing. "Sorry, Daddy. I forgot how sensitive you are."

Sensitive? Me? Try telling that to your mother.

ASHLEY WAITED at the top of the stairs for the explosion to take place. Ten seconds or ten minutes, it was hard to predict, but sooner or later her parents would start yelling at each other. They'd tried couples therapy when she was little but could never agree on a counselor. As far as she could tell, they never agreed on anything.

"It's my job, Sonya," her father said, his voice a low murmur Ashley had to strain to hear. He always started out calm and cool, but her mother knew just what buttons to push to make him raise his voice. Ashley had been terrified of loud noises—she didn't even like the movie *Star Wars* because it was so noisy, so her dad always talked softly in a low, gentle tone that made her feel safe and cherished. Even now, he rarely raised his voice around her, and Ashley knew that if she were downstairs, the argument would fizzle out before it could peak. But she wasn't in the mood to be an arbitrator for her parents. She was tired of being their referee; it didn't do a damn bit of good in the long run.

"Some job," her mother said snidely. Her mother was the queen of snide. "You gave up a perfectly fine desk job with the city—with dental, no less—to go play detective. Admit it, Matthew, a desk job could never live up to the excitement standards you require."

Ashley rolled her eyes. Her mother had hated everything about the police force—the hours, the pay, the risks, the other policemen's wives. Everything. But after the accident, when it looked as if Ashley's dad might never get to be a policeman again, Sonya had suddenly become all rah-rah police force. Grandma Irene said it was because Daddy was a hero, but Ashley doubted it. Knowing her mother, it was more a case of "I told you so." Sonya had long predicted her father would get hurt on the job, so when it finally happened, she'd been proven right. Her mother loved to be right.

"Listen, I know Hanukkah begins on Friday and you have plans," her father said. "Fine. I'll be out of town anyway, so you can have Ashley all weekend. I just want to be clear about Christmas Day."

"Hanukkah lasts eight days, Matt. We're planning—"

Her father interrupted. "Spare me the details, Sonya. It's not my fault Hanukkah overlaps Christmas."

Ashley grimaced, anticipating her mother's response. "Faith means nothing to you, does it, Matthew?"

Ashley could picture her father's frustrated expression. He never talked badly about her mother, but Ashley knew Sonya's conversion to Judaism confounded him immensely since she'd shown only the mildest interest in religion during their marriage. They'd eloped to avoid the whole church issue, and Ashley had attended an interdenominational Sunday school as a child.

"My relationship with God isn't your problem, Sonya. I'm only concerned about making sure the holidays are special for our daughter."

Ashley could picture her mother's skeptical look.

Her father went on, "I should be back by the weekend, but if something unexpected comes up, I'll have Mom pick Ashley up at noon on Christmas Day."

"No. If you're not back, then Ashley will stay here. The agreement was she'd spend holidays with her immediate family—that's you and me, not your mother and father and your sister and her kids. Besides, you know Alan and I are trying to rebuild our Jewish faith and downplay the secular.''

Her dad made a hooting sound. ''And that ten-foot pine tree in the living room is some tenet of Jewish faith?'' Her dad could be pretty snide when he wanted to be, too. ''Sonya, we've always spent Christmas with my folks. Ashley loves seeing her cousins. You'd deny her that just to spite me?'' His voice rose in volume.

Ashley sighed and shook her head. She turned away and trudged to her room. The door was open—it hadn't been when she'd left, but that didn't surprise her. Her mother ruled this household. She went wherever she wanted, whenever she wanted. Privacy was not an issue—that's why all of Ashley's personal papers, her journal and notes from friends, were in her locker at the horse barn. She knew she could keep things at her dad's without worrying, but she never knew for sure when she'd be there—her mother changed the schedule almost daily.

She closed the door on the battering voices one floor below her and flicked on the stereo. Britney Spears. Pretty. Blond. Perfect. *I bet she doesn't have to listen to her parents fight. What the hell good was a divorce if they still can't get along?*

Ashley dropped her backpack on the floor then flopped facedown on her bed. She pulled the pillow out from beneath the tasteful peach lace comforter and placed it over her head. Muffled music was all she could hear. If she closed her eyes, she could picture herself atop Jester, her fourteen-year-old Thoroughbred gelding. Riding was her escape. Circling the arena astride the beautiful sixteen-hands roan made her forget everything else.

Her mother wasn't a horse fan, but for some reason she'd championed Ashley's request to take up riding. Ashley once overheard her father tell Grandma Irene the only reason Sonya liked horseback riding was because she thought it was classy. Ashley had to admit once her mother married Dr. Al—Ashley's name for Alan Greensburg, her mother's new husband—appearances became an issue. Clothes, home, car. Everything that hadn't mattered much when they lived with Ashley's dad, suddenly became a priority.

A knock on the door made her bolt upright. A deep voice said softly, "Ashley, honey, it's Dad. I'm leaving. Can I get a kiss?"

Ashley feathered out her hair and dashed to the door. He always respected her privacy. Maybe deep down she might have wished he asked deeper questions, probed harder about her inner feelings, but in a way it was nice to know he loved her no matter what was going on in her head.

She opened the door and stepped back to let him enter. She studied his face—so handsome. All the girls thought so. Lauren Willoughby said she had a wet dream about him one night. Ashley thought that was too gross for words, but her friends were right— he was a hunk, especially for a father.

"Are you okay?" she asked, noticing the lines of tension across his forehead that hadn't been there on the drive home.

He smiled. Not his truly happy smile, but a fairly okay one. "Sure. You know how it is. We agree to disagree. The story of our marriage." He reached out and pulled her into a quick hug. She closed her eyes and breathed in his scent—leather from his jacket and a spicy smell from his deodorant. Her dad was too cool to wear cologne.

"So, kiddo, have a good day on the horse tomorrow. Tell the knucklehead I said hello and he'd better behave or I'll kick his big ugly butt."

Ashley smiled. She knew her dad wasn't thrilled about her riding; he said Jester scared the crap out him because anything that big and unpredictable shouldn't be allowed within ten feet of his daughter.

"Don't worry about Jester, Daddy. We understand each other."

He pressed a kiss to the top of her head and stepped back. "Just be careful, okay? And wear that helmet I bought you." He glanced around the room, his gaze stopping at her new Backstreet Boys poster. "I guess I should be glad you like horses more than boys. Forget I said anything."

Ashley's heart felt pinched between her lungs. She smiled but didn't dare try to talk. She'd been on this stupid weepy kick for almost a week. Bridgett thought maybe Ashley was ready to start her period, but Ashley's mom said girls who were involved in sports sometimes started a lot later than other girls. Ashley hoped so. She didn't need hormones screwing with her head; she had enough problems already.

"Hey, kiddo, you heard me tell Bo I'd do that little job for him in Atlanta, right? I plan to be back before Christmas, but if something comes up and I don't get back, you can decide where you want to spend Christmas Day—here or at Grandma's. It's up to you. And don't worry, your presents will find you no matter what you decide."

"Call me?" she said, her voice kinda squeaky.

"You bet. And you have my new cell number, too. Call anytime." He looked at her a long time, as if trying to decide what else to say, but in the end he just leaned down and kissed her cheek. "See you later, sweetness. I love you."

Ashley walked him to the top of the stairs. Leaning on the railing, she watched each carefully placed step.

"I love you, Daddy," she called out impulsively, even though she knew her mother was probably lurking somewhere nearby.

When he reached the carpeted floor, he turned around. His grin made her feel so warm and happy inside she could have cried, but she managed to smile back. "Have fun tomorrow," he said with a wave. "I'll see you soon."

"THIS PRIMA-DONNA THING isn't working for me, Eve," Barry LaPointer said, pacing from one end of the living room to the other, negotiating his way past unopened packing boxes and furnishings that had yet to be put away.

Eve, who hadn't quite recovered from her battle with some kind of intestinal disorder she'd picked up on assignment in Panama, had come down with a bout of flu the same morning the movers arrived at her New York apartment. Rather than postpone, Barry had cajoled her into letting him handle things. As a result, Eve knew where nothing was, and she was still too ill to care.

"I'm sick, Barry. Sick. Look at my tongue. Does

this look like the tongue of a healthy person?'' Eve rolled into a sitting position on the couch and leaned forward to stick out her tongue. Her vision swam and a tinsel taste made her gulp. Light-headedness was a recent addition to her list of symptoms.

Eve knew if she didn't feel better soon, she was going to have to find a doctor. No easy chore when you're in a new town and your name is Eve Masterson.

Barry stopped pacing and looked at her. ''All I see is a woman who signed a very lucrative contract and—so far—hasn't earned a dime of it.'' He stuck his hands on his hips like a coach giving a pep talk to a losing team. ''You've got the gold ring, Eve. The corner office, big bucks and people dying to do your bidding. If you'd get off your butt, we could go pick out that car you insisted on.''

Eve slowly lifted her chin. The man standing before was as handsome as a movie star. Six-three or four, slim but fit, a crown of thick, wavy hair with golden-blond highlights too perfect to be real. He'd swept in to New York in late August all southern charm and sweet-talking promises. He'd offered Eve her dream job on a silver platter. Instead of being an on-air personality following after the news, she could produce the kind of news show that informed people about issues that were vital to their lives.

Communitex, Inc., the company Barry represented, felt it was on the cutting edge of technology with its twenty-four-hour, global, interactive Internet format. They'd lined up big name media personalities to anchor these Internet news shows around the world. Eve had agreed to host the East Coast segments for six months then she would move to behind-the-scenes production.

I should have known this deal sounded too good to be true, but who knew the devil would show up wearing Ralph Lauren?

"Barry, the car was your idea. I didn't own a car in New York and I got along fine." *Of course, I was never there.* In the six months she'd worked for the network, she'd handled assignments in New Zealand, Africa, England and South America. She'd spent more nights away from her apartment than in it.

Barry pivoted on one heel and marched toward the dining alcove. "This place is a hovel, Eve. Have you looked at yourself in the mirror lately? My God! You look like a bag lady."

I met a really nice bag lady once when I was doing a story in... A wave of dizziness hit and Eve started to sway. She knew from experience that if she could just get caught up in her sleep everything would be fine.

Even as a child Eve took longer to recuperate than other kids. Her mother blamed it on Eve's "delicate constitution." But when Eve was eleven she overheard her mother and father talking about genetic conditions. It was at that moment Eve understood what it meant to be adopted—she carried someone else's past with her.

"I'm tired, Barry. I—"

He turned on her. His face contorted. "*Tired?* We don't have time for tired, Eve. I guaranteed Communitex I'd deliver your beautiful face—your very recognizable, bankable face by December first. It's almost Christmas, and you have yet to make more than a token appearance in the office. No press conferences, no glad-handing with the public, no parties, nothing. Do you know how ridiculous that makes me look?''

He'd punctuated each of her shortcomings with a Nazi goose-step until he stood directly across from Eve, his skin a blotchy red that made his Rhett Butler mustache and microgoatee stand out like white Breath Right strips.

His breath smelled of garlic. A wave of nausea made Eve shrink back to avoid vomiting on his shoes. Barry apparently read her retreat as some sort of victory. He pressed his advantage by leaning in closer. ''I took you to a doctor, Eve. He gave you pills, but you refuse to take them.''

Just the mention of those pills made Eve gag. ''They made me sick. Remember your car?'' She'd been so out of it on the trip to Atlanta, she barely recalled a moment of the ordeal, with one notable exception—emptying the contents of her stomach all over the back seat of Barry's beloved Rolls-Royce.

Barry snarled. ''That's right. You still owe me two hundred bucks for cleaning the seats and carpet.'' He snorted, ''Hell, dating you was no picnic from the start. The company ought to give me hazard pay.''

So, that's it. All that sweet-talk of love and settling down was just blue sky to hook me. To Eve's immense relief, he backed up enough to take a seat on the coffee table. He rested his elbows on his knees and eyed her gravely. ''Forget the car. I'm more worried about you, Eve. Do you have a death wish where your career is concerned? If you don't buck up and make an effort, you're going to disappear into the land of has-beens. *Entertainment Tonight* will feature you on its Where Are They Now? segment.''

Just like that, Eve's temper snapped. She hated bullies—from Saddam Hussein to Arnie Zelderman, a classmate who'd tied her to the playground swings with a jump rope during third-grade recess. Gathering strength she didn't know she possessed, Eve drew her stocking-clad feet back, placed them squarely on Barry's chest and pushed. He didn't tumble over as she'd have liked, but he was obviously stunned. And angry.

''You ungrateful bitch,'' he swore, pushing her trembling legs aside. ''I gave you the chance of a lifetime and you're blowin' it. That may be your choice, darlin', but I sure as hell don't plan to sink into this hellhole with you. It's high time I protect my derriere.''

His sanctimonious attitude fueled Eve's sense of outrage. *I'm sick, dammit. Can't you see that?* She pulled her knees beneath her and sat up straight. ''Get out, Barry. I hope Communitex fries your ass with a plate of chitlins or grits or whatever it is you southerners eat. That doctor you took me to was a quack. Those pills weren't even from a legitimate pharmacy. I told him about the Panama thing, and he didn't even call my doctor or ask to see my files.''

She had to stop to draw in a deep breath. Tremors coursed through her body—whether from fury or fatigue she didn't know. ''I'm run-down. All that over-the-counter crap you keep plying me with doesn't do a thing. I told you I wanted to see another doctor, and suddenly you just stopped showing up.''

"I had to go to Chicago. Some of us work for a living," he said snidely.

"Well, I don't know what's wrong with me, but I'm never going to get well this way."

Barry made a motion toward the kitchenette where opened cans of chicken soup mingled with cartons of orange juice and pill bottles of every size and shape. "You kept telling me all you needed was rest," he argued. "I didn't have time to find you a doctor before I went to Chicago. I couldn't call just anybody. Do you want the whole world to know about this? Weakness of any kind is a deal-breaker in this business."

She had to concede that point, but it was moot if she wasn't able to drag herself into her bedroom let alone to work. "But things have changed. I'm not well. I'm a person, Barry, not a commodity. If Communitex can't deal with that then screw them. And screw you, too. Just get the hell out of here, Barry La*Pointer*." She pronounced the word without the French twist he preferred. "You're making me sicker than I already am."

He picked up his Armani coat and walked to the door. With a haughty nod, he said, "When I'm through with you, Eve Masterson, you won't be able to show your face outside this building. And you can kiss your dream show goodbye, too," he added snidely. "Poor little Deeanna West will have died in vain. Think about that while you wallow in your illness." Then he slammed the door.

Eve toppled over and crawled beneath the fluffy comforter she'd finally found buried in one of her boxes. Her head throbbed with a hammering pain that seemed timed to her heartbeat.

Curled in a tight ball, Eve tried to block the memory of the teenager's suicide. Deeanna's story had been Eve's last assignment for the network. Then an insensitive editor had gutted Eve's in-depth piece. Eve had been furious so when Barry showed up promising that his company would let her produce a show aimed at helping teenage girls, she'd quit the network quite happily. So much for dreams. Eve knew she needed help, but the idea of finding a new doctor seemed twice as daunting as it had yesterday. *Do I even own a phone book?*

A fleeting thought crossed her mind: *call Sara or Mom.* But another voice reasoned that her friend lived too far away to be of help, and her parents were traveling in Australia. Besides, Eve had put off calling them for so long they'd probably given up on her.

Sleep, she thought, sinking into the darkness. *Just a few minutes more, then I'll figure out something...*

CHAPTER TWO

THE SOUND OF A PHONE ringing in a distant fog-enshrouded land beyond her eyes woke Eve from her thick, unhealthy sleep. For a person who once thrived on five or six hours a night, this round-the-clock slumber seemed both unnatural and dangerous.

I wonder if this is what death is like. A tingle of fear made Eve rally enough energy to open her eyes.

Nothing had changed since the last time she looked. Same neutral walls devoid of decoration. Same pile of unopened mail collecting beneath the mail slot in the door. The off-white blinds were lowered and closed, no sunlight angled through the slats so she had no idea whether it was morning or night.

All the overhead lights were on because she lacked the energy to get up and turn them off.

The phone continued ringing until the answering machine clicked on, asking in a chipper tone for the caller to leave a message.

A voice she'd never heard before spoke. "Eve, this is Matthew Ross. I'm a private investigator working with my cousin, Bo Lester. We've been asked by your friends Sara and Ren Bishop to find out if you're okay."

Am I okay? Although at some level the question made sense, the answer confounded her. As a reporter, words were her life source, her job, but now they eluded her, slipping away like ghosts in the mist. The image frightened her, and Eve reached deep for the energy to lift her head.

"I'm..." she started, but the words got stuck in her parched throat, and whatever answer she'd been trying for disappeared from her mind.

"I will be in Atlanta tomorrow and I'd like to meet with you," the voice continued. "The Bishops won't be satisfied with anything short of a visual confirmation that you're alive, so..." There was something very inviting about this voice, warm and sunny, like the beaches of Bermuda. Barry had promised her Christmas in Bermuda. Barry's promises were even less substantial than his kisses.

"If you get this message and would like to set up a time to meet, my cellular number is..." He rattled off a number the way she used to—fast, crisp and economical. Time was money. Did she have any money anymore or had Barry screwed up that part of her life, too?

A burning sensation started in her stomach. Curling on her side, Eve brought her knees to her chest. Her ribs felt as though they might poke through her skin. She needed to get up and fix something to eat, but the thought alone made her dizzy. She closed her eyes and focused on the voice. "Eve, I'm sorry to intrude on you like this, but your friends and your parents are very worried. You could save me a trip if you'd call someone and tell them what's going on."

What is *going on?*

His tone became more serious. "If this is a media thing, I promise you I won't blow it if you come clean. You're a little out of my usual realm, but I swear I'm legit here—not some screwy fan who somehow got your number. Sara and your folks are frantic. They can't enjoy the upcoming holiday unless they know you're okay. So, how 'bout it? Give one of us a call?''

The cajoling tone almost made her smile, but her mind stalled on the word *holiday*. In their big blowup yesterday—was it yesterday? Or weeks ago?—Barry had said something about it being almost Christmas, but she'd blanked it out, unable to deal with having lost so much time.

Tears slipped from beneath her closed eyelids.

''Please call if you get this message. Again, my name is Matt Ross with RBL Investigations. On the chance Sara's fears are correct and something has happened to you, I will be in Atlanta tomorrow and I'm not leaving until I find you.''

Eve opened her eyes. A single thought crystallized in her mind and stayed there long after the sound of his voice faded. *He's coming.*

A long sigh warmed the spot on her pillow. She closed her eyes and started to sink back into the comforting arms of Morpheus, but her sleep was interrupted by a second phone call.

This time the caller didn't respond immediately to Eve's invitation to leave a name and number. Instead, there was a long, ominous pause. Eve knew that pause by heart. A creepy sensation raced up her spine, making her shiver.

''I know you're there, Even Mine,'' a raspy voice said.

A pain knifed through Eve, making her choke on

a cry. She lifted her hands to her ears and pressed hard, but the sound of the voice seeped through her fingers. "You know you're mine, Eve. Why do you try to pretend you're not?"

"Leave me alone," Eve sobbed. Tears gushed from her eyes. Mucus filled her nostrils, choking her air supply. Drawing in racking, hurtful gasps, Eve welcomed the gray fog that descended over her consciousness.

"Sir?" The flight attendant leaned over to catch Matt's attention.

He blinked, pulling himself back from the brink of sleep. Reaching up, he yanked out one of his earplugs. "I'm sorry. What?"

"The pilot's turned on the Fasten Seat Belt sign," the woman said, her pretty, blue eyes both friendly and interested.

Matt fished for the ends of his belt. "Are we landing already?"

"Just a little turbulence." She reached lower to catch the silver buckle dangling in the aisle.

"Here you go." The woman had a great smile. And a nice body, a little voice added.

Wrong time. Wrong guy. Matt took the belt from her fingers and lowered his chin to focus on snapping it across his lap. "Thank you."

She straightened. "Sure. Can I get you anything?"

Matt glanced at his watch: 3:00 p.m. "Black coffee?" A beer sounded better, but he hoped to arrive in time to stop at the Communitex offices, where Eve Masterson was supposed to be employed, before five o'clock. He didn't want to show up smelling of beer.

The blonde smiled and pivoted on one heel. Matt watched her walk toward the forward cabin. He'd chosen an aisle seat in business class to accommodate his long legs, but he had to admit the view wasn't bad, either. Too bad he wasn't in the market.

Matt could almost hear Bo chiding him. *A little flirting wouldn't kill you. Pretty girls expect it. You've probably totally bummed her out.*

Matt halfway wondered if there was something physically wrong with him. He used to like flirting. He used to be drawn to women, especially attractive women with long legs.

The flight attendant returned shortly with a steaming cup and a tiny vacuum-packed snack. "Thank you," Matt said, trying to make amends.

"My pleasure. If you need anything else, just let me know."

Matt ripped open a corner of the bag with his teeth and slowly nibbled the sweetened nuts. Whatever happened to plain old salted peanuts? he wondered. Phased out for a new, improved model. Just like me.

He took a gulp of coffee, swallowing the bitterness that threatened to choke him. First, the divorce. Ten years of marriage down the drain. Then, the accident. A career—a lifetime of wanting to be a cop—gone in the time it took to ram his squad car into a telephone pole.

If it had been a movie, his selfless act—meant to keep from running over a child who'd been tossed from the moving getaway car by her junkie stepfather—would have looked heroic. Instead, the kid died from a concussion, the junkie broadsided a bus and was killed on impact, and the dope they recovered from the car wasn't as much as they'd been led to believe. Just like that, Matt's right knee had been destroyed, along with his career.

To distract himself from his dark thoughts, Matt opened the file he'd started assembling on Monday. He laid the manila envelope on his tray table and studied his computer printout. Usually, two days was more than enough time to chronicle a person's complete history, but for some reason Eve Angelica Masterson remained an enigma. All he knew was what some publicist wanted him—Joe Public—to know.

He scanned the high points. Graduated cum laude from both high school and college. Took both the Junior Miss and Miss California crowns. Her first post-college radio show, *Shake, Rattle and Roll L.A.*, went ballistic from day one thanks to the audacious claim that she and her male co-host were doing the show naked. Given her looks and ambition, Eve's move to television had seemed predestined. Then came her engagement to Ren Bishop. "A well-matched couple," the media had called them. But they'd split up—Ren had married Sara and Eve had moved to New York.

Fingering the edge of an eight-by-ten glossy black-and-white publicity photo, he slid it to the top of the stack. His seatmate to the left grunted, "Ooh, baby. Eve Masterson. Wouldn't I like to start my day off with that pretty face on the pillow next to mine. Know what I mean?"

Matt glanced sideways. The man was pudgy, in his mid-fifties and nearly bald.

"Whatever happened to her, anyway?" the man asked in a flat midwestern accent.

Matt cleared his throat. "Good question."

"Are you a fan?" the guy asked.

"I used to enjoy seeing her do the news in the morning."

The man nodded with such force, his jowls rippled. "Me, too. Especially on the weekends when I didn't have to get right to work. If you get my drift."

Matt got it—unfortunately. For the first time since he'd agreed to take this job, Matt felt a connection with his subject—pity.

"Name's Gordon. John Gordon. C.P.A. What do you do?" The guy turned slightly and extended his hand.

With a subtle flick of the wrist, Matt closed the folder and slipped it into his flight bag then returned the social acknowledgment. "Matt Jones. Writer. Freelance. I was supposed to get an interview with this Masterson chick, but she was a no-show," Matt ad-libbed. He sighed and slouched down as if utterly exhausted from his ordeal. "Celebrities," he muttered. "Whaddaya expect?"

Through his lashes, Matt saw John Gordon's pensive frown. A flicker of conscience made him regret trashing Eve's reputation, but the last thing he wanted was to be pulled into a conversation about his client. Granted, Eve wasn't his client, Sara Bishop was, but for some reason, Matt didn't like the idea of John Gordon fantasizing about Eve—even if her sex appeal was what gathered viewers.

Thinking about the little yarn he'd spun, Matt wondered—not for the first time—why Eve didn't have a staff working for her: a publicist, an agent or a secretary. She was sufficiently established that she'd need all those people, and a driver, too. But he hadn't been able to contact anyone other than Eve's former agent, Marcella Goodell, who was out of the office until January fifth. Her secretary said the agent was no longer representing Miss Masterson but refused to elaborate.

In fact, despite his best efforts, Eve Masterson was looking more and more mysterious—not at all what he'd expected. Her Web page was bright and showy—full of facts about her job and accomplishments, but it hadn't been updated in five months. Her Webmaster hadn't spoken to her personally since its inception and there'd been no return e-mail activity in several months.

Unfortunately, the week before Christmas was not the best time to try to get information from people. Eve's former secretary at the network was on vacation. Two of the names Bo listed as Eve's friends hadn't called him back—either too busy or too distrusting of inquiries.

A part of him wondered if Eve had chosen to drop out of sight because she no longer enjoyed fame and all the trappings—the negative trappings. He really couldn't blame her, but she should let her friends and family know what was going on. Unless something or someone was preventing her from making contact with the outside world.

Where are you, Eve Masterson? What the hell has happened to you?

MATT INSERTED the key into the door lock of his rented Chevy sedan and tossed his bag in the back and sat down, adjusting the seat for his long legs. He set the mirrors and turned on the engine. The defroster blasted out chilly air. Gray skies made the damp air feel colder than the thermometer suggested. He'd never been to Atlanta, but he'd studied a map of the city on the Internet and had a pretty good idea where to go.

An hour later, he finally spotted the street sign he'd been looking for and pulled into the parking lot of Communitex, Inc.

Before getting out of the car, he studied the three-story building with teal-tinted glass and tungsten-colored chrome. Pretty showy for a company teetering on the brink of disaster, he thought. Bringing Eve Masterson on board had been a stroke of genius that might have saved the company from filing for bankruptcy, but in order for her presence to work—they had to use her, flaunt her. Something that had yet to happen.

Why? Matt wanted to know. What were they waiting for? Maybe the answer would lead him to Eve.

After bluffing his way past the guard, Matt made his way to the third floor. More funeral parlor than leading-edge newsroom, he thought, looking around. Two richly appointed sound studios with state-of-the-art-looking equipment occupied half the floor space; both were dark and deserted. Matt turned to a grouping of gray-and-burgundy-walled cubicles. He picked the first one with a live body at a desk.

"Hi, there. My name is Matt Johnson. I'm here for a four-thirty with Eve Masterson," he said briskly.

The woman, a twenty-something blonde, looked up, surprise and confusion on her face. "Really? Is she feeling better?"

Matt shrugged. "I didn't know she was ill. The gal I talked to said she was eager to talk to the media."

The woman's perfectly penciled eyebrows arched severely. "I wouldn't bet on it," she said, her soft southern accent conveying scorn. "Eve hasn't been what I'd call a team player. Frankly, I haven't seen her in over a month. Rumor had it she was in Chicago with Barry, but he got back two days ago, he was alone."

"Well, darn," Matt said. "I just drove down from Nashville to do this interview. I knew I should have called first. This always happens with stars. You wouldn't believe what I had to go through to talk to Willie Nelson."

She gave him a sweet, sympathetic smile. "Do you want me to try her home number?"

"Would you?"

"Sure." She smiled coyly. "For a drink after work."

Once again Bo's cynical voice prodded him, but Matt ignored it. "I'd love that but I promised my wife I'd refrain from flirting with beautiful women on this trip—it being so close to Christmas and all."

Her disappointment seemed genuine, and while she dialed the phone, Matt took a second look just to make sure he wasn't interested. Pretty. Friendly. But too unreal. His next woman—*if* he ever got involved again—would be down-to-earth, honest—even plain. He'd married a homecoming queen and didn't plan to get involved with another beautiful woman.

"Just her answering machine," the woman said, hanging up. "I've already left enough messages to start a fire. She's either not there or dead."

A sudden jolt arced through Matt's belly. He flinched. The woman gave him a curious look. "Got a lot riding on this interview?"

"Six hundred bucks. At this time of year, that really counts."

She sighed. "That's true, but it ain't diddly compared to what we've got riding on Eve Masterson." She suddenly looked past him and said, "There's Barry. Barry LaPointer. He's the one who recruited Eve. You could ask him if he knows where she is." She lowered her voice. "Rumor has it they're involved. *Romantically.* But who knows...he's here and she's not."

Matt turned. The only person moving was a tall, fellow in an expensive suit—Armani? With blow-dried blond hair and pearly-white teeth made even whiter by his perfect tan, Barry looked like an updated version of Clark Gable—complete with slim golden mustache above his lip.

"Thanks for your help. I'll check it out," Matt said, rising.

He crossed the room in five steps and intercepted Barry before he could insert his flat key card into a door marked Private. "Excuse me. Could I talk to you a minute?"

Barry, who was an inch or two taller and twenty pounds lighter than Matt, turned with slow grace and looked him straight in the eye. "And you are?" His accent was even thicker than the woman's at the desk.

"Matt Johnson. Freelance writer. I was scheduled to meet with Eve Masterson today, but apparently she's missing in action. I was told you might know where to find her."

Barry's reaction read like the dictionary definition of the word *suspicious*. A flush crept up his throat while the skin around his eyes blanched. His gaze shot from floor to ceiling to Matt's earlobe. From years of experience interrogating crooks, Matt knew better than to believe anything that was about to come out of the man's mouth.

"Eve Masterson? The news commentator? Are you sure…?"

Matt didn't feel like playing games. "Listen, Mr. LaPointer, my assignment was to interview Ms. Masterson. Here. I know Communitex hasn't formally announced her employment, but you know what they say. It's easier to let the cat out of the bag than to put it back in. Can we cut to the chase?"

Barry took his elbow and led him to a quiet spot away from the desks. "Ms. Masterson isn't here, and I can't say for sure she ever will be. Do you get my drift?"

"Let me get this straight," Matt said. "One person said Eve hasn't been here in weeks. Somebody else said she was out on sick leave. Now you're saying she may or may not work here." Matt leaned forward conspiratorially. "Do you think she's at some kind of dry-out clinic? Or maybe she's pregnant? Either one would make a great scoop." And both were possibilities that had crossed Matt's mind.

Barry's refined features wrinkled distastefully. "Don't be ridiculous. If I see one snippet of such slander appear in…what magazine did you say you write for?"

"I freelance. This piece is for *Let's Talk* magazine—that is if I ever get to talk to Ms. Masterson."

Barry seemed to relax once he decided the piece was fluff not news. "I apologize for the inconvenience. Why don't you give me your card. If I speak with her, I'll have Ms. Masterson call you to reschedule."

"No chance," Matt said contentiously. "I drove a helluva long way to talk to her. I'm *going* to talk to her."

Barry stepped back as if repelled by Matt's ire. "I'm terribly sorry, but there's nothing I can do. I've been away. I haven't spoken with Eve in several days, and I don't know what to tell you."

If the man had a passionate bone in his body he'd probably paid to have it surgically removed, Matt thought, put out by the guy's bloodless reaction. How could this jerk have interested Eve?

"Well, ain't that just great. Merry F-ing Christmas." He turned on his heel and stalked toward the elevator. Suddenly anxious to be anywhere but in this building, Matt took the stairs. For the first time since he'd been cajoled into taking this case, Matt felt an urgent imperative to find Eve. Something was wrong. Terribly wrong. Someone as smart and savvy as Eve Masterson would never have willingly succumbed to a sleazeball like Barry. If he was behind her move to Atlanta, then she was in big trouble.

THE POUNDING IN HER HEAD kept getting louder and louder—like a really bad hangover, but Eve couldn't remember drinking anything. As she puzzled over the question, her mind kicked in on other levels. *Cold.* She was freezing. Shivers wracked her body starting from the inside out. Opening her eyes, Eve was treated to a view of the underside of her kitchen counter and a corridor of unpacked boxes edging past the confines of what was supposed to be her dining nook. Gradually, she became aware of something gritty imbedded in her cheek.

"Oh, God," she groaned, rolling to her back. She remembered walking to the kitchen for a drink of water but nothing after that. She must have fainted.

Forcing herself to move, she levered to a sitting position.

The pounding sound, which had momentarily ceased, started again with a vengeance. She put her hand to her forehead to push back a sheaf of dirty black hair that had come loose from her makeshift braid. Blinking against the dizziness that swam across her vision, she took a deep breath and tried to focus on a strange, muffled sound interspersed between thumps.

"Eve Masterson. Are you in there?"

Her name. And a question. A good question. *Am I here?*

"Eve. Can you hear me? Do you need help?"

More questions. Too many. Ignoring the voice and the questions, Eve channeled her limited resources to her most immediate need—warmth. Distantly, a part of her body suggested other needs, but the wracking chills were her first concern.

"Blanket," she whispered in a hoarse voice she didn't recognize.

She spotted a fluffy down comforter draped tent-like over her coffee table. Half of it was on the couch—her refuge.

"Eve. My name is Matt Ross. I'm Bo Lester's

cousin from New York. Ren and Sara Bishop hired me to find you. To find out if you're okay. Can you hear me?''

On her knees now, Eve crawled forward, teetering like a child just learning to maneuver. She had a flash of Sara and Ren's little boy Brady running like the wind in his miniature tuxedo at their wedding. Tears clouded her eyes. She missed her friends.

''Call Sara. She'll confirm who I am,'' the voice cajoled.

Call. Phone. A shudder passed through Eve's body and she misplaced her right hand. Off balance she fell against a tower of packing boxes. Bracing for impact, she squeezed her eyes tight. The top box fell in the other direction. Noisily.

Immediately, the pounding started again. Louder. ''I heard that. What the hell's going on? Are in trouble? Do you need help?''

Eve's lips formed the word *help,* but no sound came out.

''Eve,'' the voice said, lower but more forceful, ''I'm going for the super. If I have to call the police, I will. I'm coming in.''

Sudden panic, from a source she couldn't identify—maybe years of dealing with the public, made her cry out, ''No.''

When he didn't answer, Eve crawled forward, almost in reach of the sofa and her blanket. She drew in a breath and tried again, ''No.''

The word echoed in her head, shaky and breathless. Pitiful. That's what she'd become—pitiful, and she didn't want the world to see her this way. She clawed at the puffy blanket. Too exhausted to crawl up on the sofa, she collapsed where she was, pulling the blanket over her. A thick cushion against the world.

The metal mail flap in the middle of the door flipped open. "Eve, what's going on?" His voice wasn't muffled anymore, but it sounded strained, a little frantic. "Talk to me. I'm a friend. I'm here to help."

Eve tried to sink lower in the folds of the blanket but was stymied by the position of the couch. Like a hot dog in a bun, she was wedged between the sofa and the coffee table, snug and safe, except for the viewing hole created by the legs of the coffee table. The gap framed the door—with its little rectangular slit.

"Go away," Eve pleaded.

The pen—or whatever tool the man was using to prop open the slit—wiggled back and forth like a snake's tongue. "I will go away…just as soon as I've seen you and confirmed that you're okay. That's my job. I won't get paid if I don't."

His deep husky voice sounded anxious and a bit distraught. He probably needed the money pretty badly to be on his hands and knees talking through a mail slot. But that was his problem not hers.

"You don't believe me, right? You think I'm some crazy fan trying to get to you. But I'm not. I'm legit. I'll prove it." The flap slammed shut.

Good. Peace again. Temporary peace. Until the dreams start.

A minute or two later, a clanking noise at the door made her start. "Okay. This is what I'm going to do. I'm putting my wallet through the slot. It's got my ID in it." He paused. "And my money and my credit cards. That means you are in control of my fate because I'm flat broke and homeless in a strange city if you don't open the door and give it back to me.''

A dull thudding sound made Eve open her eyes. Six feet away, lying at the base of the heap of mail was a brown wallet. She could tell it wasn't new. It had a molded-to-the-butt look. A part of her mind she hadn't heard from in a long time wondered about the butt that had shaped it—young and virile? Or old and flabby?

''Eve?'' He sounded even more worried now. ''Are you going to help me out?''

Eve wanted to help. She was a helper. Her mother's little helper. Miss Congeniality. A team player. A trouper. But she couldn't. Not physically, or mentally. She eyed the distance to the brown wallet. *Maybe I could do it. Pick it up and put it back through the slot.*

Rallying all the strength she could muster, Eve pushed backward until she was on all fours. Dragging her blanket with her, Eve gracelessly worked her way to the marble tile of the entry.

Leaning on one elbow, she picked up the soft leather object. Inhaling, she drew pleasure from the smell. Masculine. She rubbed her cheek across the soft smooth surface.

''Eve?'' the voice whispered hoarsely. ''Eve, please answer me. Tell me you're okay.''

The man's concern touched her, and she wanted to answer him but couldn't. The exertion of crawling to the door had worn her out. She rolled to one side and closed her eyes, but her grip on the wallet didn't lessen.

MATT JERKED HIS PEN out of the viselike grip of the metal flap and plopped back against the door, his legs sprawled into the hallway. He was lucky her apartment occupied the rear corner of the top floor of the turn-of-the-century building—no one was around to witness his complete and utter humiliation.

He ran a hand through his hair and sighed. What the hell was wrong with the woman?

Matt had caught a glimpse of her through the mail slot. That is, he'd seen a person crawling. Small. Black hair. Bingo, he'd thought.

The hands-and-knees thing made him figure she was drunk, although her single response to his plea hadn't sounded drunk—just weak.

"Okay," he muttered. "Drunk or drugs. Doesn't matter. At least she's alive and she'll snap out of it sooner or later. If worst comes to worst, I can always call the super."

Matt glanced at his watch. I'll give her half an hour then go get some dinner, he thought, patting the pocket where he'd stashed most of his money and credit cards. Sooner or later, she has to open up—for more drugs, if nothing else.

Matt let his head settle back against the door and gave in to the long, fatiguing day. Not only did he hate traveling during the holiday season, he'd had to deal with Sonya that afternoon when he'd called to tell Ashley goodbye.

She'd given him the usual lament about his career then dropped a new bomb. "Something's come up, Matt. Alan has been offered a chance to relocate to a very lucrative area with a starting salary that's out of this world. We're going Monday to check it out."

"Monday? This Monday?" he'd cried. "That's Christmas. That's *my* day."

"I realize that. But all the flights are full on Tuesday. We can get a red-eye out Monday night, if you insist on sticking to the letter of our custody agreement. But Ashley will be the one to suffer. She'll be tired and moody and have a terrible cross-country flight thanks to you."

"Cross-country? Where are you thinking of moving to?"

"California."

"Like hell. I'll see you in court first."

"Alan said that's what you'd say."

Matt had been too upset to think of anything else. As things were, he barely got to see his daughter—what would it be like if she lived on the other side of the continent?

"…a million-dollar business opportunity," Sonya had blathered on. "It's a beautiful place with sunshine and great schools."

"Forget it, Sonya. I'll contact my lawyer and fight this. You can't take her out of the state without going back to court."

Sonya's voice had turned icy. "And we'll win. I'm her mother and she's entering her teen years. She needs me."

Before Matt could reply, Sonya had said, "I have to go. I've got a touch of flu and my herbal tea's coming back up. Please. Think about switching days. Who knows? Maybe the job won't pan out, but Ashley will still have a great trip. Disneyland. Universal…" She'd hung up without letting him talk to Ashley, but for once Matt didn't mind. He wouldn't have known what to say to his daughter anyway.

Groaning, Matt sank a little lower. Could my life get any worse? I'm on my butt. In a hallway. Waiting for some wasted celebrity to sober up and open the door so I can take back my ID and go home. *Ho, ho, ho.*

CHAPTER THREE

EVE AWOKE GROGGILY. Her neck was stiff, her shoulder sore. She lifted her head and gave a nudge with her chin to remove the bulky object tucked beneath her cheek.

A wallet.

A man was here. Bo's cousin. He came to save me, but I sent him away.

"Oh, God," she cried. "What did I do that for? My privacy isn't worth dying for."

Desperation gave her strength. She pushed herself into a sitting position. Her fingers gripped the wallet like a lifeline. An almost forgotten impetus—curiosity—made her draw the wallet into her lap and open it. On the right side, a clear plastic display area held a driver's license. *New York. Matthew Michael Ross.* She squinted but couldn't make out the details of his age, height and weight. Her gaze settled on the picture.

Medium-long face, uncompromising jaw. Dark hair. Dark eyes that looked straight into the camera in a manner that said, "What you see is what you get." His nose was long and straight, but fit nicely above his lips. The bottom lip was fuller than the top—both masculine and sexy. A handsome face, but real.

Eve thumbed through the wallet's plastic photo holder. Back-to-back cards. His business card—silver lettering embossed on navy stock. Matthew M. Ross. RBL Investigations. She paused at a school photo of a young girl, age twelve or thirteen. Blue backdrop. A reserved smile, as if self-conscious of having too many teeth for her delicate jaw. Big eyes. A mass of brown locks. She probably hates her hair, Eve thought, recalling how she'd begged her mother for a Farrah Fawcett cut.

At that age all you want is to fit in, Eve thought. She'd interviewed far too many young girls who had no sense of self beyond what television, the music industry and movies told them they should be. That was one of the reasons she'd been so eager to listen to Barry's baloney.

"The Internet is the medium that will connect with those girls, Eve. They don't watch television news. That's for their parents. With Communitex you'll be able to reach them and make a difference," he'd promised.

She brushed aside the memory and opened the money section of the wallet. Enough bills to make her cringe. *Did I really leave him destitute in a strange city?*

Suddenly moved by someone's plight besides her own, Eve gathered her strength. By concentrating, she rocked forward and slowly rose to one knee. Using the coffee table for support, Eve made it to her feet. After the initial dizziness passed, she unlocked the dead bolt lock that had been installed at eye level so no one could use the mail slot to secure entry.

The big brass doorknob would require both hands,

she decided. She looked for a place to put the wallet. Her grungy cotton sweats lacked pockets; the waistband was so loose it barely kept them from falling to the floor. Shrugging, she put the wallet between her teeth and bit down.

Gripping the decorative knob with both hands, she slowly turned it. To her immense surprise and horror, someone—something—was waiting outside the door. A weight pressed inward with such force, Eve toppled backward, her feet getting tangled in the avalanche of accumulated mail. Graceless as a clown, she windmilled back, landing butt first atop a stack of cardboard packing boxes, which sent the whole column and its neighbors cascading down around her ears.

When all was quiet, she braved a peek.

Crouched like a martial arts warrior ready to take on an army of villains, the man across from her scanned the foyer with eyes narrowed to dangerous slits.

"What the hell...?" His voice was deep and rich with an accent she'd grown to like during her stay in New York.

Eve watched him take in the stacks of boxes; his eyes widened at the mess in the kitchen. He was just starting to rise out of his defensive stance when his gaze zeroed in on her. For some reason, his right knee suddenly wobbled and he seemed to lose his balance for a moment.

His recovery was so smooth Eve wondered if she'd imagined it. Then she looked into his eyes and her brain forgot how to think. Her heart sped up in a way that made her feel more alive than she had in weeks, perhaps months.

His eyes—a warm shade of brown—widened. Eve tried to interpret his look. Repulsion? Disbelief? Suspicion. "Who are you?" he growled. "Where's Eve Masterson?"

Curling into a protective ball, Eve whispered, "I wish I knew."

MATT PRIDED HIMSELF on being a man of action. In a crisis, people turned to him. Maybe it was his experience in law enforcement that gave him the confidence to make tough, split-second decisions and shoulder the repercussions afterward. But, for once, Matt felt poleaxed.

Her four little words were all it took to confirm what his mind tried to deny. "Eve?" He almost choked on the word. She curled up tighter, like one of those little roly-poly bugs Ashley used to play with in the garden.

Oh, my God! How? How did this happen?

Her whimper made Matt realize he'd spoken out loud. He would have kicked himself if his knee weren't throbbing like hell. Bad enough he'd fallen asleep on the job, but his instinctive reaction to the door opening was a holdover from his karate training and not something he'd tried since his accident. *And now I know why,* he thought bitterly.

Moving gingerly, he looked around the apartment. As big a mess as he'd seen in a long time, but no booze bottles or drug paraphernalia in sight. What, he wondered, could have caused this transformation?

Baffled, he approached Eve—curled in a fetal position at the base of a jumbled stack of packing boxes. Thin to the point of emaciation, dark circles shadowed the hollows under her eyes. Her honey-almond skin was now geisha white. Her blue-black hair was knotted and partially held back in a fat, unkempt braid.

"Eve? Are you sick?"

She didn't answer.

He hunkered down in a squat, ignoring the shaft of pain in his knee. "Are you stoned? Coming off an ecstasy binge, maybe?"

"Screw you," she muttered, but her eyes remained closed.

"Have you seen a doctor? If it's not drugs or booze, then what the hell's the matter with you?"

She tucked tighter, as if trying to disappear. "Tired. Just tired."

Although heartened by her ability to answer his questions, Matt didn't like the way each response got fainter and fainter as she spoke. Was she losing consciousness?

"Eve," he said, reaching for her wrist. "Don't fade away. I need some help here. Do I call 911 or what?"

"No," she cried, batting his hand away. "Just leave me alone."

Of course he couldn't do that. She needed medical help. Matt had promised Sara he'd handle things as diplomatically as possible, but Eve was obviously very sick.

Letting out a long sigh, he stood up. "Where's the phone? You need to be in a hospital."

The word triggered an unexpected response. Eve bolted upright as if a puppeteer had suddenly jerked her strings. Swaying slightly, she pinned him with an icy glare. "I said no. I have no intention of becoming fodder for the evening gossip shows. And if you do anything to contribute to that, I will sue you into perpetuity.''

Matt wasn't even sure what perpetuity was, but it didn't sound fun. He lowered himself to one knee—his left. ''Eve, whatever's wrong with you isn't something I can ignore. Sara and Ren Bishop hired me to find out what happened to you. They're worried sick about you. I can't tell them I found you but you're wasting away to nothing and I went off and left because you threatened to sue me.''

Some of the fire left her eyes. ''Don't you understand?'' she pleaded, her voice bordering on hysteria. ''I can't be seen like this. If word gets out—and it will, I'll never work in this industry again. I'll never get another chance like this to do my show, to help...'' Her voice drained away like a wind-up toy.

Matt shook his head. ''You'd put your job ahead of your health?'' he asked, his tone dripping with incredulity.

''My job is my life,'' she answered.

Suddenly, the irony of his question hit him. In a way he'd done the same thing. Once that junkie had taken off, Matt hadn't thought twice about what might happen if anything went wrong.

Chagrined, he took a deep breath. As long as she was talking—arguing—he figured he could take the time to assess the situation rationally. Talk some sense into her. ''How 'bout I help you stand up then we talk about this calmly.'' He gently placed his hand on her shoulder. He jostled her softly.

Again, the puppet master jerked her into action. She sat up, her arms flailing wildly. The back of her hand connected with Matt's nose. Not hard, but enough to make him react as he would with any troublesome suspect. He subdued her by wrapping his arms around her shoulders, pinning her arms to her sides.

She was sideways in his arms. As she started to lower her chin toward his bicep, Eve warned with a growl, "I'll bite."

Matt fought back a grin. His leather jacket could take it, but he didn't want to see her waste her energy. "Relax," he said. "I want to help you to the couch. You're shivering. I'm afraid you might go into shock."

With a small sigh, she slumped against him. "Okay," she said. "To the couch. Not the emergency room. I hate emergency rooms." She shuddered as if haunted by something too grim to recall.

Matt had seen his share of emergency-room traumas, too. Maybe there was a way he could get her to a hospital but spare her the chaos that would follow a call to 911.

He slowly rose, assisting Eve as much as she would permit. Despite her obvious weakness, she seemed determined to do as much as possible for herself. Her grit earned his grudging respect.

"My mother is a nurse in New York City. She has a friend who works in Atlanta. What if I call my mother and ask her to find out the name of the most discreet hospital in town?" he suggested as they neared the couch. "You know, one where celebrities go."

She didn't answer until she was seated. "I have to

think about it," she said, her voice trembling with fatigue. "Don't do anything until I say it's okay."

Her order lacked force but something in the way she said it made Matt realize she expected him to honor her wishes. No questions asked.

Before he could argue, she sagged like a balloon with a leak. When her head hit the rounded leather bolster, her lips parted in a sigh. And she was asleep.

Debating his options, Matt poked around for clues to Eve's condition. Judging by the size and shape of the living room and adjoining kitchen, the apartment was fairly large—twice the size of his old place. Glancing down the hallway, he saw three open doors, one closed.

Eggshell walls. High ceilings. Oak trim around the windows that were cloaked with shades but no curtains. Not a single painting or picture was in sight— not even a calendar. Just stacks of boxes surrounded by clutter. Magazines, juice boxes, used tissues, both opened and unopened mail—scads of it.

This was so *not* how he'd pictured Eve's life. It has to be drugs, he decided, choosing the only explanation that made any sense. Bending over, he poked through the litter on the floor looking for proof. The closest thing he found was an amber plastic prescription container filled with white pills. The lack of a label raised his eyebrows.

"Eve, what's going on here? Cocaine?" he asked softly. She was thin enough, he decided, but no telltale jitters. *Heroin?* He didn't think so. Her emaciation just doesn't fit, he thought, studying her. Tiny, fragile. A lotus flower, some foolish voice said inside Matt's head.

Gently, Matt placed two fingers on the pulse point in her throat. She flinched but didn't try to pull away. Her skin was soft and cool. Dry to the touch, like rice paper. Not flushed or moist from a fever.

An odd jolt of energy passed through his fingers. He couldn't explain it since she seemed completely oblivious to his presence. With great care, Matt raised one lilac-colored eyelid, outlined by long, curly black lashes. She resisted his efforts by dropping her chin.

A soft moan slipped from her lips.

Perfectly shaped lips, he noticed, although her full bottom lip was cracked in places. Her lips, like the rest of her skin, showed signs of dehydration.

Matt's heart twisted in pity. He lifted his chin and looked around. The place was a pigsty. It stank of unwashed dishes and dirty clothes. She looked like a pathetic urchin. He'd seen cleaner homeless people. He knew how the scandal sheets would interpret this.

Torn between what he felt he should do and what Eve wanted him to do, Matt went in search of a phone. *When in doubt, call Bo,* he thought. After all, he was an envoy of Bo's company. If anybody was getting sued it was Bo.

EVE'S NOSTRILS TWITCHED.

Something was different. She sniffed, trying to place the smell. Food.

Her mouth suddenly filled with saliva and she had to swallow or choke. Her throat was dry and out of practice. She coughed.

"Beef bouillon." a voice said. "It's all I could find."

Eve's eyes snapped open. *It wasn't a dream.*

She raised her head to look around and get her bearings—hoping against hope she wasn't in a hospital room.

The sight of her four unadorned walls brought tears of relief. He hadn't turned her in. "Thank you," she said, her voice cracking.

"For what? Not calling 911?" he asked, walking to the edge of the vinyl flooring in the kitchen. From that vantage point he could look directly at her lying on the couch. *Did he carry me here?* For some reason, the idea of being held in those big strong arms made her a little light-headed.

"You won't thank me if you suddenly go into shock," he said sternly. "I know you asked me to hold off calling my mother, but I couldn't wait for you to wake up. Mom gave me all kinds of grief for not taking you straight to the emergency room, but I told her you were a litigious fool who would sue her if word of this got out."

Eve flinched. Did she really come across as that desperate and bossy?

He went on. "Mom said it's absolutely vital we get some fluids in you as soon as possible. I was just about to wake you up."

He wiped his hands on a towel and picked up a glass from the counter. It appeared to hold some kind of juice.

"Everything in your fridge had expired," he said, walking toward her. "I remembered seeing a market on the corner so I ran down and picked up a few things. This is one of those high-energy drinks. Mom said it'll help replenish your electrolytes."

Eve's heart struck up a wild tune the closer he got.

He sort of loomed over her, and she wasn't sure if her panic attack stemmed from his maleness or his size. Or both.

"Can I help you sit up?"

His tone was so gentle some of her anxiety eased. "Yes, please," she said, nodding.

He placed the glass on the coffee table, which Eve noticed was now clear of clutter. Her comforter was neatly tucked around her, and the heap of magazines and junk mail on the floor was gone from view. Lowering himself to a strip of cushion beside her, he grabbed one of the couch pillows from the far end of the sofa and placed it behind her. To facilitate the move, he looped one arm behind her shoulders and drew her forward.

Her nose just inches from his shoulder, Eve smelled spray starch. The scent evoked a memory of her father going off to work.

He eased her back. Eve was certain his hand spanned the entire breadth of her back. "You're big," she said.

He'd turned to pick up the glass but stopped and looked at her. A smile danced at the corner of his lips. She saw a faint dimple in one tanned cheek. His skin tone was a healthy, natural bronze, not the machine-groomed color Barry favored.

"I'm an inch shorter than Ren Bishop. 'Bout the same weight, though, Bo said."

Ren. Her friend. At least, she'd done something right to have friends like Ren and Sara. "Is Sara okay?" Eve asked.

He picked up the glass. He hesitated as though debating whether or not she could hold it. In all honesty,

Eve wasn't sure. Her hands didn't feel totally connected to her body. "Finish this and we'll talk," he said, lifting the glass to her lips.

Eve concentrated on the job before her—swallowing. It should have been easy, but nothing was easy these days. She opened her mouth and let the cool, refreshing liquid run down her throat. She made three successful swallows before the communication link got mixed up and she breathed in by mistake. Liquid went down her air pipe and something bitter went up her nose.

Sputtering, she arched back. His left hand slipped from the pillow, causing him to fall against her. Fighting for a breath and feeling smothered, Eve cried out in panic. Her futile struggles lasted two or three seconds at best before she'd used up all her reserves.

Instantly apologetic, he pulled back, his features showing dismay and concern. He set the glass on the table and whipped a clean white handkerchief out of his pocket. "I'm sorry. Are you okay? Did it go down the wrong pipe?" He carefully wiped her face and nose.

"Blow," he said.

"Absolutely not."

His lips quirked. "Oh, come on. I'm a dad. I've done this before."

"You're not *my* dad." Reaching deep for the energy she needed, Eve took the hankie in both hands and blew her nose. Then spent, her hands dropped to the blanket.

"You know what we need? A straw. I bet you could handle a straw. Do you have any?" He rose without waiting for her answer. A good thing, since Eve couldn't begin to predict where to find one.

After banging a few cupboard doors, he returned. "I can't believe it. I actually found one. Must have been left over from some delivery meal. Anyway, here it is." He sat down again, stripped off the paper cover and put it in the glass. "Let's try again. You have to finish this. Mom said if you don't drink it all, I have to take you straight to the hospital."

Eve wasn't sure she believed him, but the threat worked. Despite the urge to sleep, she focused on drinking and slowly finished the glass. Her stomach made ugly rumbling sounds that would have embarrassed her if she had the energy to care.

"Tell me your name again," she said as he started to rise.

"Matt. Matt Ross. Like I said, I'm Bo Lester's cousin from New York." His tone seemed to question whether or not she was mentally competent.

His brown eyes looked worried. He had beautiful eyes. The color of a fine cigar. Barry smoked fancy cigars—the more expensive the better, he liked to say.

At one time Eve had half-jokingly told Ren any child of their's would probably have dishwater-gray eyes. Looking into Matt's eyes, she thought, *If we had a child, it would have pretty brown eyes.*

His eyes widened—in alarm or surprise Eve wasn't sure which. What she did know was she'd spoken her thought out loud. To save him the embarrassment of having to reply, she turned her face to the side and closed her eyes.

What a fool! Men didn't want to marry her and

give her babies when she was beautiful—why would any man want her now?

ONCE MATT WAS SURE Eve was asleep, he walked to the extension phone in the kitchen and called his mother again.

"Eight ounces down her gullet," he reported without preamble.

"Good. But keep a bucket handy. She might not be able to keep it down," Irene Ross told him. "Is she sleeping?"

Matt leaned around the upright post to view his patient curled serenely on the couch. "Uh-huh. Like a baby."

There was a slight pause then his mother said, "In twenty minutes, I want you to wake her up and get her to try some broth. She sounds malnourished if she's as thin as you say she is."

Matt shuddered to think how thin Eve was. When he'd placed his hand behind her back to help her sit up, he'd felt every knobby vertebrae.

"If I can get her to eat, then what?" Matt asked his mother. "She seems weak, but out of nowhere up pops attitude like you wouldn't believe."

Again, there was a pause. "If I remember right, she's quite beautiful, too," Irene said, a certain tone in her voice. Matt knew his mother well enough to stifle a groan. Irene Ross was an inveterate matchmaker who was convinced Matt was bordering on depression because he lacked a woman in his life.

"Mom, this is work. She's sick. Are we clear on that?"

"I know you, Matthew. There's something in your

voice. Just like when you found that little bird when you were eight and coaxed it back to life.''

Matt smiled at the wistfulness in her voice. Gently, he said, ''Mom, that bird had the wind knocked out of it. Eve's situation is a bit more serious.''

Turning back into the health-care professional she was, Irene said, ''That's right. And she *has* to see a doctor, Matthew. When the body gets this depleted, it needs help rebuilding. In the long run, you aren't doing her any favor by keeping her from medical care.''

Matt knew she was right, and he had a feeling Eve knew it, too.

''I already called Margery and as soon as she gets back to me with the name of a doctor you can trust, I'll call you.'' Margery was his mother's old friend from nursing school. He hoped she knew how to keep her mouth shut.

As if hearing his unspoken worry, his mother added, ''Don't worry. We'll be discreet.''

''Thanks, Mom. I'd better go. The soup is boiling. I can't believe she actually had beef soup in the cupboard. There's barely enough here to keep a mouse alive.'' He started to hang up, but added, ''By the way, would you give Ashley a call later? Sonya's been sick and I'm hoping Ashley doesn't get it.''

After they said their goodbyes, Matt bagged the last of the garbage and carried it to the door. He'd take it to the Dumpster in the alley later. He had to go out to move his rental car, which he'd left directly under a sign forbidding overnight parking.

Walking to the gas range, he picked up the lid of a small saucepan. A steamy cloud of beef flavored bouillon wafted out. His mouth watered. Eve might not be hungry but Matt was. And clear soup didn't cut it. He'd whip through a fast-food drive-up window when he moved the car.

He ladled a scoopful into a plastic bowl—the kind microwave meals came in, which was all he could find. He picked up one of the three non-plastic spoons he'd found and carried both to the couch.

He set down the soup then cautiously lowered himself to the cushion near her hip. He still couldn't get over how small she was. On his television screen she'd looked larger than life. He'd watched her bungee jump, for heaven's sake. Unless she'd used a double. The thought made him frown. Was she a complete fake? Probably. She sure as hell wasn't as beautiful as her billboard.

He studied her face. True, her face still retained its basic shape—a perfect oval with high cheekbones and almond-shaped eyes that were moderated by neatly arched eyebrows and thick black lashes.

All right, he silently acknowledged, even at her worst, Eve Masterson was still the most beautiful woman he'd ever met. For some reason, that didn't make Matt feel any better. In fact, it made him a little nervous, but he put his feelings aside to play doctor. Correction. Nursemaid.

"Eve, time to eat." He lightly shook her shoulder. His hand seemed obscenely big against her thin cotton pullover.

He could tell by its wrinkles and stains her outfit hadn't been changed recently. Matt knew if he were the one lying there, he'd kill for a shower and some fresh sheets on the bed. He resolved to tackle her bedroom next.

"Eve?"

He leaned closer and said her name softly to avoid startling her. His mother had warned him that a by-product of dehydration and malnutrition was short-term memory loss. It was possible she wouldn't remember him when she woke up. Matt's earlier reaction to her asking his name probably was pretty obvious.

Eve's eyelids fluttered.

"It's me, Eve. Matt Ross. I have some soup for you. Nurse's orders." He kept his tone soft and unthreatening.

With obvious reluctance, her eyes opened. Matt had never seen such dark irises. "Are you my day nurse or night nurse?" she asked. Her small yawn removed any suggestion of banter. Matt might wish she was well enough to flirt, but that wasn't how things were.

"Both. Which brings me to a very important question. Are you awake?"

He waited until she blinked into focus. Behind those beautiful black eyes was intelligence masked by illness. He sensed the instant her mind rallied. "What?" she asked, a bit breathless.

"Do you have a car?"

The question obviously threw her. He quickly added, "The reason I ask is I have to move my rental car off the street by midnight, and I was hoping you had garage space."

She took so long to answer, he feared the question was too much for her, but before he could ask again, she said, "No car. Barry promised me a company car. A..." She struggled but couldn't come up with the name. Sighing, she said, "My parking space is the same as my apartment. Number..." Her eyebrows furrowed. Her bottom lip started to quiver.

Matt put his index finger there to stop it. "Eight. You're number eight."

The soft flesh beneath his finger stilled. Her focus turned downward, and Matt felt himself respond with something he knew wasn't pity.

Straightening up, he said, "Good. I'll move my car as soon as you've eaten."

After hastily draping a paper towel across her chest—which he was careful not to touch—he picked up the plastic bowl. It warmed the palm of his hand. "I don't suppose you know which box contains your real dishes, do you?"

Her delicate nostrils flared at the aroma emanating from the bowl. Her lips parted and her small pink tongue licked her cracked bottom lip. "No." Her attention was obviously elsewhere.

Hunching forward, Matt fed her a spoonful of warm brown liquid that smelled better than it looked. His stomach growled for equal time.

She closed her eyes and swallowed. "Brought your dog, huh?"

Her unexpected quip almost caused him to drop the bowl. His bark of laughter made her start.

"Airplane food doesn't stick," he said, giving her a second spoonful. "I'll grab a bite when I move my car."

She inhaled the soup as if it were a chocolate sundae. "My cupboards are bare," she said between bites. "Not even a dog bone."

Her wit gave him more heart than she could have known. Two hours earlier he'd been poised to call for help. Now he was starting to think she might be able to climb out of this pit without being hospitalized. He'd still take her to a doctor in the morning, but maybe they'd be able to avoid the tabloid headlines after all.

"I called Ren and Sara a few minutes ago," Matt told her, steadily plying her with broth. "Sara was so happy to hear you're alive she burst into tears and Ren had to take over."

"She's pregnant," Eve said, her lips almost forming a smile, but a small cloud crossed her face. "Isn't she?"

"Yes. She's expecting twins. Five or six months along, I think. Ren said she's been known to cry when the timer goes off on the stove."

Eve opened her mouth. Matt, thinking she was about to speak, withheld the next spoonful—until she crooked her eyebrows and looked at him expectantly. In haste, he spilled a few drops.

He used the edge of the paper towel to dab her chin.

"Doesn't matter," she said, her voice already sounding noticeably weaker. "My shirt's a mess."

"Understandable," Matt said. "When I get back from the car business, I'll change the sheets in your bedroom. Maybe you'll feel up to a shower or soaking in the tub before bed."

She took the last spoonful and sank back with a sigh. "That was good," she said. "Very good."

She was silent a minute, but Matt had the feeling she wasn't asleep yet so he waited. "Thank you. A bath sounds like heaven. It might *be* heaven, you know."

Matt took that for a yes. After making sure she was comfortable and snugly wrapped in her blanket, he dimmed the lights and picked up his jacket. At the doorway, he paused and looked back. The place wasn't quite the mess it was when he first arrived, but it still remained a long way from what he'd been expecting.

He stared at the woman lying on the couch to make sure she was still breathing. The thick comforter rose a fraction and Matt let out the breath he'd been holding.

Ill and frightened, yet strong enough to fight for what she wanted. In a way, he admired her, but at the same time he couldn't comprehend why she would put her life at risk to protect her image. Matt shook his head. He'd never understand celebrities. He just hoped like hell he'd made the right choice on her behalf.

CHAPTER FOUR

EVE DIDN'T WANT to be disturbed. She'd been enjoying a pleasant dream about a man with chocolate-brown eyes and a kind heart. She pushed the hand away. "Not now," she muttered.

"Eve, it's getting late. If you want a bath, you'd better wake up."

A bath? That's what the man in her dream had promised her, too. And he'd even joined her in a big, round tub.

"Eve."

The dream evaporated. Irritated, she snapped, "Oh, all right." She opened her eyes, then blinked, not quite certain whether she was awake or dreaming.

"It's you," she said in a throaty whisper she didn't recognize.

He nodded as if she were mentally challenged. "Yes. It's me. Matt Ross. From New York. Remember?"

The way he spoke in a slow, deliberate cadence made her want to laugh, but she didn't want to hurt his feelings. He'd been kind—in her dream, anyway. The rest was a little vague.

"I remember," Eve said, sitting up. She was surprised to find she actually had the strength to do so without feeling light-headed. "I feel better."

"Good. Do you feel strong enough to take a bath? I drew some water."

Suddenly the urge to be clean, to submerge her withered body in warm water took on a need akin to lust. "Yes. A bath sounds wonderful." Taking a deep breath, she attempted to rise, but Matt stopped her by placing his hand on her shoulder.

"If you don't mind, I think I should carry you."

His suggestion was so formal, so polite; she didn't know what to say at first. "Why?"

"To help you conserve energy. Mom's worried about the bath. She actually suggested I give you a sponge bath, but I told her I didn't think that was a good idea."

The heat from his hand soaked through the fabric of her sweatshirt, like a hot-water bottle wrapped in a towel—her grandmother's way of warming the bed when Eve was a child.

"Right," she said dumbly.

"Just relax," he said. "Let me get my feet under me and we'll be in fine shape."

Fine shape, she silently repeated as her fingers lightly skimmed the breadth of his shoulders. He'd changed into a faded gray T-shirt adorned with the letters NYPD.

He slowly straightened, gathering her to his chest like a heroine in a romance novel. Unfortunately, Eve felt anything but sexy.

His first step was accompanied by a slight shudder.

She frowned. For one so athletic, he seemed to carry himself a tiny bit off balance. When he walked, there was a definite hitch in his gait. Eve would have asked about it, but she was suddenly overcome by emotion. She closed her eyes to keep her tears at bay and pressed her cheek to the crook of his shoulder.

"Are you okay?" he asked, pausing.

"I'm sorry you have to do this, Matthew Ross," she said, concentrating on recalling his name from his driver's license. Eve had always prided herself on her ability to remember names.

"I don't have to do anything, Eve. I'm here partly as a favor to a friend and partly because I'm getting paid for it," Matt said, turning toward the hallway.

The words clicked in her head, bringing back Barry's candid admission that he'd wooed her for profit not love. "Yeah," she muttered, "there's a lot of that going around. I'll try not to be too much of a nuisance."

His scoffing sound made her tilt her chin back to look at his face. His grin seemed self-deprecating. "As if there aren't half a million men who would kill to be in my place."

Eve understood what he meant, but that only applied to the old Eve. "What man in his right mind would volunteer for invalid duty? Helping a stranger."

His low chuckle thrummed through her chest. "*I* may be a stranger, but you're not, Eve. I used to have breakfast with you every morning."

She glanced up and saw him smiling down at her. A genuine smile. The kind of smile you could trust, but then, she'd thought that about Barry at first, too.

"Are you okay?" he asked again, apparently sensing her tension. "I bought a few groceries, parked the car and changed the sheets on your bed." He carried her—effortlessly, it seemed—toward her room. "After I removed all the shoes," he added, wiggling his narrow black eyebrows in a playful manner.

"The shoes?"

Suddenly, she remembered. In a snit, Barry had dumped an entire packing box of shoes on the bed while trying to find a pair of slippers Eve had requested. "Sorry about that."

"No problem," Matt said with a grin. She could smell his breath—coffee and something aromatic. Some kind of gum. She recognized the brand but couldn't come up with its name. *Think, Eve. You know this.*

"Dentyne," she exclaimed triumphantly.

A muscle twitched in his cheek. He had that look again—as if her mind was functioning at half power.

"Do you have any gum?" she asked as casually as possible.

He stopped in the middle of the hallway. The overhead light cast his features into a dramatic relief of shadows and angles. *He is a very handsome man,* Eve thought. *I wonder what his wife would think of him carrying me to my bath.*

He shifted Eve in his arms. Her breasts brushed against his chest. The sensation was enough to create an automatic reaction she couldn't believe still existed. Her nipples puckered. Without a bra, they felt slightly chafed by the fabric of her sweatshirt.

If Matt sensed her response, he was gentleman enough to ignore it. "I just bought some," he said, producing a small flat package that he flipped in the air. It landed on her belly. "Help yourself."

She tore her gaze from the new growth of beard shading his jaw, which worked his gum with serious force, and picked up the glossy package. In order to open it, she was forced to raise her right hand to her left—in essence wrapping her arms around his neck. The situation felt slightly loverlike and Eve blushed as she hastily unwrapped a small rectangle, then popped it in her mouth.

His color changed ever so slightly and he swallowed hard, as if his gum had become lodged in his throat, then he resumed walking.

Eve bit down on the small soft morsel. The taste of cinnamon exploded in her mouth. A veritable flood of saliva swamped her throat muscles. Between swallows, she choked out, "Thank you."

As they passed through the doorway of her bedroom, Eve twisted her neck to check out her room. The shoes were nowhere in sight. "Wow! You're not just a nurse. You're a genie."

He shrugged. "I moved your suitcase to the closet, hung up the clothes that were in it and put your cosmetics bag in the bath. The shoes are in the box in the corner."

He headed toward the bed.

Bending at the hip, he eased her down on the clean-smelling linens. "Wait," she cried. "I'm too grubby to touch clean bedding. Can you take me to the bathroom?"

"Sure. It should be nice and steamy in there by now."

He had to juggle her again to finesse the doorknob, and then he quickly slipped inside the warm, fragrant room. Eve inhaled deeply.

"Lavender," Matt said, answering her unasked

question. "I found a little bottle of bath oil by the tub so I put some in the water."

Lavender. A memory flickered. *A bad sunburn. With Ren? In Maui?* The memory fled like a rabbit down a hole. What was wrong with her?

"I can't remember things," she said abruptly. "What if my mind is going...like Reagan's?" she asked.

He slowly lowered her to the ground.

"Reagan has Alzheimer's," he said firmly. "That's not your problem."

"What *is* my problem?"

"I don't know. I'm not a doctor, but it isn't Alzheimer's. Okay?" His gaze—intense and alive—held hers captive until she nodded.

He added, "Mom told me short-term memory loss is a common side-effect of dehydration and malnutrition. It'll come back once you're better."

Eve hoped he was right.

He released his hold on her shoulders and stepped back. "I'll be right outside if you need any help. Just holler." He started to open the door then paused, apparently noticing a switch on the wall. "Great. A heat lamp." He gave the knob a twist and suddenly the room was bathed in a bright, warm glow. "This way we can keep the door open a tiny bit and you won't catch a chill." Glancing over his shoulder, he told her, "I promised my mother you wouldn't get your hair wet, okay?"

Eve nodded, eager now to get to the water. Without even waiting to see if he was gone, she struggled out of her top, barely finding the strength to lift her arms. Her loose-fitting bottoms puddled at her feet. Her thick wool socks were troublesome, but she finally got them off and stepped into the large, pale pink tub.

The heat was a shock at first, but Eve slowly lowered herself into the fragrant water.

Closing her eyes, she rested her head on a built-in cushion and sighed, "Oh…heaven. I finally made it to heaven."

A chuckle made her smile. It was comforting to know she had someone looking out for her—even a total stranger. A man. A part of Eve warned it was foolish to trust a stranger, but at the moment, he was her link with survival.

"This feels so good. You have no idea. My skin is like sandpaper. Worse than when I was in Saudi…I think I was in Saudi."

"Do you need me to turn up the heat?" Matt called from the doorway. "It seemed a little chilly in here for someone who wasn't moving around much, but I'm not good a judge. My body runs warm."

Does it ever. Just being in his arms had been enough to thaw the block of ice inside her. "I think it's okay. It's like a spa in here. I may never come out."

"Not even for Christmas?"

His tone was light and teasing, but the reality of his words struck her like a sucker punch. "W-what day is it?" she asked in a small voice.

"Wednesday. The twentieth."

"Of December?" Panic grabbed her by the throat, cutting off her breath. She'd lost more than a month of her life.

"Let it go, Eve." His stern tone cut through her rising hysteria. "When you're sick or laid up, there's nothing you can do about lost time. Believe me. That's just the way it is.''

The old Eve would have argued, but the old Eve hadn't been around for months. The new Eve lacked the energy even to consider why Matt knew such truths so intimately. Sighing, she closed her eyes.

''I don't remember much since I left New York on November first,'' she said. ''I know I was sick the whole way here,'' she said. Images of the trip appeared like frames from a 1950s B movie. A big car with a chrome nude on the hood. Barry—smoking a cigar in the front seat. Eve shivering under piles of blankets in the back. Nauseated.

She'd thrown up all over his precious car, and Barry had complained about it to the movers when they arrived here with her stuff. ''If I'd known she was the type to get car sick, I'd have made her ride in the back of the moving van,'' he'd joked.

Or maybe he was serious. He'd never displayed a single iota of concern for her health and well-being. Unlike this man, this stranger.

Matt Ross.

Eve was sure she'd never known a man as kind and caring. His actions could be considered motherly, yet he pulled them off without sacrificing an ounce of masculinity. In fact, there was something incredibly sexy about the way he fed her soup.

''It's kind of quiet in there,'' Matt said from the doorway. ''You're not going to pass out or fall asleep, are you?''

Eve shook her head from side to side, but it was an effort to say, ''I'll try not to.''

''Maybe I should keep you talking. Just in case.''

He paused a second then asked, "Why were your shoes all over your bed?"

"Barry. He has a short fuse."

"Barry LaPointer?"

Eve concentrated on washing her legs. She truly didn't want to talk about Barry. Who knew what kind of mischief he might come up with before she could find the energy to defend herself?

"I met him this afternoon," Matt said when she failed to respond. "And I hate to say it, Eve, but I wasn't impressed."

"You saw him?"

"At Communitex. I told them I was there to interview you."

"How did you find out about Communitex? I didn't tell anyone where I was going. Barry wanted to pull a big publicity coup."

"It wasn't easy, but that's what I do. I told them I was there to interview you. Rumors were thick, but no one seemed to know what happened to you—not even Barry."

Eve closed her eyes. "He knows. He says it's my fault I'm sick."

There was a dull thud, as if a fist had collided with the wall. "He knows you're sick? And he just left you here? Alone in a strange city?" Matt's scorn was nothing compared to the contempt she felt for herself for getting involved with Barry in the first place.

Eve closed her eyes. *What a fool! Why did I let myself...?*

She hadn't intended to give voice to her anguish, but Matt's reply proved she'd done just that.

"Who knows why any of us make bad choices when it comes to our love life?" He made a sound of disgust. "If we were smarter, there'd be a lot less divorce, right?"

"My parents have been married for thirty-six years," Eve said, trying to recall when she'd last seen them. They'd stopped in New York in July on their way to...somewhere. Her energy was dwindling fast. She should get out of the tub while she still could, but the water was so warm, so pacifying.

"Mine just celebrated their forty-third," Matt said. "My older sister threw a big party for them. She says they're the reason she's so happily married." He laughed bitterly. "I don't know...it didn't help me."

"Why not?" Eve asked, curious about why any woman would give up a man like Matt. So caring, so real.

"My ex-wife wanted a different kind of life from the one I was capable of providing."

"'Capable'? You seem capable of anything."

"I guess maybe she wanted something other than what I *chose* to provide. I chose to be a cop. She opted to be a doctor's wife."

Suddenly, a wave of fatigue overwhelmed Eve. She sank back; her butt sliding against the porcelain made a squeaking sound.

"Eve? Are you okay?"

The concern in his voice made her focus. "I'm going to try to get out now," she said, gathering her strength to lift her body from the tub.

"Eve?" He sounded poised to rush to her aid, but Eve was determined to salvage at least one shred of dignity. Hand over hand, elbow over elbow, she slowly clawed her way to a shaky stance in front of the vanity. Her reflection was obscured by the misty condensation on the mirror.

"I left a bunch of towels on the toilet," Matt volunteered.

She looked at the door again, but it faced away from the vanity, so she knew he couldn't see her. After wrapping herself in a fluffy sea-foam green towel, she said, "I need a clean nightgown."

"You're right. I should have thought of that. Tell me where to look."

"Oh, dear. I don't have any idea. Wasn't there anything in my suitcase?

A couple of minutes later a hand shot through the open crack. "Uh...will this do?"

Eve looked up from brushing her teeth. A frilly black silk and lace number she didn't even remember buying dangled from the end of Matt's fingertip. Eve felt her face flush.

"No," she sputtered, sending toothpaste froth everywhere.

The scrap of fluff disappeared.

Drawing on her innermost strength, Eve managed to complete her ablutions. By the time she finished, she'd resorted to leaning on one elbow. The clean mint taste in her mouth made her smile, but the sight of her hairbrush—thick with tangled black hair— wiped it from her lips.

She used the hand towel to clear away a spot on the mirror. She stared at the unfamiliar image peering back at her a moment then averted her gaze. All her adult life, Eve had traded on her feminine appeal. Without her looks, who was she? Eve Nobody.

Choking back tears, she dropped her head, wavering to keep her balance.

"Matt...I can't...stand up any..." The words were barely past her lips before the door rocketed open and he was at her side.

"Lean on me," Matt said gruffly. He looped one arm around her shoulders to keep her steady.

"Thankyouforthis." Her words ran together as a wave of gray passed across her line of vision.

"Damn," Matt muttered. Anchored by his strong grip, Eve's toes barely touched the floor. Rotating her one hundred and eighty degrees, he kept his hands on her arms then hoisted her up. Her bottom sank into the eiderdown-feather mattress.

"Nice," she said with a sigh. He'd turned down the covers. Her fingers flattened against the smooth, clean bedding. Somehow he'd found her Neiman-Marcus sheets. Four hundred–thread count. Better than silk.

Sleep beckoned like an old friend, but she couldn't fall over sideways and curl up—not wrapped in a damp towel. Without warning, tears spurted from her eyes.

"What's wrong? Are you in pain?" Matt asked, bending over to see her face. Even given the height of the bed, the top of her head barely reached his shoulder.

Ashamed of her helplessness, she kept her chin down. "Can you help me with the towel?"

He gulped. Loudly. "Sure. I can do that." She heard him take a deep breath. "This is probably pretty awkward for you, Eve, but just think of me as a nurse. Okay?"

"Okay," she whispered.

In the end—thanks to him—the whole maneuver was fast and effortless. Almost before she knew what had happened, she was lying beneath her silky sheets, the down comforter pillowed at her chin.

Eve wanted to express her thanks—tell him that she appreciated his kindness and respectful manner. She meant to offer him the guest bedroom for the night, but her goodwill faded beneath the pressing urgency of sleep. Fatigue hit like a tornado and whisked her into a black abyss.

MATT CLOSED Eve's bedroom door with a low, long sigh. He'd been called upon to do many odd, unimaginable tasks in his years on the force, but if anyone had ever suggested he might one day be asked to remove Eve Masterson's wet towel and help her to bed, he'd have laughed in their face.

And even sick, she was lovely. Pale as a marble statue but beautiful.

Matt smacked the heel of his hand against his forehead. As his nervous tension began to dissipate, he tried to focus on a plan of action. Pushing off from the wall, he made an effort to shake off his edginess. *Why the hell couldn't I find a nightgown? Something in flannel.*

While hunting through one box, he'd run across what his sister used to call "unmentionables" of all shades and fabrics—from red silk thongs to leopard-print bras. His fingers tingled, imagining Eve wearing the frilly underthings.

"This is nuts," Matt muttered, stomping past the

kitchen to the living room. "She needs a doctor, and I need a psychiatrist."

Glancing at his watch, he detoured to the couch. It was three hours earlier on the West Coast. He wanted to speak to Bo, but first he had to give his mother an update.

Irene picked up as though she'd been waiting for the phone to ring.

"Hi, Mom, I got her to bed. I think she was asleep before her head hit the pillow," he said.

"Good," his mother said in a hoarse whisper.

"Are you in bed?"

"Of course. You need to get some sleep, too. Does she have a couch you can sleep on, honey? You really can't leave her alone, you know. Not until we get her checked out by a doctor."

Matt had surmised as much, but it surprised him to hear his mother suggest the same. His suspicions began to percolate anew. Did his mother see Eve's situation as an opportunity for a little long-distance matchmaking?

Sighing, he closed his eyes. He loved his mother dearly, but she didn't understand how hard it was to go from a long-term marriage to being a bachelor again. Matt was nowhere near ready to get involved again. And even on her worst day, Eve Masterson was miles out of his reach.

But that didn't change the concern he felt for her. Tomorrow, he would take her to see a doctor. More than likely, she would need hospitalization. After that, Matt would be free to book a flight for home. *For the holidays. Without Ashley.*

After wishing his mother good night, he dialed a

memorized number. As he listened to the phone's muted ring, he idly picked up a pair of discarded slippers. Leopard-print scruffs made of fuzzy material, like a stuffed animal.

After just two rings, a female voice answered, "Hello?"

Matt recognized the voice of his cousin's fiancée's. "Hi, Claudie, it's Matt."

"Hiya, Matthew, long time no talk. How's the Great Eve Hunt going? My money's on you, big guy."

Claudie sounded jovial. "Smart pick. I'm at Eve's now. Didn't Ren or Sara call you?"

"Dunno. I just got home from a county supervisors' meeting. Did Bo tell you we're starting to lay the groundwork—budgetwise—for a second halfway house?"

Claudie's renovated Victorian home in Folsom, California, known as One Wish House, was where she helped prostitutes find new lives off the streets.

"Very ambitious. I thought you were holding off until after the holidays. And don't you have a wedding to plan, too?"

Claudie snorted. "Nag, nag, nag. You sound just like Bo. He should be home any minute by the way. Meanwhile, what's the deal with Eve?" Claudie asked. "The girls at One Wish House are betting alien abduction."

Matt's lips twitched. "We haven't ruled that out." He tried to keep his tone light. "I found her, but she's not exactly the same old Eve."

"Really?" Claudie's voice went low and serious.

Matt regretted his jest. "She's sick, Claudie. I don't

know exactly what's wrong, but I plan to take her to see a doctor tomorrow. Mom says it sounds like she's suffering from malnutrition and dehydration. What brought it on is anybody's guess."

Claudie was silent a moment. "God, Matt, I feel like such a schmuck. Sara's been upset about this for weeks, but I kept telling her it was some kind of publicity gimmick."

Matt felt the same way. "Hey, you're not the only one. Remember how much I fought coming here?"

"We call that hindsight, Matt." She paused. "Hold on a sec. I think I hear your cousin." She set the phone down with a clanking sound.

Matt heard the low murmur of voices in the background then Bo came on the line. "You found her?"

"Yup. Wasn't all that tough. By the looks of it, she's been in her apartment the whole time. Sicker than a dog."

"Wow. That's a shame. Must be bad if she couldn't even call her family or Sara. Didn't she get any of our phone messages?"

Matt had glanced at the answering machine. A readout showed the number: thirty-four. "I'd bet yes, but she's pretty much out of it, Bo. At first, I thought drugs, but it's not that. My impulse was to call 911, but she flat-out refused, so Mom's been holding my hand long distance."

"What does Aunt Irene think it is?"

"Hard to diagnose over the phone. I should have the name of a reliable—*discreet*—doctor in the morning, then I'm taking Eve to see him no matter what."

Somehow, Matt doubted Eve would protest. That little episode in the bedroom couldn't have been too pleasant for her. Matt knew how humiliating it was to ask for help undressing.

"So where are you now?" Bo asked.

Matt frowned. "I'm staying here—just in case she needs anything."

"Man," Bo said with feeling. "How did this happen? Where are her friends? What happened to that guy who wooed her to Atlanta?"

Matt stretched out, letting his head sink into the cushion. "I can't tell you, Bo. I met Mr. LaPointer this afternoon, and my first impression was he's an arrogant SOB who wouldn't lift a finger to help someone else unless there was something in it for him."

Bo was silent a moment. Matt opened one eye and saw he had a chokehold on Eve's defenseless slipper. Frowning, he tossed it to the floor. "Do me a favor, cuz. Run a check on Barry LaPointer. I didn't bring my laptop with me."

Matt heard Bo scramble for a piece of paper, then Bo said, "Will do, but here's an idea. Why don't you bundle Eve up and bring her back here? We've got clinics. Hell, Hollywood must have a place that specializes in helping skinny showbiz types."

Matt was faintly offended by Bo's callous attitude. "Well, for starters, Eve threatened to sue my butt off if word of this got out."

"Really? Now, that sounds more like the Eve we all know and love. I was just thinking that you could plug her into some hospital then meet Ashley in la la land."

Matt's stomach turned over. "What are you talking about?"

Bo made a funny noise in his throat. "Please tell

me I didn't just step in a big pile of dog doodoo. You heard about Sonya and Alan's plans to go to L.A., right? Some job offer with a high-profile clinic.''

Matt's stomach wrestled with the burger and fries he'd consumed earlier. ''Sort of. How do you know about it?''

''Your mom told my mom and my mom told Claudie who told me.''

Matt could imagine the uproar the news had generated. With the exception of Sonya, these women were all on his side. ''Hey, cuz, I'm sorry. That bit about seeing Ashley was stupid...'' Bo's voice trailed off, and Matt heard someone in the background. ''And insensitive,'' he hastily added.

There was another pause and Matt heard Bo speak to Claudie. ''Here,'' Bo said loudly. ''If I'm such an insensitive jerk, you talk to him.''

''Matt?''

''Claudie?''

''Sorry about that. We haven't seen each other all day and sometimes things get mixed up on the phone. When I talked to Bo's mom, she'd just gotten off the phone with your mom. Apparently, Ashley was pretty upset about missing Christmas with you. Irene said she'd promised Ashley you wouldn't let that happen.''

Matt groaned. ''Great. A sick celeb and a pissed-off ex-wife I can handle, but not my little girl's broken heart.''

''Matt, I haven't met Ashley, but kids today are smarter than we were at that age. I'm sure she'll understand no matter what happens. Just be honest with her." She paused. "She knows you love her, Matt. That's what really counts."

Matt hoped she was right. "Thanks, Claudie. I'm glad Bo's got you to keep him from making a complete ass of himself."

Her light laugh made him smile.

They said their goodbyes, then Matt decided one more call was in order. To hell with the time. He needed to talk to his daughter.

ASHLEY POUNCED on the phone on the first ring. Her mother was such a grouch lately. She'd probably have a cow if it rang more than once this late at night. Ashley didn't know who might be calling—her stepfather's service probably, but she hoped it was Bethany calling to tell her Neil Brickman would be riding with them Sunday. He was by the far the cutest boy in school and rumor had it he was getting a horse for Christmas. Of course, there was no guarantee her mother was going to let her go to the stables on Christmas Eve since they were flying out West the following morning.

"Hello," she said, her voice cracking a bit.

"Hi, hon, it's Dad."

"Daddy," she squealed in surprise.

"Did I wake you?" He sounded serious. Too serious.

Ashley's heart rate sped up again. Her stomach tensed. "No. I was writing in my journal. But it's kinda late. Are you okay? Is anything wrong?"

"No. Not at all. I had an interesting day. Met Eve Masterson. Remember? You asked me about her."

"You met her? In real life? Like face-to-face? Wow!"

"Yep, face-to-face," he said, but there was something funny about the way he said it. It made her curious.

"Do you like her? Is she hot? Are you going to date her?"

His spontaneous denial was so like him, Ashley burst out laughing. Her dad hadn't dated anyone in six months—not since he and that physiotherapist, Karen, broke up. Ashley had known from the start that wouldn't last—no sparks.

"I told you before I left, hon, this is business. She's not well, and I'm here to make sure she gets some help."

Ashley read the *Enquirer*; she knew what that meant. "A dry-out clinic, huh?"

"No. Absolutely not. She's ill, not on drugs."

Ashley wasn't sure she believed him, although she'd never known him to lie to her. But celebrities were always messed up on drugs or booze.

"So, what then? You'll, like, take her to a hospital and then come home?" If her mother had her way, Ashley wouldn't get to see her dad or any of the Ross family before she left for California.

He didn't answer right away. "Honey, I know you're worried about Christmas. I barely had a chance to talk to your mother about this, so I don't know the whole story—"

Ashley interrupted him. "The story is, Dr. Al's got a chance to make a zillion bucks doing chin tucks on Hollywood's fading beauties. So I may have to leave my horse and my dad and move three thousand miles away.''

His low chuckle made her wish she could crawl into his arms and cry. "Did I just get second billing below a horse?''

Ashley choked on her laugh. "Sorry, Daddy. You know I love you and Jester the same,'' she teased.

He made a gasping sound as if he were having a heart attack.

More serious now, she said, "I might not get to go to the arena Sunday because Mom said if she could talk you into switching, we'd fly out Christmas Day.''

"Where do *you* want to spend Christmas, honey?'' He paused a second then added, "And don't tell me what you think I want to hear. I'm a grown-up, I know all about disappointments and reality. You're the kid and you get to be selfish. So you tell me what works for you.''

Ashley sighed. She halfway wished he wasn't so darned accommodating. Part of her wanted him to fight for her, demand equal time. But she also knew she had to live in *this* household—her mother's house—and when Sonya was upset, everybody was upset.

"I don't know, Daddy. I guess I'm kinda sick of this turning into a big deal. Maybe what would be best is if I could see you and Grandma and Grandpa Christmas Eve.''

"Done.''

"Thanks, Daddy.''

"And tell your mother I said I was willing to share my day with that big ugly horse of yours. Go riding in the morning, and either Grandma or I will pick you up at the stables at two, okay?''

Ashley's throat was tight, and her voice cracked again. ''Okay. Love you.''

''I love you, too, Ashley. Sweet dreams.''

CHAPTER FIVE

MATT WENT from sleep to total awareness in under a second. His sleep pattern had become erratic since the accident—some nights were a gruesome recounting of crash sounds and flashing lights. But the noise that woke him now wasn't a memory.

He rolled to his back and opened his eyes, letting his pupils adjust to the dimly lit room. He'd left a light burning in the bathroom across the hall to provide enough illumination to navigate to Eve's room if she needed him. Was that where the sound had originated?

Holding his breath, he strained to hear.

Click. The noise, though faint, reverberated in his awareness. Something metal. A key in a lock.

Nerves primed, he sat upright and drew on the T-shirt and sweatpants he'd laid out. One ear cocked toward the foyer, he squatted by his flight bag for his gun, but after a few seconds of fruitless searching, remembered that he'd left it behind—not wanting to be hassled by airport security.

"Damn," he muttered under his breath.

Barefoot, he rose and silently walked to the doorway. Little bits of packing material stuck to his feet. One foot at a time, he brushed them off while peeking around the doorjamb. The position of the hallway gave him a clear view of someone entering the apartment.

A man dressed in black pants and a bulky parka. At least Matt hoped that buff silhouette was the product of down stuffing, not muscle. He hadn't tried hand-to-hand combat in quite a while. But his instincts were still sharp. Like a cat targeting an unsuspecting mouse, Matt watched the intruder.

Out of habit, he checked the time. Three-sixteen. What kind of hospitality was expected at three in the morning?

Not the purely social kind, for sure, he decided.

The man paused beside the bar area where Matt had piled the mail. The intruder pushed it aside with a negligent shrug. *I've seen this guy before,* Matt told himself, but he didn't have time to think about it because the fellow started down the hallway. His size blocked the light from the bathroom, but Matt decided, friend or foe, the guy was going down. When the man was even with him, Matt reached out, grabbed a handful of ski jacket and yanked him sideways. Off balance and startled, the man crashed clumsily to the floor. Two seconds later, he bounced to his feet like a yo-yo, sputtering, "What the hell..."

Matt flicked on the light switch. Since he was prepared, Matt wasn't blinded the way the other man was. Barry LaPointer danced skittishly. Blinking in panic, his jaw hinged open and shut like a bigmouth bass. Matt slugged him in the gut.

Barry doubled over with a loud grunt and dropped to one knee.

Matt smiled at his knuckles. Any jerk that'd run

off and leave a sick woman all alone deserved a punch.

Cursing like a street punk, Barry lumbered up. "Who the f...? Wait. I remember. You're that reporter. What are you doing here? Why'd you hit me?"

Matt stepped back. He rested one shoulder negligently against the door frame. "One reason and one reason only—Eve. How could you leave her here, you low-life bastard."

Barry put an extra two feet between them.

"What are you talking about? She was getting better when I left for Chicago," he said, his voice taking on a whining, self-righteous tone. "She had pills."

Matt said nothing.

"When I talked to you at the office today, you got me thinking. I became worried so I came to check on Eve."

"At 3:00 a.m.," Matt said dryly.

Barry shrugged. "This was the first chance I had."

"Well, here's a news flash—she's asleep. So... crawl back into the same hole you slithered out of. And don't forget to leave your key on the counter."

Barry's eyes narrowed haughtily. "Who the hell are you to give me orders?"

"I'm Eve's new best friend."

"Says who?"

"Says me," a small voice said.

Both men reacted as if a bomb had gone off beside them. Eve stood directly behind Matt, one hand on the doorknob, the other at her throat, gripping the fabric of her robe, which Matt had run across while hunting for her medical records. He'd draped it on the foot of her bed.

"Eve, you shouldn't be up," he gently scolded, noting the grayish color around her cheekbones.

She shifted her gaze from Barry to look into Matt's eyes. Fatigue was there, but so was an element he recognized as pure Eve. Newscaster Eve. The Eve who could make a president sweat.

She lifted her chin, then looked at Barry. "This won't take long."

She took a breath. Matt saw her knuckles whiten on the doorknob. "You're scum, Barry. You lied to me. Get out of here and don't come back. If Communitex wants to sue me for breach of contract, then so be it. I could care less."

LaPointer snorted. "Don't try to make me the bad guy here, Eve. You snapped up Communitex's offer faster than a catfish in my daddy's pond. 'Give me editorial control and I'll follow you anywhere,' you said." His nasty falsetto made Matt want to punch him again. "You're a *face*, Eve, a very famous face. But that wasn't good enough for you, was it? You had to have your little dream show—the story behind the news. Like that would ever fly."

Matt saw Eve shudder. Before he could say anything, she regrouped. Her eyes narrowed and she said, "You wouldn't recognize the truth if it flew out of your nose and danced for you. Get out of here. Now. If you ever try to contact me again, I'll invite one of my journalist friends to sit down and listen to the horror story of your business practices and your personal cowardice."

Her voice faltered slightly. Matt moved to her side

and wrapped his arm around her shoulders. Hopefully, the move looked more like a gesture of friendly support than a move to prevent her from crumpling to the ground.

"Well said. Let's step over here so the man can vamoose."

They walked to the bed Matt had been sleeping in. When he was confident she was seated comfortably, he turned and faced the man who seemed to be preparing some kind of verbal defense. Matt wasn't interested. "In case you're not familiar with Eve's background, Barry," he said, "her ex-fiancé is a judge. A man of considerable power and influence. In fact, I'm not a reporter. I'm a private investigator.

"Judge Bishop hired me to find Eve. The judge is very upset by all this, and believe me, once Eve's well enough to give a deposition, he'll be asking for a full investigation into your role in this matter."

Matt caught the look of surprise on Eve's face and hastily stepped in front of her. "No decent human being," he said as snidely as possible, "walks off and abandons a person who's too sick to even call a doctor. I don't know what the hell you're doing here tonight, but I wouldn't mind calling the police and letting them figure it out."

Barry put on a good show—all puffy indignation and self-righteous denial, but he pitched his key on the bed on his way past. "This isn't my fault. It's Eve's," he snapped, pausing in the doorway of the bedroom. "She's the one who made promises she couldn't fill. She told me she'd picked up a bug. She'd also mentioned she suffered from anemia and all she needed was a little R&R. I'm the one who's been juggling nervous executives and irate producers for the past two weeks.

"I went to Chicago to finesse an extension, Eve. A reprieve so you could salvage your career. But do you take those pills I got you? No. You have to play the prima donna—just like every other beautiful woman I've ever met."

His lips curled back in a grimace. "Only now, you're not even beautiful. You're a scarecrow. Who the hell would want to watch you on the news? You're enough to make me puke."

Matt's fist curled, but Barry backed out of reach. "You can tell Judge Bishop that if anybody does any suing around here, it'll be Communitex." He looked at Matt and sneered. "So help me, if I go down, I'm taking her with me."

Matt started toward him. "Great. If we're going to court anyway, I might as well rearrange your face first. Whatta I gotta lose?" Matt faked his best Bronx accent.

"No, Matt." Eve's soft whisper made him halt in his tracks. "Let him go. He's not worth it."

No doubt recognizing a lucky break when he saw it, Barry fled. The door slammed with enough force to make Eve shudder.

"I'll be right back," Matt told her. "I want to make sure it's locked."

MATT CLICKED the dead bolt, making a mental note to get the locks changed before he left town. He hurried back to his room and found Eve curled on her side, sobbing. His heart twisted in his chest.

"Eve, don't cry. You said yourself, he isn't worth it." He walked to the bed and sat down beside her.

She curled a little tighter, her chin tucked against her knees.

"Are you upset about what he said? The heck with Communitex. Once you get better, you can probably get your old job back." His tone sounded falsely bright—which it was. He'd caught the morning show twice this week. In Eve's place was a stunning new anchorperson—too blond and cute and chipper for his taste, but Matt knew she'd appeal to a lot of viewers.

Eve took a deep breath and rolled to her back. Her cheek was less than an inch from his hand. Eyes closed, arm across her forehead, she sighed, "Some of what he said was true. This is my fault. I refused to see my doctor in New York because I was afraid he'd tell me not to take the Communitex offer."

"I still don't understand how you could risk your health for a job."

Her lips trembled and her long lashes fluttered against her cheeks. "I thought it was my chance for the whole ball of wax. Barry was so sweet and persuasive when we met. I actually believed we had a shot at something together, both professionally and personally."

For some reason, the thought made Matt ill.

She shook her head. "When he first called me in New York, I thought he was a headhunter who lived in Atlanta. It wasn't until later that I found out he not only works for Communitex, but his father is CEO. Snagging me was some kind of coup to show Daddy how brilliant his son could be."

Matt still didn't get it. His image of Eve as the

savvy news anchor just didn't jibe with a woman who would bank on the slippery promises of a glib salesman. "Didn't you check him out?"

"Yes." She nodded then frowned. "Some." Her bottom lip trembled. "Obviously not enough."

It took her a few seconds to master her emotions, then she said, "I saw the risk, but at that point in my life, I was willing to gamble." She looked at him, her eyes pleading. "I'm not normally an impulsive person, Matt. But something...a report—an issue I cared about—was edited badly and when Barry promised me editorial control of my own stories, I jumped at the chance. Physically, I was run-down. But I was just plain tired, too. Tired of my life, all the traveling. I listened to what I wanted to hear—blue skies, friendly people, editorial control, a chance to make a difference."

Two tears slipped from the corners of her eyes. Matt realized if he lifted his thumb, he could catch one tear before it landed on the mattress.

Shaking his head, he took a gulp of air and forced himself to move. This wasn't good. Totally unprofessional. He rose and walked to the door. "Can I get you something? Warm milk? Tea?"

"No. Come back. Please. I need to talk to somebody and..."

Her tone held such yearning Matt was powerless to resist. Since she was angled sideways—closer to the head of the bed than the foot, Matt took the lower half and sat down. He sank backward, using his elbows for support.

"Hey, this isn't over," he said, trying to sound

positive. "Tomorrow, we'll get you hooked up with a doctor. If it is anemia, you can lick it. Right?"

She sighed. "I don't know. It was never this bad. The first time it happened was when I started my period. I think my poor mother thought I was faking it to get out of gym class or something. She kept sending me to school, then I fainted in English class and whacked my head on a desk." A tiny smile touched her lips. "The next time was in college. I had pneumonia one spring and couldn't seem to get over it. They had me in the hospital for three weeks. They told my parents it might be leukemia. Finally, they gave me a transfusion and the next morning I was dancing on the bed. This time it could have been caused by the bug I picked up in Panama and couldn't seem to shake."

Matt frowned. "If you knew what the problem is why didn't you get help?"

She looked at the ceiling and let out a long sigh. "Part of the Communitex deal involved a huge publicity push. Barry said if word got out about my illness I'd be viewed as a liability, and it might adversely affect the stock value." She turned her face away. "And I really thought I'd bounce back once I was rested. So why risk everything? The public is fickle, Barry was right about that."

Her casual acknowledgment of her industry's shallowness baffled him. How could anybody work in that kind of business?

As if reading his mind, Eve said, "That's one of the reasons I wanted this job. I saw it as an opportunity to make changes, enlighten people about the faces behind the camera images they see."

Matt winced sheepishly. He was just as guilty. He'd callously pigeonholed Eve right up to the minute he met her.

She sighed. "My main goal was to reach girls and young women. They're the biggest demographic in the industry, but we fill their heads with complete and utter crap. Nobody talks about inner beauty, values, morality, health issues. When I was thirteen and I..." Her voice petered out, like a wind-up toy that had run out of steam.

"I'd better get you back to your bed," Matt said.

Yawning, she said, "Maybe I should stay here. In case Barry comes back. He's probably got a second set of keys." She turned her chin to look at him. There was nothing flirtatious about her suggestion. Just something sad and lonely.

Matt told himself the smart thing to do would be to carry her to her room and pray nothing else happened until he could get her to a doctor. But, heedless of his better judgment, he reached out to brush a stray lock of hair from her eyes. It refused to cooperate. He inched a fraction closer and used the tip of his finger to nudge the strand behind her dainty ear.

"Okay," he said. Matt twisted to his side, resting his cheek in his palm. Once Eve was asleep, he decided, he'd carry her back to her own bed.

A smile flickered across her lips. She closed her eyes. "Thanks, by the way."

"For what?"

"For punching Barry."

"What makes you think I punched him?"

Her eyebrows constricted. "Maybe I dreamed it." Her features relaxed and her voice started to fade like a bad connection on a cell phone. "A good dream...for a change."

Matt studied her lips. He wished he had some balm to heal them, but he didn't. Tomorrow. He'd add that to his list.

Her robe, a thick purple thing made of the nubby material he associated with bedspreads, exposed a V of pale white flesh that rose and fell with each breath. His blood stirred in a way that annoyed him. He had no business looking. He rolled away, sliding his elbow under his head as a pillow. He closed his eyes to plan the coming day's agenda. *First, I talk to Mom and get the name of the doctor, then...*

THE FOLLOWING MORNING, Matt set the ball in motion —once he'd recovered from the shock of awakening with Eve Masterson in his arms. He wasn't sure how that had happened, but he promised himself a stern lecture once he got Eve settled. He called his mother for the number of a specialist, then made that call. The doctor wanted Eve to come directly to the hospital—a small, private facility that was known for its discretion. The man sounded gravely concerned about Eve's condition.

"Eve," Matt said, squatting beside the bed where he'd left her sleeping. "I brought the car around out front. We need to go now."

She roused herself enough to blink, twice. Her color was wan, her eyes bleary. "No." She shook her head. "Not out front. Might be press. Paparazzi."

Two thoughts hit simultaneously: even sicker than hell she's worried about her image, and she was right about the risk.

Damn. Why didn't I think of that? Matt's only thought had been to warm the car, and he'd left it running out front where the doorman could watch it.

"Sweetheart, I'm sorry. We don't have time to move it. I'm going to wrap you up in this blanket and carry you. No one will see you," he told her, pulling a pair of heavy socks onto her feet. "It's damn cold out this morning."

She accepted his help without comment, but he could feel her unease.

"Besides," he said, trying to lighten the moment, "it's three days till Christmas. Nobody's going to be looking at you."

His tone must have come off sharper than he'd intended because she seemed to shrink into the blanket. Feeling like a heel, he picked her up. She clenched the blanket to her chest and kept her chin tucked tight as they exited her apartment.

Thankfully, the elevator was empty. The only sound came from the overhead speakers—a jingly beat of an updated version of "O Christmas Tree." The seasonal carol must have touched a chord with Eve because she looked up at him and smiled. "Shouldn't you be somewhere else? With your family?"

Matt experienced a sudden unexplainable urge to kiss her. Fortunately, the doorman greeted them the instant the elevator doors opened. "Good morning, Miss Masterson. So sorry you're under the weather. Please let me know if we can be any help," he said, escorting them across the lobby.

Eve nodded and tried to smile, but Matt could tell

her strength was gone. He picked up the pace, praying his gimpy knee would hold.

With formal dignity, the doorman held the exterior door open, wishing Eve a ''speedy recovery'' as they walked past.

As he neared the car, a sudden niggling sensation made Matt lose focus on his step. His knee wobbled but he was able to right himself without stumbling. Concentrating on reaching the rental car, he limped to the street. Within seconds, she was tucked in the car. Matt tipped the doorman then hurried around to the other side of the car and got in.

''We're almost home free,'' he told her, ignoring the nervous glitch in his belly—his cop's instincts. ''I'll have you at the hospital in no time, then all you have to concentrate on is getting well.'' At least Matt hoped it would be that easy, but something told him nothing about Eve Masterson's life was ever quite that simple.

CHAPTER SIX

MATT TWISTED the lid off his two-dollar bottle of water with enough force to decapitate a chicken. He'd run out of patience five hours ago. His usual calm resignation had been replaced by impatient pacing in the hallway. He wasn't sure why, but it had something to do with the fact that Eve Masterson looked so ill in the big sterile hospital bed. His heart hadn't been able to take it—especially seeing the array of tubes attached to her thin, white arm.

"Sir? Your wife's blood work is back," a nurse said, dragging Matt off his restless loop.

"Is it bad?" Matt asked.

The woman, a forty-something brunette with a large faded burgundy birthmark on her cheek, glanced at the chart then said, "Whoops. You're not married."

"No, but we're planning on it." Matt didn't consider that a lie. He might possibly remarry someday, and he was sure Eve planned to be wed sometime in the future—just not to him.

"Well..." She shot a sideways glance to her associate—a pert, Meg Ryan–ish redhead with a lilting accent. The other nurse shrugged. "Hemoglobin's at four. And her platelets are down. Way down."

"What does that mean?"

She frowned. "The doctor will discuss it with Miss Masterson when he comes back."

"When will that be?"

Her bemused look seemed to say "whenever." Matt understood. "I get your drift. My mom's been a nurse in New York for twenty years."

The two women looked up with interest. He fed them a few nursing stories that made them laugh, and they shared a few bits of inconsequential trivia with him. Then the redhead said, "I was so surprised to see Eve Masterson on our patient list. The last I heard, she was going to be Communitex's golden girl." She made air quotes with her fingers. "It was all very hush-hush, but my husband golfs with Dag LaPointer, the CEO."

Her friend pointed at Eve's chart. "You can't do much of anything when your hemo's that low. I'm surprised she's still functioning."

Matt's heart bottomed out near his stomach. "She's going to be okay, isn't she?"

The two nurses looked at each other before the redhead said, "She'll be fine. She's a lucky gal to have you sticking by her side—even if the hospital is a lousy place to spend Christmas."

Despite the tasteful holiday decor in the hallway and waiting room, the holiday's proximity hadn't sunk into Matt's consciousness.

Frowning, he walked to Eve's room.

SOFTLY CLOSING THE DOOR behind him, Matt glanced at Eve—still asleep. Wrung-out, no doubt, from the battery of tests and X rays and the MRI she'd had that morning. Matt had spent much of the time in the cafeteria or outside making the requisite calls to Sara, Bo and his mother.

Sara—the only who'd been home to take his call—had been weepy, gushing on about how heroically Matt had saved Eve's life.

"I'm nobody's hero, Sara," he'd said shortly. "This is my job. You'll get a bill."

Of course, no job in the past had included opening his eyes to find a famous television star curled up beside him. Matt had yet to figure out how that had happened. *The chilly temperature combined with the gravitational pull of two warm bodies?* But that didn't explain the attraction he felt toward her. Something not only unprofessional but also unrealistic.

As Matt approached the bed, he tried to tell himself the only thing he felt for Eve was pity. And maybe a little bit of awe. After all, he'd never met a celebrity before. He was entitled to be a little impressed, wasn't he?

Coming to a stop at the foot of her bed, Matt thought—not for the first time—that even ill, Eve was one of the most beautiful women he'd ever met. Desirable. Unattainable. *Totally out of my league.*

He crossed the room to the pair of armchairs situated near the window. He glanced outside at the iron-gray clouds pressing low to the earth. In the distance the sound of a siren seemed to grow in volume, but he couldn't see any flashing red light. Before sitting down, he stripped off his sweater—a remarkably dignified navy-and-hunter-green-striped crew neck Ashley had given him last Christmas.

Thinking of Ashley made him pull his cellular phone from the pocket of his leather jacket, which was draped over the back of the chair. He punched in the code then took a sip of water.

"Hello."

He closed his eyes in gratitude. Ashley, not Sonya. "Hi, it's me. How ya' doing?"

"Hi, Daddy! I'm okay, but I have the hugest zit on my nose. It's so gross and now Bridgett's invited some boys to her Christmas party tonight. And her brother's home from college."

"You're beautiful—zit or no zit," he told her.

"Oh, Daddy, you don't understand."

That was true. His daughter was perfect in every way that counted, but she seemed to run herself down at every opportunity. Any glitch in her clothes or body was cause for grief.

He just didn't get it, and probably never would. But he had a feeling Eve would understand. Unfortunately, despite her own conviction, the message her profession gave was that looks were everything. Matt didn't want his daughter believing that. Ashley was so much more than that.

"Is everything working out with Eve?" she asked, her tone too disingenuous to be real.

"Not exactly. She's in the hospital, honey. That's for your ears only, by the way."

Ashley made a sympathetic sound. "Will she have to stay there over Christmas?"

He hoped not. "I don't know, hon, they're still running tests."

"Oh. That's too bad. Did you call to talk to Mom? She's not here. You know, Daddy, I'm starting to get a little worried about her. She hasn't felt too hot lately."

Matt shrugged it off. Sonya pushed herself—and the people she loved—to the limit. "It's probably stress. Your mom wants everything to be perfect."

"I know. Especially *me*," Ashley wailed.

"You *are* perfect." He smiled at her happy laugh.

Glancing toward the bed, Matt saw that Eve was awake and looking at him. A funny hiccup in his chest made him rub the fingers of his free hand over his breastbone. "Ashley, I have to go. I'll call as soon as I get back to town. Forget about the zit, and have fun at the party. I love you."

He turned off the phone and put it back in his jacket pocket then rose and walked to the bed.

"Hi," he said. "Feeling any better?"

She aligned herself a little straighter, fussing with her pillow. Without asking permission, Matt pressed the arrow key on the control pad attached to the bed rail. A motor hummed as the head of the bed lifted. He stopped it at forty degrees.

Eve smiled. "Typical guy. Get within ten feet of a remote and they have to press buttons."

"Humor is encouraging," he said, crossing his arms to keep from touching her.

She sighed. "You mean there's hope I'm not brain dead? I don't know if that can be determined until after an autopsy. What other reason could there be for getting involved with Barry?"

Her self-disgust was obvious. Matt hated to see her beat herself up over one slip in judgment. "So you made a little mistake. Big deal. I heard the doctor say that bug you picked up in Panama really zapped you and is probably to blame for the anemia." He rested his hip on the bed—far enough from her to be discreet. "If that's true, then you can't be held account-able for anything you said or did in the last few months. It's the law," he added, trying to keep a straight face.

"The law according to Matthew Michael Ross?" Her eyes seemed to sparkle with a hint of her re-nowned wit.

"Hey, your brain is back online."

She sagged. "Enough to know I owe you a huge thanks."

Matt shifted uncomfortably. "Let's hold off on that until the book's closed on this case, okay?" Maybe his tone was too stiff and businesslike. She looked a little hurt.

"I talked to Sara," he said, changing the subject. "She sounded relieved to hear you're getting the care you need. She said she'd contact your parents in Aus-tralia and tell them you're okay. I gave her this num-ber and she promised to call tonight after Ren gets home."

"I keep thinking about what might have happened if Ren and Sara hadn't sent you to find me. I might be dead if it weren't for you, Matt."

Matt felt himself blush, but he didn't reply because she closed her eyes and sighed. Her energy seemed to retreat like an ocean tide. He depressed the down arrow of the control pad then tugged the soft woven blanket around her shoulders. He studied her face sev-eral minutes before making himself turn away.

Give it a rest, Ross.

He picked up his jacket intending to head outside for a walk when the phone in his pocket jingled. He pulled it out and pressed the talk button.

"Hey, cuz," his cousin said, his natural exuberance echoing across the line. "I just talked to Sara. Sounds like Eve's in good hands. I guess you can head home."

Matt grimaced. Somehow he'd known that was what his cousin would say.

"I'm not sure I can do that," he said sheepishly.

There was a small pause, then Bo asked, "Why not?"

Good question. "I don't know exactly. I guess I feel sorry for her. You wouldn't believe the mess in her apartment. Boxes everywhere. And I've got to do something about the lock situation. I don't trust that jerk Barry not to have another key." He paused. "By the way, what'd you find out about him?"

"I'm still working my way past the basics. Gimme a break. You're the computer geek, not me."

Bo made an odd sound—sort of a strangled laugh. "But I think it's safe to say he's no prize. I'm sure Eve would feel safer if you stick around. We don't have anything pressing in New York until after the first of the year."

Matt frowned. "I don't plan on staying *that* long. I can't miss Christmas Eve with Ashley, but I may hang around here until Saturday."

"Okay," Bo said, drawing out the word as if following another train of thought. "That's cool." He cleared his throat, then added, "Um, cuz, you're not by any chance falling for her, are you?"

Matt blew out a harsh sigh. "Dammit, Bo, number one—this is my job. She may be famous, but I'm not some starstruck teenager. Number two—she's ill. She's not the same woman we used to see every morning on television.'' He made sure by his tone Bo caught his meaning. ''Mainly, this is Christmas, and I can't help feeling sorry for her. All right?''

''Okay. Okay. I get it. Don't bite my head off. You just sounded different. My mistake.''

They said goodbye then Matt pocketed his phone. Glancing over his shoulder, he was relieved to see Eve still asleep. He hadn't been entirely truthful with Bo, but it was better than admitting to the world the depth of his foolishness. He might be attracted to Eve in the worst way, but with any luck nobody would ever know it.

EVE LAY as still as possible, her heart hammering in her chest. She'd been asleep until the sound of a low voice had entered her dream. Matt's voice. At first she didn't try to make sense of the words. It was comfort enough to know he was near. He was her anchor to reality, which, if she stopped to think about it, was an odd thing since they'd known each other less than twenty-four hours. But then, the phrase ''This is my job'' sank in.

The sleepy fog disappeared.

She missed some of what followed but understood what wasn't said. *Not the same woman...*

A heavy weight pressed on her chest making it hard to breathe. *Why did I think he was different?*

She strained to catch the rest of his words, but made out only something that sounded like, ''I can't help feeling sorry for her.''

A deep sadness seeped through her bones. Numb, she remained motionless until she knew he was gone, then she rolled to her back and stared blankly at the ceiling.

When did everything go haywire? she wondered. *When did I stop thinking with my head and let my heart lead me astray?* Tears threatened, but she was too tired to cry.

What does it matter? she mused. So, he pities me. Why not? I'm pitiful. I brought all of this on myself. If I'd paid more attention to my health than to Barry's promises, I wouldn't be in this mess. Maybe that's the lesson I needed to learn—to put Eve first.

But who is *Eve?* A little voice asked. *The beauty queen? The celebrity? Or a woman with two pasts and a questionable future?*

Sighing, she closed her eyes and welcomed the gentle oblivion of sleep.

EVE COULDN'T GAUGE how long she'd slept, but when she opened her eyes she still felt far from rested. "When am I not going to feel so tired?" she muttered.

"Soon," a voice said.

Eve lifted her head from the pillow. A man in a white lab coat stood in the doorway. Something about his dark complexion, receding hairline and thick glasses looked vaguely familiar. "You're my doctor."

He awarded her with a smile. "Yes. How are you feeling—besides tired?"

He walked to the bed and took her wrist in his hand. While he did "doctor things"—like flashing a light in her eyes, examining her tongue and throat, and listening to her heart, he explained the test results that had returned. Eve caught about a third of what he was saying.

"You think the anemia is a result of the bug I caught?" she asked.

He patted her hand. "It's a possibility, Eve. But we still don't know for sure."

"What did you say about a blood transfusion?"

He ducked his head as if trying to avoid being pinned down for an answer. "Again. A *possibility*. We need to run a few more tests."

Eve frowned. "How can you expect my body to build up blood when you keep taking it from me?"

He smiled as if pleased by her little show of testiness. "You need to rest and let your body tell us how to fix what's wrong. Time will tell."

She scowled. "That's easy for you to say. You get to go home for Christmas."

His sigh sounded sympathetic, but it was interrupted by a commotion at the door. Something green and bushy waltzed into the room. A tree. A five-foot fir was doing some kind of two-step with Matt, who peeked around its aromatic branches.

"Have tree will travel," he said, grinning.

"Matt," she exclaimed. Eve was thankful she wasn't attached to a heart monitor—it would have drawn a brigade of nurses with a crash cart. "What's all this?"

He gave her a droll look. "It's a Christmas tree, of course."

"It's beautiful," Eve said, eyeing the healthy green specimen. She spotted a telltale cord. "Does it have lights?"

Matt pretended to be surprised. "Uh-oh. Maybe

this was the display model." He gave her a roguish smile. "Too late now. It's yours. Where should I put it?"

As he glanced around, he suddenly stiffened, apparently spotting her doctor. He set down the tree, making sure its plastic stand was properly aligned, then walked to greet the man.

"Matt Ross."

"Ahmed Krist."

They shook hands. "I can come back later," Matt said. "Didn't mean to interrupt."

Krist beamed. "No, no. We're done here. Aren't we, Eve? Or do you have other questions?"

If she did, they were lost in the ozone.

He smiled and nodded, then started to walk away. He stopped by the door, and—as if it was an afterthought—added, "I'll check in with you tomorrow. I've faxed your blood tests to a hematologist at Johns Hopkins."

Matt cleared his throat and said, "Um, Dr. Krist." Eve had never seen him out of his element, but he looked decidedly uncomfortable. "My mother is a nurse in New York. I was just on the phone with her and...if Eve approves, I'd like to keep Mom in the loop. She's volunteered to act as Eve's advocate to help her understand what's going on." He held up his hands in a conciliatory manner. "Nothing official. Just for moral support." He shrugged. "She said even the most savvy patient can use an outside opinion to maintain some perspective. And Mom has a lot of great resources, too."

He glanced at Eve as if asking for her take on his suggestion.

"That's really generous, Matt," she said, slightly overwhelmed that a stranger would volunteer her time so freely.

The doctor took a moment to consider. "My only hesitation would stem from your celebrity status, Eve, but if you're comfortable with it, I have no objection." He looked at Matt. "Give the nurses all the details and we'll see what we can do."

Once the doctor was gone, Matt walked to Eve's side. "I'd planned to run that by you first, but I hated to pass up the opportunity to talk to him. Are you sure it's okay with you?"

She reached out and touched the back of his hand. "Are you sure your mother wants to do this? I feel like such a nuisance."

He pulled his cellular phone out of his pocket and punched in a number. A second later, he held it out to her. "Here. Ask her yourself."

Eve gulped and hesitantly put the phone to her ear. The voice that greeted her immediately put Eve at ease. After introducing herself, Irene Ross explained about the advocacy idea and her years of experience. "I'm just an extra set of eyes," Irene said. "A friend. Nothing more."

Eve watched Matt fussing with an extension cord he'd pulled from the pocket of his flight jacket. "I truly appreciate your volunteering to help," Eve said, "but it's the holidays. Surely you're too busy—"

Irene cut her off. "Nothing is more important to me than family. My Matthew is worried about you. If he worries, I worry."

"But, it's his job to worry."

There was a pause. Then Irene chuckled. "Dear

girl, you don't know Matt very well, but I can assure you, you're more than a job to him—even if he doesn't realize it himself yet.''

Eve started to protest, but his mother added, ''Matt hasn't shown this much interest in a woman since his accident. Well…there was that physical therapist, but when you've cheated death, you're entitled to one mistake.''

Eve felt her face heat up and a tingle of emotion spin through her body. Matt slipped the phone from her weak grip. He studied Eve's face as he told his mother sternly, ''What did you say to her? She looks ready to faint again.''

Whatever Irene answered, it didn't appear to sit well with Matt who turned away so Eve couldn't hear him. She sank back against the pillow and let out a long, slow breath. Matt's mother was wrong. He had no interest in Eve outside of work, and that was a good thing. The best thing for both of them, really. Eve's life was a shambles—both healthwise and careerwise. Romance was out of the question.

''Are you okay?'' Matt asked, cutting into her train of thought. ''Mom has great heart—she's the most loving, accepting person I know, but she's also a mother. She…meddles a little—actually a lot.''

Eve nodded. ''I understand. Ren's mom was the same way. Her name is Babe. What a character! She had us married before our second date.'' She sighed. ''We haven't spoken in ages…just lost touch somehow…''

He smiled and reached out to take her hand. A soft squeeze. Supportive. Reassuring. Nothing more, she told herself. It lasted a heartbeat, and then he released her and walked toward the tree.

"Okay," he said, his voice catching. He cleared his throat and started whistling a Christmas carol. "Let's plug in this baby and hang some ornaments."

"You bought ornaments?"

His grin reminded her of a little boy on Santa's lap. "Nope. But I managed to find some of the classiest ones I've ever seen."

For the first time, Eve noticed a brown paper bag sitting on the floor near the tree. Matt picked it up and opened it with a flourish. "Voilà!" he exclaimed with a magician's drama. "Is this one pretty or what?"

He produced a four-inch porcelain ballerina in a faded pink-net tutu. He held it by its golden string, and the dark-haired dancer began to twirl.

Eve's eyes filled with tears. They were *her* ornaments. Ones her mother had sent years before.

"Mom started a tradition of buying my brother and me a dated ornament each year. That one was when I was twelve, I think."

Matt turned it upside down to check the date. "That sounds about right," he said. "Did you do ballet?"

She closed her eyes and pictured those early years. "Ballet, tap, jazz—you name it, I did it all. Mom thought it would give me poise." She looked at him and grinned. "Puberty was hell for me, and I was a terrible klutz in my younger years."

"Me, too. Then I discovered football and I had something else to worry about—like getting pummeled by two-hundred-pound tackles."

Eve laughed. "What position did you play?"

He made a face. "Quarterback. High school, only. I wasn't good enough for college. Besides, by then I knew I wanted to be a cop. I've always been an all-or-nothing sort of guy." His broad, powerful-looking shoulders rose and fell. "Guess that's just the way I am."

He turned away and carefully hung the ballerina on a prominent branch, then glanced at Eve for approval.

She nodded enthusiastically.

The next one was a little house with glittery snow on the roof. "My first home. Mom gave it to me when I bought my condo in Roseville."

Eve sighed, suddenly missing her parents. "I haven't put up a tree in years. Just too busy. December's a horrible time of year for a holiday."

Matt smiled. "I stumbled across the box—and I mean that literally, when I went back to your apartment to meet the lock guy." He stopped what he was doing and fished a shiny new key out the pocket of his denims. "By the way, here's your new one. I'll put it in the drawer for now, okay?"

Eve nodded, but just barely. Fatigue was creeping back.

She forced her eyes to stay open. He moved to her bedside and back in what looked like slow motion. "When I saw the box, I took it as a sign," he said. "I stopped at a tree lot on my way here." His hands made a so-sue-me gesture. "Hey, everybody sends flowers when someone's in the hospital. I just like to be different."

Eve's chuckle got trapped in her throat; its humming sensation passed through her body, reminding her of how she'd felt when Matt touched her. "You are that, Matt Ross. Different from any other man I've ever known.''

There was a moment of awkward silence, but Matt banished it by plugging in the cord. Tiny white lights twinkled to life. The tears in her eyes made them look like crystal moonbeams. She wanted to stay awake and supervise the placement of ornaments, but she couldn't.

''Thank you, Matt. For everything.''
For saving me, she silently added.

THREE DAYS LATER, Eve gazed at her little tree with renewed appreciation. Since putting it up Thursday evening, Matt had added something new each time he visited her. This morning—Christmas Eve morning—he'd brought an angel for the top. Not your traditional angel, either, she thought, a warm feeling spreading through her.

''I can't believe you found a dark-haired angel,'' she said, chewing on the last of her breakfast croissant—another gift from Matt.

''I found it in a shop in Little Five Points,'' he said, glancing at the tree. ''Ray, your doorman, knows everything there is to know about this city.'' A smile lifted one corner of his mouth in the rueful way she liked so much.

She was going to miss him something fierce, but she knew better than to tell him that. ''When does your flight leave?'' Eve asked, trying to sound upbeat. Now that she was feeling stronger, it didn't take too much effort. ''You can't be late.''

''I have time. I'm taking a taxi. I left the rental car

in your garage. Like I told you, I'll be back as soon as they give you walking papers.''

His light chuckle settled just below her tummy. "Who needs to walk?" she said impulsively. "I feel as if I could fly."

His eyebrows lowered as if something was bothering him.

"What?" Eve asked.

"I just can't quite believe this miracle recovery. I mean, yesterday morning you looked a little better, but you were still..."

"Sickly," she supplied.

Eve sat up a little straighter. She took a deep breath and rolled her shoulders, reveling in the action. She couldn't quite believe it herself. Within thirty minutes after her transfusion she was sitting up in bed; two hours later she was standing. By the time Matt returned from his shopping excursion, she was walking—with help.

"Even my mother was surprised," he said, running his hand across the back of his neck.

She loved watching him move—the simplest gesture seemed so healthy and sexy. But she made herself look past him to the bright scene outside the window. The sun was shining; a gusty wind batted around the treetops. Matt's cheeks had been pink when he came in.

"Looks like a good day to travel," she said. She started to get out of bed, but Matt stopped her.

"Have you been cleared to walk alone?"

His concern touched her, but she ignored the feeling. He pitied her; he was probably worried that she'd have a relapse, and he'd have to spend more time in

Atlanta. "I'm taking it easy," she said a bit testily. "I was only going to the chair."

"Sorry," he said, a sheepish look on his face. "Can I help?"

Yes. Of course. Let me lean on you. "No, thanks."

Eve pulled the edges of her robe together and swung her legs over the side of the bed. She tossed her head, enjoying the feel of clean hair brushing against her shoulders. The motion undermined her equilibrium. Bright lights flashed behind her eyes and she felt herself wobble.

"Eve," he said, suddenly at her side. "Don't push it. You're not a hundred percent, yet."

She knew that. "It's not my fault they gave me the blood of a sixteen-year-old," she grumbled in jest. "I have energy to spare."

"If you lie back down, I'll let you open your Christmas presents," he said, his tone teasing.

"Presents? Oh, Matt, no," Eve wailed. "You've done so much already." She felt pressure building in her sinuses. She couldn't cry; she'd vowed to be positive and strong so he wouldn't feel sorry for her. "And I don't have anything for you. I tried. This morning. But I couldn't find anyone who'd deliver today. Even for double or triple their normal rates. They laughed at me."

A dark look passed across his face, and he turned to walk to a large shopping bag that he'd set just inside the door. Eve hadn't even noticed it until now. In his navy cords and festive sweater, he looked so incredibly handsome. How could she possibly care so much for someone she'd known less than a week?

Drawing on years of practice, Eve put on a public

facade to hide the ache inside. She knew Matt's true feelings about her, and she would make this leave-taking as easy as possible for him. It was the least she could do.

Matt kept his back to Eve long enough to corral his wayward emotions. He simply hadn't expected her to look so...vibrant this morning. Yesterday afternoon, he'd had his first warning of how beautiful her hair looked when it was clean and brushed. But this morning the silky black tresses draped over her shoulders like a veil—a shiny contrast to the teal velour fabric of her robe.

Matt had been commissioned the day before to locate Eve's *favorite* robe and nightgown—even if he had to "open every damn box in the place." He peeked over his shoulder. She sat on the bed like a queen. Chin high. Hands folded in her lap.

Regal. Remember that. She's not your type, and you sure as hell aren't hers.

Her comment about trying to get gifts delivered sounded like the Eve he'd been expecting to meet when he arrived in Atlanta. Well, not quite. She didn't come off bossy or demanding; but she was a person who knew what she wanted and had the money to back it up.

There wasn't anything wrong with that, he told himself. But it made his gifts seem a bit—cheap. *Oh, well, bite the bullet and get it over with so you can fly home,* he told himself.

"I got you a couple of things. Little things. Silly things," he said, rising with care. His knee had been throbbing all morning, and he wasn't looking forward to his cramped commercial flight, but Ashley was expecting him. And he wasn't about to disappoint his daughter.

Blinking as if to refocus her thoughts, Eve looked at him and smiled. Something was different about this smile. It seemed practiced. Artificial.

He almost changed his mind, but then she spotted the little gift bag dangling from his fingers. Her smile blossomed. Her eyes lit up. "Isn't it adorable?" she exclaimed, reaching for the bag adorned with a goofy-looking moose with a string of colorful lights tangled in his antlers.

"It reminded me of my Christmas lights back home," Matt said, pleased by her girlish laughter.

Grinning, she fished inside and withdrew a plump tube of lavender-scented body lotion.

"It's supposed to be calming," she said, looking at him with a smile that rocked him off center.

She snapped open the lid and rubbed a dab on her arms and at her neck. "Mmm, I love it," she murmured, closing her eyes to inhale. Her eyelids still retained a purplish hue. "What do you think?" She extended her arm for a sniff.

Matt frowned. The scent brought back the memory of her sleeping beside him that first night.

"Am I taking too long?" she asked, apparently seeing his expression.

"No," he answered. Too sharply. "Take your time."

She smiled tentatively and peeked over the lip of the second bag he handed her. "Hmm...this looks promising," she said, withdrawing a gift-wrapped rectangle. She worked her fingernail under the flap, extricating a slim book with a colorful cover.

Silently she read the title then quickly flipped it over to scan the back blurb. "*A Map of Your Night World.* A learner's guidebook to dreams." She looked up, a slightly stunned expression on her face. "Did I tell you about my dreams?"

He shrugged. "You mentioned something. I know when I was coming off medication..." He caught himself. Now wasn't the time to get into his history. "I had some pretty heavy dreams for a while. I thought this might help make sense of them."

Her expression of wonder made him uncomfortable, so he reached behind his back for a box wrapped in shiny blue and gold foil.

She shook her head in an innocent gesture that made her hair shimmy provocatively. "Ooh, this one's too pretty to open."

"It's just paper. Dig in."

She sighed in defeat and ripped it down the middle. Paper flew in every direction. Matt held his breath as she removed the lid of the box. Nestled on white tissue paper was a set of mohair mittens, hat and muffler. Ruby red. Soft as kittens.

"Oh, my goodness. Matt," she exclaimed, pulling on the hat. Red on black—just as dramatic as he'd envisioned. She tossed the muffler around her neck with verve then plunged her hands in the mittens. "Absolutely gorgeous."

He shrugged, trying not to show how pleased he was that she liked his gift. "I thought the color would look good with your hair. And you're going to need something to wear home besides a blanket."

Unshed tears made her eyes luminous, and it was all Matt could do to keep from kissing her.

"Oh, Matt, this is all so special. Come here. Let me give you a hug."

Hug, Ross. Got that?

He tried. But the touch of her hand cloaked in mohair, the scent of lavender. Maybe the fact this was Christmas and she was in the hospital. But when she put her arms around his neck and pulled him down for the obligatory hug, Matt moved incrementally to the middle. Instead of a kiss on the cheek, she delivered his kiss on the lips.

Her warm, wonderful lips. Almost healed. Soft and full. A gift he hadn't asked for, and most definitely couldn't return.

Matt made himself back away. He shrugged on his jacket.

"Umm…Merry Christmas," he said inanely.

Eve smiled, looking as radiant as the angel atop her tree. "It is—*very merry*—thanks to you."

Feeling as giddy as a thirteen-year-old, Matt shoved his hands into the pockets of his coat and encountered a piece of paper. "By the way," he said opening the folded sheet of stationery. "I copied down the messages on your answering machine. The majority were calls from your parents and Sara, but some were from friends. See?"

Leaning down, he placed the sheet on her lap. "There were a few—four to be exact—that bothered me. Same voice. Raspy. Sounded mechanically altered." Although nothing in the messages was explicitly threatening, the general tone had given Matt the creeps. "The voice kept referring to you as 'Even Mine.'"

Eve didn't answer. She pushed the paper away and rolled to her side facing the wall.

"Eve," he said, placing a hand on her shoulder. "Don't shut me out. Could this be Barry...or maybe a stalker? Maybe we should notify the police—"

She shivered. "No, Matt. It's not Barry. It's...it's just a prank. Let it go. Please."

The desperation in her plea made him agree. How could he fight her? But Matt hated loose ends and he planned to tie up this one the minute he returned to Atlanta.

CHAPTER SEVEN

"SO, BROTHER DEAREST, what's this about Sonya and Alan moving to the West Coast?" Deborah asked, ambushing Matt before he could shrug off his jacket. Ashley had raced in ahead of him and was nowhere in sight.

Matt inhaled deeply. He loved the smell of his parents' home at Christmas—it smelled like family. From the sporadic cries of glee coming from the direction of the family room, Matt could tell Ashley had made contact with her cousins. Deborah had four kids—sixteen-year-old Andrew, eight-year-old Delia and the twins, Kevin and David, who were five.

"Surely you aren't going to let Sonya get away with that," Deborah insisted.

Matt took off his gloves and crammed them in his pockets. "Merry Christmas, sis," he said, kissing her warm cheek. Deborah was six years older than Matt and built like their father—stocky and compact.

Never known for her tact, Deb's blunt, cut-to-the-chase attitude had earned her the vice presidency in her union job.

"It's nothing definite," Matt said, taking a wooden hanger from the closet. After he closed the door, he took another step into the foyer and inhaled deeply. "I smell pumpkin pie." His stomach rumbled. "I've been on the run all morning and a bag of stale nuts on the airplane just didn't cut it. Are there any appetizers?''

Deborah waved toward the kitchen. ''A zillion. But I want to know what you're going to do about this. You can't let Ashley go without a fight. I just read that schools in California—''

Matt cut her off by looping his arm around her shoulders and squeezing. He loved his sister, but she was famous for producing off-the-wall statistics that could never be proven. ''Sis, I appreciate your concern but don't start worrying about something that might not happen. You know what Grandpa Ross always said, 'It's gotta rain before there can be a flood.'''

She made a face. ''I can't help it, Matt. I'm worried about you.'' She patted his cheek and sighed. ''Mom thinks you'll turn into a hermit if Ashley moves. We hardly see you as it is.''

Matt shrugged. ''She's our mother. It's her job to worry. But I'm fine. Truly. In fact, I'm too busy to do my laundry, let alone brood.''

She looked curious. ''Really? Whatcha doing? Are you seeing anybody?'' Matt knew that look. Her matchmaker look. She'd set him up so many times Matt had lost count.

''I'm on a job for Bo at the moment,'' he said, steering her toward the kitchen. ''But I'm not at liberty to speak about it.''

''Because it's someone famous,'' Ashley said, suddenly materializing at his side. She threw her arms around his waist and hugged him fiercely. Matt slipped his free arm over her shoulder and squeezed. *What will I do if Sonya moves?*

"Who?" Deborah asked, eyes wide with curiosity.

"It's a secret. She's sick, but not rehab sick. Right, Dad?"

Matt wasn't comfortable talking about Eve. It was bad enough that she'd stayed in his mind the whole flight home. Even when he watched Ashley complete her final series of maneuvers on her horse, Matt's mind had been rehashing their goodbye kiss. A mistake for sure.

"She's a celebrity. She's been sick and needed a little help. Let's go find the grub. I'm starved."

Deborah balked. "No fair. Ashley knows. I wanna know."

Matt snickered. "You sound like a five year old. Speaking of which, where are your kids?"

"I won't tell anybody," Deborah wheedled. "Please."

"Don't feel bad if he won't tell you, Aunt Deb. I only know because I was eavesdropping, which—" she smiled impishly "—is a very bad thing to do. Right, Dad?"

Matt cuffed her hair lightly. "Terrible. Good thing Santa was too busy to check his list twice or you'd be out of luck this year."

She laughed and raised on tiptoe to kiss his cheek.

Deborah said, "Speaking of gifts, kiddo. Would you round up the rest of the bunch? We're going to let each child open one gift before dinner."

Ashley's lips formed a perfect O. "Awesome! I know which one I want to open first. The big one from you, Dad."

She dashed away, her long legs getting caught up in her floor-length black velvet skirt. A white satin blouse with full sleeves would have given her a Victorian look—but for the Doc Martens on her feet.

"Isn't she something?" he asked softly.

Deborah nodded, her eyes filling with tears. "We'll all miss her so much if she moves away. It'll break David's and Kevin's hearts," she said.

Not as badly as mine. Matt shook his head. He'd told himself he wouldn't be melancholy. "It's Christmas Eve, sis. Let's just enjoy the moment. At least we're together. We could be alone in a hospital like—" He bit off the word *Eve.*

Deborah jumped on his oversight. "Like *who?* Tell me, Matthew. I'll make you tell. I know how to get it out of you, little brother."

She needled him all the way to the kitchen, where Matt grabbed a plate of goodies and a glass of wine. Her pestering came close to breaking down his resolve, but the image of Eve, alone in her hospital room, solidified his silence.

Later, when the family gathered around the six-foot tree to watch the children, Eve's secret was still safe. But how safe was the woman herself? There was still that matter of the mysterious caller she'd refused to tell Matt about.

"Daddy," Ashley called, drawing him back to the festivities. "I'm going to open this one from you, okay?"

Matt glanced at his mother who'd been watching him with a knowing smile. He'd hear about this later. "Go for it, sweetheart."

Wrapping paper flew, followed a moment later by

a squeal of joy. "My own laptop. Oh, Daddy, thank you so much. This is so awesome."

Matt let out a sigh of relief.

"We'll get it plugged in while we eat and maybe you can take Grandpa online after dinner. Scare the pants off him."

Jacob Ross—a silent, stalwart man of sixty-four—gave his son a dark look. "Hmmph."

Ashley hugged Matt. "I love you, Daddy."

"Me, too, hon," he whispered, his throat tightening. "Now you can keep in touch with me no matter where you are. E-mail." Matt tried to keep his tone light, but inside he was losing it. E-mail wasn't even a close second to seeing her, watching her ride her big ugly horse or sharing microwave popcorn while enjoying a video. He felt like a man watching his whole life slide down a hillside. All he could do was pray there'd be a few pieces to pick up once it stopped.

"YOU'RE IN LUCK, Eve," Joy, the night nurse, told her. They'd already joked about the irony of women with their names being stuck in a hospital on Christmas Eve. "The cook went all out—clam chowder and pecan pie. Not bad, hey?"

Eve was ravenous. She could feel her strength building each hour. After Matt left, she'd even walked to the window. "Great. So far, the food's been wonderful. Maybe I should do a piece on five-star hospitals."

"Public relations would love you, but some people come to us because we're so private." Joy set the tray on the movable table and waited while Eve positioned herself correctly.

"Like me," Eve said softly.

Joy shrugged. "You're not the first celebrity whose been here—won't be the last. With an NFL team in the neighborhood, you get all kinds of calamities popping up. Don't even ask."

Eve smiled. "Don't worry. I'm pretty much out of the news business at the moment." She spoke flippantly, but a part of her despaired at where her career was going.

"You're kidding. I loved watching you in the morning. What are you going to do?"

Eve busied herself with tucking her napkin into the neckline of her nightgown—the nightgown Matt had found for her. She knew she was stalling but Joy waited for an answer. "I'd like to try producing. I once had an idea for a talk show for young girls. Something that would help them work on self-esteem issues."

Joy's brown eyes lit up. "Oh, man, could my little sister use some of that. She's really into makeup and shopping, and the fashions out there make her look like either a hooker or a biker. And skinny," she said with a shudder. "Why do they think they have to be size zero?"

She seemed to catch herself a second and a blush claimed her pudgy cheeks. "I d-didn't mean," she stuttered.

Eve made a backhanded gesture. "Forget it. I'm probably a subzero right now. And this is not a good size to be. Trust me. Because of my job I've always watched my weight, and when I got sick, I didn't have much of a reserve to fall back on.''

Joy seemed to relax. "With your face, you could be a size twelve and men would still be interested.''

"Maybe. But that's not necessarily a good thing.'' At Joy's look of confusion, Eve said, "Why does it always have to be about looks? I've traded on mine my whole life and what has it gotten me? I'm alone on Christmas Eve. What does that tell you?''

Joy made a face. "I hadn't thought about it like that.''

Eve didn't want the kind woman's sympathy. She wanted to change things. She sat forward and drummed her fingers on her knee. "You know what I really want to do? Create a show that reaches young women. The teen years are so important, yet they've been reduced to a marketing target. In retail, if you're a hit with young girls, you've got it made.''

"Wow,'' Joy exclaimed. "You just light up when you start talking about that. I wish my sister could hear you.''

They chatted a few minutes longer then Joy returned to her rounds. Feeling restless and a tad melancholy, Eve toyed with her pie. Although she hadn't mentioned it to Joy, Eve could pinpoint the exact minute she'd made up her mind to do a show for young girls. It started with Deeanna West's obituary. Sixteen years old. A chubby, pimple-faced girl who'd stepped in front of an express train.

Deeanna's story had been Eve's first assignment after her return from Panama. Still suffering from the effects of the virus, Eve had visited Deeanna's home. The instant she'd walked into the young girl's bedroom, Eve had been overwhelmed by a sense of futility. From the posters on her walls to the glossy glamour magazines by her bed, it was obvious Deeanna had dreamed of an image far beyond reach.

But for the grace of God, so go I, Eve thought. Her junior-high years had been hell. Her dark, exotic features had made her stand out when all she'd wanted to do was fit in. If her mother hadn't encouraged her to participate in her first pageant—Eve had come in third, ahead of four blond girls—who knows what might have happened?

But that had been then, and although success in the pageants had improved Eve's self-esteem, she longed to be able to teach young women like Deeanna that beauty is way overrated. People need to be judged from the inside out, not the other way around.

The jingle of the phone startled her. Maybe it's Matt, she thought, unable to prevent the rush of emotions that came with his name. *Dumb, Eve. Give it a rest. He's not looking for a relationship and you sure as heck shouldn't be.*

"Hello. Merry Christmas."

"Eve!" her mother exclaimed. "We finally got through. It's been a nightmare trying to find you. God bless Sara Bishop."

"Hi, Mom," Eve said, reclining her bed a few degrees. "Is Dad there with you?"

There was a slight delay in the transmission before Kathleen Masterson's answer came across the line. "He's right here beside me. Sara said you're doing great, honey. Do you need us to come back?"

"No, Mom. I'm fine. Really I am."

Her father's booming laugh caught her in the middle of the chest with the impact of a Ford truck. "That's my girl. Your mother was going bonkers, but I told her you were made of sturdy stuff like your old man. You'll be back on your feet in no time."

Like your old man... Eve didn't usually dwell on the past, her fate, her adoption. But this near-death experience had changed her somehow.

"I feel good, but I've had a lot of time on my hands and I got to thinking...if you had it to do over again, would you still adopt me?"

In the two-second transmission delay, Eve's heart constricted to the size of a pea. Her lungs couldn't fill with air and she felt woozy.

"Oh, Eve, we're coming back right this minute. I knew we should have come as soon we found out you were sick. If you have to ask me something like that then you're in worse shape then you let on and you need your parents."

The answer had come in one long breath and Eve smiled, her own breath releasing with a sigh. "No, Mom. It's okay. Really. Don't come. You and Dad have waited your whole lives for this trip. I was just having weird dreams and then there were a few calls on my machine from...you know who."

Her mother let out an impatient snort. "I wish that woman would give up and disappear. Just ignore her, Eve. You're our beautiful little girl and we love you. Don't ever doubt that."

Even if I'm not beautiful anymore?

Her parents broke into an off-key Christmas carol that made Eve smile, then they both told her goodbye. Blinking back tears, she replaced the receiver.

Joy came in a few minutes later to collect Eve's

tray. "Have a piece of candy? Your *fiancé* left a big box of See's candy at the nurses' station."

She and Eve shared a smile. Eve had told them Matt wasn't truly her fiancé. "By the way, where is he tonight?" Joy asked.

"In New York with his family. He has a twelve-year-old daughter."

"Really? Is he divorced?"

Eve nodded.

Joy made a thoughtful sound. "Do you like kids?"

"Are you none-too-subtly playing matchmaker?"

"Hey, the guy's crazy about you. He brought you a tree. I've never had a man even offer to help me decorate a tree. Do you know how special that is?"

Eve knew. But the truth was he was in New York and she was here. Alone.

That word annoyed her. It kept popping up trying to spoil the mood she was trying to maintain. She picked up the remote control and turned on the television. Maybe with any luck, she could find a cheerful holiday movie—preferably something that didn't include hearth, home and family.

She flicked through the stations—right past *It's A Wonderful Life* and the ubiquitous *Miracle on 34th Street.* She settled on a Hollywood gossip show because she thought there was a chance someone she knew might be having a worse holiday than she was.

Absently staring at the muted screen, she nearly choked on her chocolate treat when a familiar face caught her eye. Matt? The grainy black and white image obviously was taken with a telescopic lens. Eve's apartment building was in the background. In

Matt's arms was a bundled form with a pair of life-less-looking feet dangling over one arm.

''Oh, no,'' she groaned, flopping back on her pillow.

She hit the volume button. The commentator—a woman Eve once met at a fashion dinner came back on the screen. ''Who this mystery man is is anybody's guess. Where he took Eve Masterson also remains a mystery. A spokesperson for Communitex, the Internet giant that reportedly hired Eve Masterson away from this station two months ago, told *Spotlight on Celebs* that Ms. Masterson's whereabouts was a mystery to him. As far as he knew, Eve was on sick leave. A mysterious illness, perhaps? Until we find Mr. Mystery Man, it will remain just that—a mystery.''

''Quality journalism,'' Eve snarled. ''Five frigging lines and you used the word *mystery* six times.''

Her head began to throb as adrenaline flooded her system. Her pulse raced. Was this Barry's handiwork? Maybe he figured that by starting a firestorm of bad publicity around her he could deflect from himself any blame for her nonappearance as Communitex's star.

She grabbed the phone. Maybe she couldn't save herself, but she sure as heck could warn Matt. She hated to interrupt his Christmas with his family, but she'd never forgive herself if some reporter showed up on his doorstep and she hadn't given him some kind of heads-up.

She punched in the number he'd scribbled on the back of his business card.

''Ross residence. Deborah speaking.''

Matt's sister. Eve took a breath and asked for Matt. The woman called him to the phone. "Hello?"

"Matt, it's Eve." She hated the breathless quality in her voice. Her heart wouldn't stay steady. "Something's come up. Barry's dirty work, I imagine."

He listened attentively while she explained about the show and the possible fallout that might come from it. "I'm going home in the morning," she said. "I won't feel—"

He interrupted. "Did your doctor give you the okay?"

"Not yet, but he will. I know my body, Matt. I'm on the mend. I can feel it."

"Aren't you the same person who refused to see a doctor because you knew your body and thought you could fix it yourself?"

Eve's face grew warm. "Hey, this is still Christmas Eve, Mr. Ross. Watch the attitude or Santa will put a lump of coal in your stocking."

Matt cleared his throat. "I'm sorry. That wasn't called for. But this sounds like a rash move, Eve. The hospital deals with security issues all the time. They'll keep you safe until I get back."

Eve liked the sound of that, but she wasn't some needy child, and for some reason it was important to make Matt believe that. "Don't worry, Matt. I'll hire a private nurse, if the doctor insists. I'd just feel safer at my apartment. Barry told me it was a veritable fortress. Nobody can get in without permission, so once I get home, I'll be safe."

"And we all believe everything Barry has to say," Matt said snidely.

Eve rolled her eyes. "I read the brochure. The security system at my building is state-of-the-art. Now, get back to your family and have a wonderful holiday. If you still want to come back and check up on me, you know where to find me. Tell your mom I said hi." She swallowed against the tightness in her throat. "Bye."

She put the phone back on the nightstand and let out a long, slow sigh. She'd made up her mind and knew what she had to do.

Half a dozen calls later, the plan was in motion. Exhausted, Eve turned off the lights and snuggled beneath the covers. She rolled to her side to gaze at her little Christmas tree. The miniature white lights sparkled like fireflies.

Matt isn't going to like this, Joy had predicted.

Eve knew that for a fact. He'd already called back twice and even put his mother on the line once to try to talk Eve into staying put. But what the Rosses didn't understand—couldn't understand—was Eve's deep-rooted insecurity. There was no way in hell she was going to be photographed looking the way she did at the moment, especially in a hospital bed.

The Eve Masterson that millions of people saw on television each morning was an amalgamation—a product of thirty years of work. The hair. The smile. The rapier wit. Eve couldn't help frowning at the contradiction her life had become. Here she was protecting her own image but wanting young women everywhere to know that outward appearances aren't everything.

She squeezed her eyes tight and wrapped her arms around her knees. Her world was on the verge of imploding, and there was very little she could do about it except hunker down and wait.

Earlier that morning, when Matt had asked about the strange caller on her answering machine, Eve had panicked. What was she supposed to say? She wasn't ready for him to know the truth.

Eve's head ached and her heart felt old and tired. She considered buzzing Joy to ask for a sleeping pill but decided against it. She'd need her wits about her in the morning.

Where was Santa when she needed him?

"DON'T WORRY, Ashley, I kept the receipts," Deborah said as Ashley carefully eased her thumb under a piece of tape. Her aunt always took her gifts to a fancy wrapping center. "Last time we talked, you were into LL Bean, so I did the catalog thing this year."

Ashley's excitement increased. There were cool things in that catalog. In fact, that's where she'd ordered her dad's sweater last Christmas. And she knew he liked it because he wore it a lot—and not just when he knew she was going to be around.

She looked at her father. He occupied one of the two matching recliners—Grandpa had the other one. Although his eyes were trained on the scene before him, Ashley sensed his mind was somewhere else, and she had a feeling it was because of Eve Masterson.

"Hurry up, slowpoke," Ashley's cousin Andrew said. He was four years her senior and full of himself.

Ashley purposely drew out each movement.

"Mother," Andrew groaned. "She's being a brat."

That seemed to get her father's attention. He sat forward, the footrest of his recliner folding beneath the seat. "Hey, who you callin' a brat, mister? You wanna talk about it outside?"

Andrew leapt to his feet. "Snowballs to the death!" he cried.

Aunt Deborah, who was holding Delia on her lap, intervened. "I don't *think* so. Sit down, both of you. Ashley, honey, speed it up. The little ones—" she nodded at Andrew and Matt "—are getting antsy."

Snickering, Ashley whipped open the box. She found a fabulous cream-colored fisherman-knit sweater and black, cuffed hip huggers. "Your dad gave me the sizes," Deborah said.

Ashley reached across the distance and hugged her aunt—pesky little cousin and all. "Thanks so much. I love them both. Truly. I'll wear them on the plane tomorrow."

Suddenly everyone went quiet. The air felt charged and awkward. Ashley held her breath waiting for someone to say something.

"Whoa. It's like someone farted in church," Andrew said.

Ashley slugged him.

Her grandmother leapt to her feet and made a motion with her arm. "Come on, everyone. Pie and coffee in the kitchen."

The entire crowd piled out of the room—all except Ashley and her dad. "I blew it, didn't I?" She couldn't look at him. Her heart squeezed against her chest like someone was standing on her back.

He crossed to where she was still kneeling and put his hand on top of her head. It felt as warm and comforting as a hug. She knew it was hard for him to get up and down, so she jumped to her feet and wrapped her arms around his middle. Tears gushed from her eyes for no reason.

"Don't cry, baby," he said, stroking her hair. "It's Christmas."

"I know, and it sucks," she cried.

He made a father sound. "Such language. What would Santa say?"

She cried all the harder. "What if I have to move, Dad?" she blubbered against the fabric of his corduroy shirt—her gift to him, along with a new wallet. "I won't fit in out there. All the girls are skinny and blond and perfect. I have big teeth and frizzy hair and a fat butt."

"Baby doll, what's this all about?" He pressed a kiss to the top of her head. "You're the most beautiful girl in the world. And that includes California," he added dryly.

She tried to smile for his sake. "Oh, Daddy, you don't understand. You're not a girl."

He frowned, his face full of worry. "Grandma and Aunt Deb are—"

"Old, Daddy," she whispered tersely.

He looked as if he was trying not to laugh.

"I'm serious, Dad. Mom thinks I should be able to adjust just because she wants it to be so. But I'm afraid. I won't know anybody out there. It's not like here. I have friends, my riding friends. We're different from the perfect girls. But out there, it'll just be me. And I won't fit in."

Her father made a funny sound in his throat. "I

think I know somebody who would understand, Ash. Eve."

"Eve?" Ashley hooted. "Oh, puh-leeze. She's gorgeous. What would Eve Masterson know about being dumpy and shy?"

"Eve Masterson?" Deborah chirped as she walked past with one of the twins. "Is *she* your client, Matt? Ohmygod. Jimmy, guess who Matt's working for in Atlanta?"

Ashley grimaced. "Sorry, Dad."

He gave her a stern look. "I wonder if it's too late to take back that laptop." A wink told her he was joking.

Laughing, she took his hand and led the way to the kitchen. "You're crazy. I'm going to call Eve and warn her that she's hired a crazy man."

"Oh, trust me, honey, she already *knows* that."

Ashley wasn't sure what he meant, but she knew better than to ask for details. His work was private and she'd already pushed her luck far enough for one night.

CHAPTER EIGHT

MATT FINISHED PACKING and checked his watch. Still early. The house was quiet. He hoped to slip out and be on his way without waking his parents. Deb and her family had returned home last night; Alan had picked up Ashley a little before midnight. Matt and Ashley had managed to get in a little quality time playing video games before her stepfather had arrived. Since his parents were spending Christmas with Bo's parents at the rehabilitation center, Matt had decided to return to Atlanta.

Walking softly, he carried his briefcase and carry-on bag to the kitchen to microwave a cup of coffee. To his surprise his mother was standing at the stove. The image of her in a thick robe and slippers, her silver-threaded brown hair uncombed, brought back fond memories of Christmases past.

"Hey, lady, what are you doing up? This is your chance to sleep in," he said softly. Walking up behind her, he looped his arms around her middle and gave her a hug.

The smell of bacon sizzling in the pan made his mouth water.

"I know what airplane food is like. The least I can do is send you off with a good breakfast."

Matt glanced at the white enamel clock above the

sink. "I should have time. Traffic can't be that bad yet. It's Christmas morning. Thanks, Mom."

He took a seat at the counter and watched her crack eggs into the pan. For as long as he could remember, his mother had been in his corner. She'd cheered him on after his accident, consoled him when his marriage fell apart. But lately, he'd sensed a bit of strain between them. "Mom, are you upset with me?"

She whirled around. "Of course not. Should I be? What'd you do?"

He snickered at her tone. "Nothing. I just wondered if you blamed me for Sonya's decision to take Ash to California."

Irene sighed and went back to ladling hot grease over the glossy yellow yolks in the pan. "Son, life throws us a few wrinkles from time to time. All you can do is get past them and keep going. Sonya and Alan seem very happy. You and Sonya were never a good match. If you ask me, Ashley is better off with two happy parents who don't live together than two miserable parents who do."

Matt buttered the toast she put in front of him. "I agree, but how do we work it when we're on opposite sides of the country? I barely see Ashley now and we're in the same city."

Irene slid the eggs onto a plate then added six slices of bacon.

"Perfect. As always. Thanks, Mom."

After refilling their coffee cups, she sat down on the stool across from him. "Matt, I'm no seer. I can't tell you what will happen next week, let alone next year. But I do know that Ashley will grow up and make a life for herself, maybe thousands of miles from where you live. That's the way life works. All you can do is give her the support she needs to make good decisions wherever she chooses to live."

Matt agreed with a nod as he ate.

Neither spoke for a few minutes, then Irene said, "I have great faith in Ashley. She's a pretty level-headed girl, even if she worries more about her looks than I like, but I guess that's the way with young girls today." She made a dismissing motion with her hand. "I'm more concerned about you than Ashley. She, at least, seems happy *some* of the time."

"I'm happy, Mom. Last night was great. Didn't I smile enough?" he teased.

She snorted then rose and walked to the far counter where a vast array of sweets was assembled. After dinner last night, the children had gathered to frost Christmas cookies with their grandmother—a tradition Irene had started when Andrew had been a toddler.

"I don't mean laughing and smiling. Those are short-term happy. I mean joy. The kind that comes with loving someone and being loved in return."

Matt's appetite vanished. He pushed his plate away and picked up his coffee mug. "Mom, that isn't the kind of thing you can conjure up just because you want it."

She looked at him over one shoulder. "No, but you have to be open to it or you might miss it when your chance comes." She put the lid on the Christmas tin she'd been filling and turned to face him. "You've closed off your heart, Matthew. That young physical therapist who fell for you was a case of bad timing.

You had too much healing to do, but *now,* Matt. Now you could let yourself feel again.''

Matt knew what she was talking about—*whom*—and he didn't want to discuss it. He moved back from the counter and stood. ''Mom, it isn't going to happen.''

Hands on hips, she faced him belligerently. ''Why not? I like her. She's not so uppity-up the way you described her. She's a real person in an unreal job.''

He walked to his mother and pulled her into an embrace. ''Mom, you're the best. I love you. And I appreciate everything you've done for Eve. I know she does, too. But drop the matchmaking. I'm flying back there today because she's upset about some news story that broke.'' He forced a chuckle. ''If she's that bent out of shape over the media finding out about her hospital stay, do you really think she'd date a private eye?''

Irene sighed and shook her head. ''Son, for a smart man, you are sometimes very obtuse. Did it ever occur to you she might have called just to get you back to Atlanta?''

Matt stepped back. ''No.'' *Maybe.*

She smiled then, and reached up to pat his cheek. ''You'd better go. Eve needs you.'' There was something smug about the way she said the latter, but Matt ignored it. ''I want you to take these cookies to her. Tell her I said Merry Christmas and to get well soon.''

Matt wedged the tin into his flight bag then gave her one more hug before leaving. She was wrong, of course. She only knew Eve through their telephone calls, which had been quite productive until Irene had suggested sending Eve's chart to a geneticist doing research in the area of chronic anemia and other blood disorders. For some reason, Eve had declined. Adamantly.

MATT'S FLIGHT from La Guardia was fast and relatively painless. He spent most of the time reading a new techno-thriller his father had given him for Christmas. Before he knew it, he was back in Atlanta.

The weather was balmy—the high forties compared to the twenty-degree temperature he'd just left. His first dilemma was whether to go straight to Eve's. He called the hospital, but someone new was on the desk at the hospital and refused to disclose any information about anything. The answering machine picked up at Eve's.

When his cab pulled to the curb of the apartment building, Matt paid the driver then stepped beneath the green and silver awning. He stood for a moment and took a deep breath. The air felt invigorating. He hadn't been to the gym in weeks and really felt out of shape. *My New Year's resolution,* he thought, turning toward the entrance.

As he did, a small crowd surged out of nowhere. Before he could blink, two women with loud voices approached Matt asking questions he couldn't hear. They were flanked by two men with cameras.

Matt put his head down and shouldered his way to the steps. The doorman opened the door for Matt alone, blocking the others from gaining access.

"Good Lord, Ray," Matt exclaimed. "What the hell was that all about?"

Ray gave a resigned shrug. "Started showin' up

last night. Lookin' for Miss Masterson. Don't know how they got this address. Big pests, if you ask me. Like I told Miss Masterson this morning, they won't get past me,'' the doorman said firmly.

Matt's stomach turned over. Had Eve been subjected to this circus? After handing the doorman a healthy tip, he hurried to the elevator.

When he reached her floor, Matt used the extra key the locksmith had given him to let himself into the apartment. He opened the door quietly, not certain what to expect. The apartment was silent, except for the faint hum of the heating unit and the drip he'd meant to fix in the kitchen faucet.

Stepping into the foyer, he closed the door and locked it. He bent down to place his bag on the floor, and as he straightened, he saw her. Asleep on the couch. The familiar old comforter pulled up to her chin. Her long black hair—clean and glossy—fell in messy disarray from the fuzzy red knit cap. Her hands—swathed in red mohair—were folded, beneath her cheek.

Matt glanced at the answering machine. Four new messages. He took off his coat and walked to the leather recliner across from the sofa. He tucked his gloves in one pocket and sat down, draping the jacket across his knee. The apartment was warm. Something smelled different. Pine.

Her little Christmas tree stood squarely in front of the fireplace. It wasn't plugged in, but its cheerful greenery and bright ornaments gave life to the otherwise bleak room.

With a long sigh, he kicked out his feet, easing the

chair into a reclining position. A nap sounded just about right. He'd earned one.

Through partially closed eyes, he stared at Eve a full minute.

She liked my Christmas present, he thought, closing his eyes.

EVE ESCAPED from her dream with remarkable ease. One minute she was alone in a dark hallway, lost and terrified. The next, she opened her eyes to a landscape of red fuzz.

My mittens. The ones Matt gave me. She stretched as she yawned. She knew where she was.

"Good to be home," she muttered.

"Huh?" a voice grunted.

Eve's adrenaline factor shot off the scale. Her panic dissipated the instant she saw Matt's familiar shape in the chair.

"What are you doing here?" she asked, her voice coming out in a peep.

He pressed the chair into an upright position. "Merry Christmas," he said, yawning. "I could ask you the same question. Did you have to move heaven *and* hell to get here so fast or just one?"

Eve almost grinned, but his teasing had a peculiar edge to it. "There was a Medi-cab available so I grabbed it."

His eyebrows rose and fell. "Were the media sharks circling out front when you got here?"

Eve's stomach clenched. "Yes, but I'd called ahead and the garage attendant kept them out. I didn't see anyone." Frowning, she asked, "Is it bad?"

Matt shrugged. "I have no idea. Nothing to compare it to since I've never been mobbed by reporters before. But it wasn't pleasant.''

Eve looked at her hands. ''No. It never is.''

Matt rose and walked into the kitchen. Eve watched him go. Each time she saw him, she was struck anew by his size and grace—the combination seemed incongruous, but in Matt it worked.

He returned a minute later with a glass of water. ''Drink. Mom said you need lots of fluids. Preferably milk shakes and power drinks to put on a few pounds, but there's nothing in the fridge.''

Eve accepted the glass, her fingers brushing his as the exchange was made. Even that simple, innocent touch made crazy things happen in her extremities— toes, fingers, scalp—the works. She dropped her gaze to keep her emotions hidden. ''Thanks,'' she murmured between swallows.

He returned to his chair. He hunched forward, apparently preparing to lecture her.

Eve beat him to the punch. ''I know you think I should have stayed in the hospital, but I couldn't. You don't know these people like I do, Matt. They're tenacious. Driven. Somehow—bribery, treachery, flat-out bullying—they'd have gotten into the hospital, and I'm just not ready for the world to see me.''

Matt looked truly baffled. ''So what if someone sees you? You're recovering from a serious illness. It's not your fault you got sick. You're human.''

Eve shook her head. ''There's no way I can make you understand. You don't live in this world. You don't know what it's like when your face shows up on the cover of every scandal rag at every checkout counter in America with questions about alien abduction or mystery diseases or drug problems.''

Matt frowned.

''I am my image, Matt. That is the awful truth. And I have to protect it, if I want to stay in this business.''

He sighed. ''Your image won't do you any good if you're dead.''

''I know that. We should think about ordering in some groceries. I'm getting kinda hungry.''

Matt leaned over the arm of the chair for the handle of his flight bag. From its dark recesses, he pulled out a red and green tin box. ''Mom sent you some cookies.''

He stretched across the coffee table to hand it to her.

''Cookies?'' Eve's heart constricted. Her contact with Matt's mother these past few days had blossomed into friendship. Irene was a caring, generous woman who loved her son immensely. This gesture felt like an endorsement of sorts.

''Thanks.'' She accepted the tin without making eye contact. She didn't want Matt to guess what she was thinking. It was probably a silly thought, anyway. What mother would want someone like me for her son? I've got too much baggage—even more than Matt or his mother know about.

TWENTY MINUTES LATER, Matt set the teapot—a smart-looking black enamel number—on a hot pad in front of Eve. He left enough room for her to play solitaire with her cookies, which is what she appeared to be doing. The dozen or so sugar cookies were lined up like cards in columns.

"Is there a system to this madness?"

"Yes," she said, looking up. There were little white crumbs at the corners of her lips and Matt had to lace his fingers behind his back to keep from brushing them away. "They're ranked according to beauty and whimsy. I plan to eat them in order."

"Best first?"

"Of course," she said, reaching for one Matt recognized as Ashley's contribution. The bell-shaped sugar cookie with ornate swirls of green, pink and purple frosting made his teeth hurt just looking at it.

He poured tea into her mug.

"Mmm," Eve said, closing her eyes as she chewed. "Beautiful and tasty."

"You know, Eve, taking into account your beauty-queen background, Dr. Freud might find this whole cookie-thing *very interesting,*" he said.

She brushed away the idea like a pesky fly. "Freud-schmoid. What did he know about cookies?"

She chewed, accenting the movement with moans of ecstasy that made Matt's throat—not to mention other parts of his anatomy—tighten. "Absolutely delicious. Tell your daughter I said so."

"What makes you think Ashley decorated that?"

Eve opened her eyes. "Cookie decorating is like any other art form. Each artist has his or her signature style." She leaned forward to rearrange the remaining cookies. "I would say these three are Ashley's. There's a free-spirited joy to them. The four more traditional ones are from an adult. Your mother?"

Matt nodded. "And the wild ones were done by a younger hand—or someone on drugs."

Matt hooted. "I'm glad to see you've got your cognitive processes back. Very good deductions. You're right about them all, except one."

He selected one from the "child's" pile—a particularly bizarre mishmash of lines and squiggles that resembled an out-of-control doodle. "I made this one." He bit down and chewed.

Eve frowned. "Are you serious?"

He nodded, trying hard to keep from smiling. She looked so consternated he almost burst out laughing.

"Were you on drugs at the time?"

He laughed, and almost choked on his cookie. Eve passed her cup to him. The tea was still hot but he swallowed a gulp then gave it back to her. The heat from the cup mingled with the warmth of her fingers in a way that seeped deeper than seemed possible.

She started to say something, but the phone rang before she could get the words out. Matt didn't like the fear that flashed into her eyes. He considered letting the machine pick up, but opted to answer it.

"Hello," he said sharply.

"Matt?" a female voice exclaimed. "Hey, everybody, it's Matt."

"Sara?"

"Oh, Matt, thank God you're there. Here's Bo."

After a moment of dead air, Bo came on the line. "Hey, cuz, what a break! We were calling your place next. This makes things so much simpler."

Matt cut in. "What the hell are you talking about?"

"You've gotta get out of Atlanta, Matt. All hell's breaking loose. Even Ren and Sara have gotten calls—on Christmas morning, for heaven's sake. So Ren worked it out that you two will fly to Cancún, Mexico, this afternoon. We'll have a rental car waiting for you. Ren's buddy has a great beach house in a resort near Tulum, and the people who were renting it over the holidays bailed at the last minute. Can you believe it? Is that luck or what?''

Luck? Try ludicrous. ''What about work?'' Matt asked. ''I'm supposed to be lining up new jobs.''

''This *is* your job, man. Hell, I'd jump at it in a heartbeat—'' He broke off to speak to someone else. ''No, of course, I'd rather be here with you. I didn't mean *I* want to go to Mexico,'' Matt heard him say.

Matt couldn't keep from grinning. Claudie could keep his cousin on his toes like nobody else could.

''Matt,'' Bo said, his tone tense and impatient, ''just do this, okay? Eve needs the help. You're getting paid. Ashley's gone for the week. You're the only person for the job. Got it?''

Eve cocked her head and mouthed, ''Mexico?''

''Let me get this straight. You want Eve and me to sneak out of the apartment, catch a plane to Cancún, then spend a week at some guy's beach house just to avoid a few reporters?'' Matt had to admit it didn't sound like a *bad* idea—just ridiculous.

''It's worse than that. Here. I'll let Ren explain.''

Ren Bishop, cool and levelheaded, as usual, said, ''Communitex is suing Eve for breach of contract. It's pure and utter bull—legal posturing to create a smoke screen that might keep Communitex solvent through the end of the year. That check you had Bo run on Barry showed how shaky things are there. My friend in the market says there's talk of a buyout.''

Matt had to assume Eve didn't know this part of the story. "The suit is completely bogus," Ren said. "But, in the meantime, you need to lie low. Barry will turn this into a media circus if he gets his hands on Eve."

Matt's resolve solidified. He'd never let that slimeball anywhere near her again.

"The beach house is stocked with beer and goodies. I went online this morning and arranged tickets," Ren said. "All you need is your passport. And Bo said you always carry it when you travel."

Matt looked at Eve. "Do you have your passport?"

She nodded, her eyes round and unblinking. "It's probably still in my Panama bag. I don't think I ever unpacked."

"Good. Don't bother. Looks like we're heading to Mexico."

"Trust me," Matt whispered in Eve's ear as he opened the door leading to the garage. "This is going to be a breeze. We drop off the car, take the shuttle to departures and we're home free. Your own mother wouldn't recognize you in that getup."

Eve reached up to align her wig—a blond bob that had been part of a flapper costume she'd worn one Halloween. Without spirit gum it didn't fit well. Somehow it seemed symbolic of her life—nothing fit anymore. Without warning, she burst into tears. "I'm so sorry to put you through this."

"Sweetheart," he said, the endearment one he undoubtedly used with his daughter, "I don't think spending a week in the Mexican Caribbean is such a bad thing."

Sniffling, she looked up. Even in the dimness of the garage, the humor in his eyes was impossible to miss. "But I know privacy is important to you—especially in your line of work."

His expression changed. "This is my job, Eve. I'll deal with the flack as it comes. Hopefully, we'll dodge the bulk of the hoopla."

It was the word *job* that shut her up. She had to remember that. Matt was doing this as a favor to Ren and Sara. Bo's company would be paid for Matt's time. This wasn't personal, even if there were those who might try to build a romance around it.

When her step faltered, Matt lifted her and walked briskly to the car. Eve kept her chin tucked against her chest in case any photographers were lurking in the shadows. She was exhausted. All she wanted to do was sleep. Preferably with Matt—something she knew wasn't likely to happen. The night in her guest room had been a fluke, but she'd slept nightmare-free. And she wanted that again.

Maybe I could bribe him, she thought. He sure as heck wouldn't do it for sex, but he might take money.

"Would you sleep with me?" she asked, the fatigue making her words slur. "I'd pay you."

He almost dropped her. His arms double-clutched, and Eve liked the way she wound up pressed even tighter to his chest.

"How many of those pills did you take?" he asked, coming to a stop. Eve felt him lean down to open the door of the rental car.

"It's not a pill thing. I just sleep better when you're around. That's what I meant."

He gently deposited her into the passenger seat then

depressed a lever, which made the seat recline. Eve opened her eyes and stared straight ahead, too embarrassed to look at Matt. No doubt her face was as red as her mittens. "Forget it. That was a stupid thing to say. I'm sorry."

She scrunched down until the downy muffler touched the bottom of her lips, and closed her eyes.

This left her wholly unprepared for the touch of Matt's lips on hers. A quick kiss, but friendly.

"We'll be sleeping in the same house for a week," he said, his breath touching her cheek. "You're there for rest and relaxation, but I could use a little of that, too. It's been a tough year."

Eve opened her eyes and looked into his. He was smiling. Really smiling. She wanted to reach out and touch his cheek. Maybe kiss him again and see if they could go beyond *friendly*. But she knew that wouldn't be smart.

She forced a smile. "You're right. This trip is just what the doctor ordered. Maybe there really is a Santa Claus."

CHAPTER NINE

"THIS PLACE HAS CHANGED a lot since the last time I was here," Matt said, taking in the looks of the Cancún airport as they exited the plane. A steward was waiting with a wheelchair. Although Eve had argued against it, Matt noticed she sank into the waiting seat with a sigh. He was worried that this trip was going to be too much for her fragile reserves, but fortunately she'd slept quite a bit of the flight, her head on his shoulder, which was both a good thing and bad.

Although the steward offered—in English—to push Eve, Matt handed him their two carry-on bags instead. "No, *gracias*."

With a cheerful smile, the man directed them to the elevator.

"When were you here?" Eve asked, peering around like a child at a circus. From his vantage point Matt saw that her wig was mussed in the back. Its brassy, ash-blond color made her look washed-out. Her khaki pants and long-sleeve, denim blouse two sizes too big accentuated her thinness.

"I don't remember exactly. Ashley was seven or eight. We left her with my folks," he said, wishing she would sit still. The oversize blouse made it far too easy to look where he shouldn't.

"A second honeymoon?" she asked, her gaze fixed on a splashy travel poster beckoning jungle tours and archaeological sites.

More like a last-ditch effort to save our marriage. "Something like that," Matt lied. At the time, he had termed their problems "a few bumps in the road." Not long after that trip, Sonya had become involved with her plastic surgeon and the road crumbled. "They were just building this place then. We landed at the old airport."

"Hmm," she said, looking down when a young girl offered her a coupon booklet.

"No, *gracias,*" Matt said, shaking his head. The elevator doors opened and he pushed the wheelchair across the threshold.

"Customs," the steward said, pressing the down arrow.

Matt wasn't looking forward to the upcoming ordeal. Their plane had been filled with excited American tourists ready to party for the final week of the year. He feared someone might recognize Eve.

By the time the elevator door opened, the lines of eager travelers had stalled to a tangled V of ants funneling into two or three slots. "Oh, dear," Eve murmured softly.

The young attendant at his side motioned for Matt to follow him. The detour took them to a makeshift gate blocked by a table. An official-looking fellow in a tan uniform met them. After a brief discussion too swift for Matt to catch, the customs officer took their passports and forms and walked to a nearby desk.

Seconds later, the documents were stamped and the barricade moved. Astounded by their good luck, Matt pushed Eve through the gate, but his jocularity vanished when the man asked Eve for her autograph. She did so with a smile, then motioned for Matt to hurry.

He couldn't say what disturbed him the most—the fact she was recognized or the fact he felt like her hired hand.

Which, he reminded himself, *I am.* His job was to get Eve to a safe place where she could recuperate. That did not include kissing her. Or anything else of that nature.

She's a client. Don't ever forget that. You saw the movie The Bodyguard. *You know what happened to Whitney Houston and Kevin Costner.*

"Do you think that could be us?" Eve asked, cutting into his thoughts. Her question stymied him until he followed her outstretched finger. A small intense-looking man with a placard stared at them, smiling hopefully. Matt read the name on the sign and sighed.

"That's us, all right. My stupid cousin has a warped sense of humor."

Eve's low chuckle made gooseflesh appear on his bare forearms despite the muggy heat that enveloped them the instant they passed from the air-conditioned building.

"Señor *y* Señora Matthew Goodfellow, welcome to Cancún," the man said, rushing up to greet them. "Your car is right over here. In the back is a cooler. Ice, *agua, cerveza,* juice."

The car, a four-door sedan, seemed fairly new and reliable. Matt was pleased to see it had air-conditioning. He settled Eve in the passenger seat then put their bags in the trunk. After tipping the wheelchair attendant, he signed the rental car agreement.

The agent gave Matt directions to the nearest shopping area along with a flyer with directions to the beach house where they'd be staying.

"Casa Rosa," Matt said, glancing at the glossy brochure. The two-story rose-colored house looked very inviting. He passed the papers through the window to Eve, then walked around the car to get in.

"It looks heavenly, doesn't it?" Eve said, opening the folded brochure. "I wonder—"

Matt glanced sideways. She was nibbling on her bottom lip—a sure sign she was nervous about something. "You wonder what?"

"I don't want you to be bored. That wouldn't be fair. Maybe we should check into one of the hotels here in Cancún. That way, you could get out and have some fun instead of just hanging around watching me sleep."

I can think of worse things to do, Matt thought.

He didn't answer until he'd negotiated his way through traffic to a huge gray building with the familiar Wal-Mart logo. After he pulled into a parking spot, he turned to face her.

"This isn't about me, Eve. It's about getting you somewhere safe so you can recuperate in peace. That's what I'm getting paid for, okay?"

She didn't answer.

Matt pulled off his sweater and tossed it in the back seat then checked his hip pocket to make sure his wallet was in place. Despite the air-conditioning, his jersey turtleneck was sticking to him like wet paper.

"Are you sure there's nothing *you* need?" he asked.

She started to shake her head, but suddenly reached up and yanked off the wig. It flew over her shoulder like a dust mop to land on top of his sweater. Leaning forward, she worked the pins out of her hair in a feverish frenzy.

Matt watched as bobby pins dropped like spent ammunition. She sighed with pleasure and shook her locks free, then she vigorously massaged her scalp.

"Ahh," she breathed, righting herself with a backward flick of her chin. "I couldn't stand that a minute longer." Shifting in the seat to face him, she removed her sunglasses and looked at him. "I could use some really good hair conditioner." She rattled off several brand names, but they could have been in Spanish for as much sense as they made.

Matt's gaze remained fixed on the intoxicating glimmer of her trademark hair. His fingers itched to draw one glossy section to his cheek.

"Matt?"

The throaty purr added to the intimacy of the moment, but it held enough of a question to draw Matt back to solid ground. He coughed nervously and gracelessly stumbled out the door. "Conditioner. I'll see what I can find."

As he marched to the building, he sternly went over the list of reasons he couldn't get involved with Eve. They were too different. She came with too much baggage. Matt had Ashley's welfare to consider. The list seemed endless.

Maybe I should have Ashley's name tattooed on my forehead, he thought, chuckling under his breath. An in-flight magazine had carried an article about henna tattoos. Supposedly, they wore off after a few weeks. *That would give me enough time,* he thought. Or would it? Something told Matt, Eve Masterson might be in his head for a long, long time to come.

"HOW MUCH FARTHER?" Eve asked, waking up to find the sky fading to a silvery gray. "Did I miss anything?"

"You sound just like Ashley," Matt told her, his tone teasing.

She really liked it when he lightened up and relaxed. During the entire flight he'd seemed poised to jump in front of her anytime anyone looked at her sideways. Eve appreciated his dedication to duty but now that they were out of the rat race, she hoped he'd loosen up.

"I am a kid—at heart. Most people think I'm a workaholic with no sense of humor. But a lot of that is due to demands of the business."

Matt made a funny sound in his throat and she turned to look at him. They hadn't really talked since he'd returned with two overflowing shopping bags and a thick wad of pesos. He'd cracked open two ice-cold juice drinks then they'd been on their way out of town.

"How'd you get into TV?"

Something about his tone made her say, "Don't you mean *why* did I get into broadcast news?" There was enough residual light from the setting sun to see him blush.

She made an offhand gesture and accidentally brushed her fingertips against his arm. Touching was not a good idea. It led to more touching, or at least, wanting more contact. "You get a lot of media exposure when you make it to a certain level in state and national beauty pageants. I actually enjoyed talking with reporters, and one day—at the Miss California, I think—one of the radio deejays got sick and they asked for a volunteer to fill in." She rolled her eyes. "It was a hoot. I was hooked."

"Radio?" he repeated. "Isn't that like feeding caviar to cats? I mean, with your looks…"

Eve blushed. "You have to start somewhere to learn the business. I switched my major to journalism, with an emphasis in broadcasting. My first major gig was in L.A."

"Oh, yeah, I read about that in your bio." The smirk on his lips made her slug his shoulder.

"Hey," he complained.

"Hey, yourself. It was our gimmick. *All Nude— Live!* It was a spoof. You know, like who could tell— because it's radio, right?"

His chuckle felt like a feather tickling her insides.

"Was your other host naked or just you?"

She slugged him again. "We were never naked. My cohost, by the way, was an overweight gay man."

"Sorry," Matt said sheepishly. "I was just kidding. You've always been a class act, Eve. I can't fault you for that. What I don't get is why anyone would want the job. Is fame and fortune worth what you have to give up?"

Eve turned her gaze to the road. A year ago, she'd have said yes. A year ago, she'd had all her ducks in a row, her foot in the big pond and she couldn't have been happier. But now? Now she didn't know what she wanted or why.

Except maybe one thing, but that she wasn't likely to get.

"Right now, all I want is to go swimming," she said in a small voice.

Matt made a peep—as if he'd just pricked his finger on a tack. She glanced sideways. "What?"

"Nothing," he said, meeting her gaze for a fraction of a second. "I just hadn't thought that far ahead. You're supposed to take it slow and easy, remember?"

"Your mother said to listen to my body," she reminded him. "And my body says swim." Seeing his grimace, she added, "Don't worry. I won't drown. Maybe you could outfit me with little water wings until you trust me not to sink."

"I trust you," he said, his voice stern. "But I don't want you to relapse. My Spanish isn't good enough to deal with hospitals and doctors."

Eve settled back in the seat and looked at the scenery flying by.

"I visited two emergency rooms when I was in Panama," she said, trying to suppress a shudder. "Believe me, Matt, I plan to take it very easy."

Matt's shoulder muscles appeared to relax a bit, but she could see his jaw grind.

"Is something wrong?" she asked.

"No. I was just thinking about Ren and Sara doing all of this. The house, the car." He glanced sideways, his expression puzzled. "I can understand why Ren wants to help you, but I still don't get how come Sara is okay with this. I mean, you were engaged to her husband.''

Eve chuckled. ''You haven't met Sara, have you?'

Matt shook his head. ''We've only talked on the phone.''

''The first time I met Sara I pegged her as a sweet, spineless little Goody Two-shoes.'' Laughing, Eve shook her head. ''I think Ren did, too. Sara's the kind of person you overlook until your boat's sinking. When everyone else is running around in a panic, Sara is passing out life jackets—cool as a cucumber.''

''Bo said she's been a little volatile lately, but that might be due to her pregnancy,'' Matt said.

Eve shifted in the seat to face him. ''Oh, I'm not saying she's not extremely passionate about things— Brady, Ren, Claudie's halfway house—but she's so focused and organized she sometimes comes off as laid-back. Believe me, I found that out the first time I returned to Sacramento after moving to New York.''

''This was after you and Ren broke up?''

Eve nodded. ''We parted friends. I knew he was in love with Sara before he did. And I'd just been offered the network job, but from the minute I landed in New York I felt as though I'd grabbed hold of a tornado. It was hang on for dear life or crash and burn.''

We know how that turned out, don't we?

''I used to watch you every morning. You were great,'' Matt said quietly. His words were just what she needed to hear. Straight, simple and, she hoped, sincere.

''Thanks. It was quite a ride. Short, but at certain moments very sweet.''

Eve wasn't ready to think about her career. "As I was saying about Sara, I flew home for my dad's retirement party, and Sara called. She insisted we get together. That was my first glimpse of her grit and determination."

Matt's low chuckle seemed to confirm a similar impression.

"We met at Bo's houseboat of all places. We had the place to ourselves, and we hung out—like a couple of guys."

In truth, Eve couldn't explain how it had happened or why Sara had made the effort, but the two had bonded that afternoon and Eve counted Sara's friendship among her blessings.

"Sara's the reason I came to Atlanta, you know," Matt told her.

"Persistent, isn't she?"

Matt's chuckle touched her like a warm breeze. "She just wouldn't let up—steady, friendly persuasion."

An odd thought entered her head. One she hadn't considered before. Was Matt sent to Atlanta for another reason as well? Could Sara be playing matchmaker?

Before Eve could voice her suspicion, Matt said, "I think we're getting close. Can you read that sign?"

Eve squinted. Her vision was improving, but the headlights of an oncoming car gave the billboard on the side of the road a halo effect. "I think it said Casa something. "

He stepped on the brake and applied the signal to turn left. "Keep your fingers crossed. This looks like a leap of faith to me."

The road—no more than a crushed limestone shoulder—led past a locked, unattended guard house to a lane bordered on each side by a mangrove swamp. "Oh, this is exciting," Eve said. In the past few years, she'd never stayed at any venue less prestigious than the Hilton. "Do you think it's the right place?"

Matt grimaced. "I hope so. I timed the distance on the odometer. We've got to be close."

The car dipped and swayed in birdbath-size potholes—some filled with pale gray water that made a sloshing sound as they oozed through them. Eve was close to suggesting they turn around, when a cinderblock fence appeared with the number five painted in ornate lettering.

"*Cinco.* That's us," she exclaimed, shaking the flyer in triumph.

The tires made a crunching sound as they turned into the driveway. The headlights didn't reveal much of the landscaping aside from neatly groomed palm trees and scattered bushes bearing fist-size flowers. "It looks nice," Eve said. "Downright palatial. Are you sure this is the right place?"

Matt nodded. "It looks like the picture."

He turned off the engine and lights. Quiet, sudden and complete, enveloped them. Without the air conditioner running, the air in the car became stultifying. Despite everything, Eve felt an almost tangible sense of peace. "This might be heaven, you know," she murmured.

Matt glanced at her a second then opened the door and got out. He stretched and looked around. "Do you have the key?'' he asked, squatting beside the door.

Eve fumbled in the outer pocket of her purse. ''Right here.''

''Great. Stay put until I turn on the lights. I'll be right back.''

He took off before she could reply. She collected her purse and bobby pins and sunglasses then opened the door. The air smelled of ocean and plant life. Using the car door for leverage, Eve stood. Her legs still felt slightly disconnected from her body.

The coarse gravel underfoot crackled beneath the soles of her tennis shoes. Eve couldn't wait to take off her shoes. She hoped there was a sandy beach somewhere nearby.

A porch light snapped on, highlighting the rear entrance of the house. A metal screen door sprang open and Matt charged out, a big grin on his face. ''Ohmygod, wait till you see this place.''

His infectious joy took her breath away. She'd never seen this side of him, and it was a hundred times more attractive than his brave, serious businesslike self, which already made regular appearances in her dreams. *Uh-oh, I'm in big trouble now.*

Eve's qualms doubled when Matt picked her up and carried her over the threshold like a new bride. He didn't make a big deal of it, but Eve's heart was barely back to normal when he paused midstride to ask, ''Nice, huh?''

Her chin swung from side to side. Whitewashed walls, wicker, pottery accents of cobalt blue. ''Homey,'' she said, dropping her cargo on the broad rustic dining table. ''Beautiful.''

"Oh, honey, you ain't seen nothing yet," Matt said, grinning. He hefted her a bit higher in his arms and plunged through the airy living room and out a sliding glass door. Eve barely caught a glance of the thatch-covered veranda as he marched ahead.

"Hold on tight," he whispered, his lips close enough to her ear to move a lock of hair. "This sand is tricky."

Eve looked down. Sure enough, white sand. Everywhere. The path Matt followed was lined with six-foot palm trees, bushy and black in the moonlight. "Where...?" The question died on her lips as they crested a slight rise that gave way to a horseshoe-shaped lagoon.

"Oh," she gasped on an inhale.

The moon, which had been drifting in and out of black-bottom clouds, broke free to illuminate the scene. Even though well short of being full, its radiance sparkled on the waves like silver confetti.

"Is this paradise or what?" Matt asked, grinning like a boy.

His joyful tone drew her gaze from the ocean. She lifted her hand to touch his lips in wonder but caught herself in time. Her heart was thudding so loudly she doubted even the sound of the wind and waves could muffle it.

"Yep, it's paradise all right," she muttered with a sinking sensation.

She squirmed to be set down. Matt complied without question. In fact, he seemed a bit embarrassed—as if he'd forgotten he was carrying her.

Spotting a weathered log half buried in the sand, Eve walked to it and sat down with a sigh. She couldn't say for sure why she suddenly felt so troubled.

"Do you need a sweater?" Matt asked solicitously.

Then it struck her. He thinks I'm an invalid. *Good grief. I'm in paradise with the man of my dreams, but I look like the scarecrow from* The Wizard of Oz. *Oh, Sara, what have you done?*

"JUICE?" Matt asked, approaching the half-buried log where Eve was still sitting—unmoved since he'd left her there half an hour earlier.

His eagerness to share the beauty and wonder of their hideaway had been enough to make Matt forget all his lectures about keeping his distance. He'd been quite content to hold her in his arms—right up to the minute he'd felt her withdraw.

She'd seemed so absorbed by her thoughts that Matt backtracked to the house and unloaded the car. He'd even changed into a tank top and shorts—a pair of baggy, knee-length shorts in a gaudy Hawaiian print he'd never wear outside of Mexico, then snagged a couple of drinks from the cooler before seeking her out.

Eve gave a little shudder and sat up straighter. "Oh, hi. What did you say?"

Her tone—slow and weary—troubled him. He handed her the orange soda and sat down beside her. "Are you okay? You need food, don't you?"

She took a drink, tilting her head back to swallow. In the moonlight, her neck resembled an alabaster sculpture. She wiped her mouth with the back of her hand, and smiled when she caught him staring at her.

"I'm not hungry but I should eat something. We need to unpack, too. But, I just...it's so ..perfect."

The moonlight glinted on her hair like silver on satin; her eyes showed fatigue, but something else, too. A sadness that made Matt ache to take her in his arms. He would have if she were anyone else. But she was Eve. Maybe it was time to clear the air.

"Eve, I think we should discuss our relationship."

Her eyes opened wide.

"I don't mean *relationship* relationship. I mean our working relationship."

Her lips formed the word *oh*, but no sound came out.

"Since Bo and Ren set this up, I have no idea who's paying for what, but more than likely you're my boss." Her lips quirked in a near smile. "And I'll do whatever you want, but since I'm the healthy one, I think that puts me in charge."

Her smile grew. Matt liked her smile. A lot. "We've only had a couple of days to get to know each other and here we are sharing a house. So, what I'm proposing is—we just kick back and hang out."

"Like friends?"

Matt attributed the tremulous quaver in her voice to fatigue. "Right. We'll divvy up tasks. I'll do the cooking and shopping. You rest and read."

That made her giggle.

"That's your job, Eve," he said seriously. "To get well. The brochure says there's maid service a couple of times a week, so aside from eating, what's there to do?"

"Won't you be bored?" she asked, burying the toes of her Nikes in the sand.

Instead of answering, Matt wiggled his beer bottle into the sand beside the log then leaned over to draw her foot closer. His fingers felt big and awkward, but he managed to loosen the laces. Then he pulled the shoe off—the sock, too. He did the same with the other foot and placed both shoes on top of the log.

When he looked up, Matt caught a glimmer of tears in her eyes. "Thank you," she said in a husky whisper.

"Okay, but that's the last one," he said after taking a hearty swing of beer.

She blinked. "The last what?"

"The last thank-you. No more until we get back to the States, then you can put them all into one, big fat thank-you." He decided a *little* flirting couldn't hurt. She would be healthy someday. And as Bo often told him, pretty women expected it. "In the form of a kiss, I think. Yep, that sounds fair."

Her smile told him that his flirtation had hit the spot. Unfortunately, those lovely upturned lips also sent a flurry of male hormones off on a mission impossible. Matt took another hasty swallow of beer. Sitting in the moonlight is off the list of things to do with Eve, he decided. It wasn't smart. She tempted him without even trying.

Matt polished off his beer then rose and extended a hand to her. "How 'bout a quick bite then we call it a night?"

That she didn't argue seemed to confirm her fatigue. They walked slowly, and Matt looped his arm around her shoulders—just in case.

"I put your bags upstairs. There are three bedrooms on the main floor, but the top floor's got a killer view," he said, resisting the urge to pull her into his arms and kiss her. *Is there something in the air that's messing with my libido or what?*

"Stairs?" she wailed thinly. "I can't do stairs."

"Not at first. But gradually you'll be able to gauge your improvement by how many stairs you climb." Matt had employed the same principle during his recovery. "Believe me, it's a good exercise. And you can always use one of the other bedrooms during the day, then sleep upstairs at night. Sound fair?"

He felt her nod.

"Why don't you stretch out on the sofa while I whip up some scrambled eggs? We have fresh flour tortillas and avocados and cheese. Will you try a burrito?"

She nodded again.

Twenty minutes and a quarter of a burrito later, Matt carried Eve upstairs. He could feel her trying to rally her strength, but he pressed a light kiss to her nose and whispered, "Go ahead and sleep, sweetheart. In the morning you'll wake up in paradise."

Her sigh warmed his chest. She felt so right in his arms. She'd looped her arms around his neck as if it was the most natural thing in the world. Her hair fell over his arm like satin rain. His gut knotted recalling her suggestion they share a bed, but he knew she was too wiped out to care where she slept, let alone with whom.

Fighting his baser instincts, he deposited her in the marble-walled bathroom instead of her bed—that would have been tempting fate. She turned and hugged him, her chin down. "Thank..." she started to say, but Matt shushed her.

"Save it for my kiss," he said as gently as possible then walked away.

After her light clicked off a few minutes later, Matt restlessly explored the house. He discovered a journal written by former guests. Many left detailed messages about possible excursions and points of interest. Others named local restaurants to try.

Good, Matt thought, mentally taking note of several ideas. With any luck, Eve would recuperate in record time. The sooner she got well, the sooner she'd be up for a little sight-seeing. Not that that was his thing, but, maybe, Matt thought, if he and *Señora Goodfellow* could play tourist, this little vacation would seem less like a honeymoon.

CHAPTER TEN

MATT DECIDED to gamble. Eve had been a perfect patient for four days. Almost perfect. It wasn't her fault she was so damn beautiful in her colorful swimsuit and gauzy cover-up that he was forced to spend most of his daylight hours in the water to keep from doing something unprofessional.

A picnic on a public beach ought to be a safe bet, he decided.

"Are you up for an outing today?" he called, hearing Eve's slow descent to the ground floor. By their second day at the house, she'd mastered the stairs on her own—although Matt still kept a close eye on her just in case she got dizzy.

"Really?" she asked, rounding the corner to peer into the kitchen.

Her eager smile almost caused him to drop the egg he was about to crack into the sizzling pan. Frowning to regain his focus, he said, "I thought we might pick up some *carnitas* and have a picnic. There's a great public beach near the ruins, if I can find it."

"Oh, Matt, that would be wonderful," she said, sliding onto one of the stools at the counter. He'd already set out plates and silverware and two glasses of pineapple juice. "I didn't want to complain, but I have been going a little stir-crazy."

Matt glanced sideways when she made a little bubbling sound. Her mischievous grin made him glad he'd donned an apron.

"I know you'd be happiest if I'd confine my waking moments to reading in the hammock, but after a couple of days that can get a little boring."

Her smile softened the complaint. They both knew she'd spent the better part of those hours asleep in the hammock.

"Hey, I rigged that chair for you in the surf."

In lieu of swimming, he had persuaded her to lounge in a plastic lawn chair that he equipped with an inflated mat to keep her feet floating. Sitting chest deep in the warm surf, she'd giggled with delight when little fish had nibbled on her fingers.

"True, but you spent the whole time hovering on the log behind me."

She'd teased him about being her "strong silent lifeguard" comparing him to the large brown pelican that occupied a roost on an exposed rock a few yards away, but Matt had pretended to be engrossed in his book. It was the only way he could keep from giving in to the insane urge to take her in his arms and make love to her—right there on the beach.

He blamed it on the way her damn hair floated on the water like a mermaid's locks.

"What were you reading, anyway?" Eve asked, taking a sip of juice.

Matt felt his cheeks heat up. He didn't have a clue. "Uh…some mystery." He whipped the pan off the stove and slid two perfect eggs on her plate. The tortillas were already warmed and in a basket beside the tin of butter.

"Aren't you joining me?" she asked as he added a helping of fried potatoes to the plate.

"My mother taught me to cook eggs two at a time. Three max. Perfect eggs require patience and finesse."

Eve ate in silence a minute then said, "Your mom's a cool lady. I really appreciate all she's done to help me."

As his eggs steamed, Matt recalled his mother's parting warning. "Make her rest, Matthew. I mean it," Irene had stressed. "If you care about her, you'll see to it she gets a nap every day."

Matt *cared for* Eve, but not in the way his mother hoped. He wasn't as foolish as he used to be. He no longer believed that love conquered all. Even if he came to adore Eve, to treasure her, he wouldn't commit his heart to a relationship that had no chance of success.

"Since we're going out later, maybe you should rest this—"

"Oh, Matt," Eve groaned. "Couldn't we take a drive? Please."

Her plea got to him. "Okay. We'll go exploring then check the faxes and pick up lunch." He served up his eggs and sat down beside her. "There's a great little shop that sells barbecue pork dinners that come with tortillas, salsa, beans and cabbage salad. I'll put the cooler in the trunk, and I found a big umbrella in the closet. How's that sound?"

He took a bite of eggs and potatoes. When she didn't answer right away, he glanced sideways. It was obvious she was trying to cope with her emotions. His throat tightened and he had to wash down his food with a gulp of juice. The bittersweet taste seemed fitting.

THREE HOURS LATER, Matt was pleased by how well his plan was unfolding. Eve had seemed content to stay in the car while they toured the nearby town of Akumel and barely complained when he wouldn't let her swim with the dolphins at Playa del Carmen.

"Can we visit the ruins sometime?" she asked as they passed the turnoff to the national archaeological site. "I read about Tulum in the travel guide at the house. The Mayan culture was amazingly advanced in some areas."

"Particularly in competitive sports."

"What do you mean?"

"When I was here, our tour guide showed us a stone chopping block where the captain of the losing team lost his head. Literally. I think it was some ancient form of a salary cap."

She looked both amused and skeptical but remained quiet the rest of the way to the beach. That suited Matt since he was having a hard time recalling the exact turnoff. He let out a sigh of relief when he spotted a parking area with half a dozen cars present. "Okay. Here we are."

Three armloads of gear and a gallon of perspiration later, he collapsed on the blanket beside Eve. The umbrella created a teal-blue shelter that for some reason seemed relatively private, despite the scattered groupings of people up and down the beach.

"It's beautiful here," Eve said, shading her eyes with her hand. "Look at the color of that water. Isn't it amazing?"

"Amazing," Matt repeated. Only he wasn't looking at the ocean. He was dazzled by Eve. Each day she seemed to blossom a little more. The brightly patterned cover-up she wore made her resemble an exotic bird—rare and priceless.

She glanced down and caught him staring. Matt scrambled into action, serving their lunch. The aroma of barbecue pork and spicy salsa made his mouth water. He passed Eve a plate.

With a bemused smile, she politely accepted his offering. They ate in silence. Matt had just popped his last bite in his mouth when Eve made a curious sound. He tucked his right leg beneath him and leaned forward to see what she was looking at.

A man stood ten feet away. His back to them, the man's pale skinny buttocks were clearly visible. A hunk of pork became lodged in Matt's throat. Between coughs he said, "Good Lord, this must be a clothing-optional beach now."

"Is this what you meant by sight-seeing?" Eve teased, tearing off a bite of tortilla with her teeth.

Matt took a swallow of beer. He wasn't a prude but a sudden flash of memory—helping a very naked Eve into bed—triggered an uncomfortable reaction.

"Time to go," he said, handing Eve a paper napkin.

"It's not a big deal, Matt. I've been on nude beaches before."

Matt didn't want to think about that. Eve. Nude. On a beach somewhere with hunky guys surrounding her. It was bad enough that he was lusting after Eve, he didn't want to think about all the other men on the planet who had the same thoughts.

"Power-nap time. Nurse's orders."

She didn't argue, but Matt could tell she was disappointed. So was he. It was time to cross picnic lunches on the beach off the list of things he could do with Eve. Matt was beginning to think there wasn't anything he and Eve could do that wouldn't wind up with him in dangerous waters.

EVE EXPELLED a long, noisy sigh the following afternoon as she adjusted the binoculars for a better view of the person snorkeling a couple of hundred yards offshore. Her elbows tingled from the rough surface of the balcony wall. A large floppy hat shaded her nose and eyes from the brilliant sun that warmed and, hopefully, tanned her bare back.

The new color was helping to take the edge off her terminal-patient look, she'd decided that morning when she looked in the mirror. One of the good things about her ambiguous heritage was the generous supply of pigment that turned tan rather than red.

The starved-waif look was another story. Maybe if she weren't so pathetically thin, Matt would be interested in spending time with her instead of communing with the fishes.

A distant splash caught her attention. "Where'd he go?"

The crystal water reflected the brilliant blue sky, making the submerged patches of coral resemble big purple blotches. Matt's long tanned body disappeared beneath a froth of turbulence kicked up by his fins then reappeared moments later. He expelled a blast of water from his snorkel like a whale's spout.

"Damn!" Eve muttered. "I want to be out there, too."

Worse than a mother hen, Matt strictly regulated her activities, but she hated to complain. In truth, he was the perfect...*nursemaid? Housemate? Companion?* She wasn't sure how to label him. He cooked, cleaned, shopped, pampered, praised, scolded and fussed over her. The only problem was, he kept things very businesslike.

Frowning, she studied him in the water. A truly magnificent body—long and lean, but not thin. He was substantial in every sense of the word. Smart and well read, he entertained her in the evenings with board games and crossword puzzles. They'd played two marathon rounds of Yahtzee—each winning one.

Their only major disagreement stemmed from their isolation. Eve was by nature a people person and she liked action. Which was why she'd been so enthusiastic when he'd suggested yesterday's picnic.

"And we all know how well that turned out," Eve muttered, turning from her outlook.

She set the binoculars on the ledge and stepped back, her bare feet tingling from the heat of the terra-cotta tile. The private, walled second-floor patio lacked the shady roof of the lower veranda.

Dashing to her padded chaise, she flopped into the towel-covered chair. The heat imparted a sense of well-being, but Eve knew she was a long way from being completely recovered. One look at her bra told her that. Glancing down, she frowned. You could fit two fingers in that gap, she thought, tugging on the orange and pink flowered material.

"Poor Matt," Eve said, sighing. "No wonder we

didn't stay on that beach very long. He was probably afraid I'd want to get naked, too.''

Sighing, she pulled the brim of her floppy hat a little lower. On the table beside the chair was a sheet of white paper that Matt had handed her before heading for the water—a fax from Sara. He'd passed her the wrong fax accidentally but caught the mistake almost immediately.

''Is that from your daughter?'' Eve had asked, trading papers.

When he'd nodded, Eve's gaze had been drawn to his hair, uncombed and ruffled with a boyish artlessness to it. ''Yeah. With the cell phone out of commission—'' his phone hadn't worked since their arrival in Cancún ''—I decided to fax her hotel.''

''Is she having a good time?'' Eve had asked, curious about the girl Matt obviously adored.

''She loves room service, and she liked Knott's Berry Farm and Universal Studios, but not Disneyland. Too many bratty kids,'' he'd said with a small smile. ''She didn't say anything about her stepfather's new job.''

Sinking back against the sun-warmed pad, Eve took off her sunglasses and picked up the fax. She'd been reluctant to invite the outer world into her oasis but knew she couldn't put it off forever.

The first paragraph was a quick update on her legal situation. Eve smiled at the line that read: *Ren is confident he can serve you Barry's male reproductive organs on a platter when you return.*

Eve didn't want anything from Barry—even something that small. She accepted her part of the blame for the present situation, although the media fiasco was all Barry. He should be held accountable for that.

But the Communitex deal was entirely her fault. She'd assured Barry that she would recover from the virus she'd picked up in Panama. Except for two earlier bouts of anemia, Eve had always been healthy as a horse. Because of that, she'd kept telling herself—and Barry—she could bounce back in time to make everybody happy—right up to the moment she no longer had the energy to pick up the phone and call for help.

Sara's last paragraph made Eve's throat close up with wistfulness:

Brady is growing up so fast—he's into everything.

Eve didn't have much experience with kids, but a part of her yearned for a baby. Maybe that had been Barry's meanest trick of all. While wooing her for his father's company, he'd also courted her heart, promising a long-term relationship, complete with hearth, home and family.

Maybe I will take those genitals, she thought.

"Whoa," a voice said from the doorway of her bedroom. "Do I dare come out there or not? That's a pretty fierce frown you're wearing."

Eve looked up, grateful for the distraction. "I was reading Sara's fax."

"Bad news?" Matt asked. He opened the screen and stepped outside. He was wearing navy blue, boxerlike swim trunks, leather huaraches, and an unbuttoned Hawaiian-print shirt that looked as if he'd donned it without drying off completely. His glossy hair was finger combed off his face. No hat, just sunglasses that were pushed to the crown of his head.

He carried something draped over one arm, but she couldn't make it out because of the glare of the sun—and the fact that she couldn't take her gaze off the slender V of curly black chest hair.

"Not really. I was just thinking about that rat Barry."

"Ah," he said stepping forward. "That's enough to make anyone frown. So..." He paused. "I thought we might try another outing. Something closer to home."

"Really?"

He nodded. "There's something I want you to see."

"Great. Let's go." She swung her legs around, discreetly slipping her cover-up across her shoulders.

"Don't you want to know where?"

She shook her head. "Anywhere. You have all the fun—swimming, snorkeling, seeing all the great fish." She looked toward the reef. "And all I can do is watch. It's not fair."

His grin made her start to stick out her tongue at him, but discretion prevailed.

"Here. See if this fits. It was the smallest they had." He held up a bulky black object.

"A wet suit?"

"A shorty. No sleeves, but it should help keep your body heat in since you don't have an ounce of fat on you, and it will be good buoyancy."

"You're taking me snorkeling? Really?"

He handed her the neoprene suit as she passed

through the door then followed her inside and closed the screen. Eve was a certified diver, but the last time she'd donned a wet suit was three years earlier in Maui with Ren.

"In the cenote," Matt added.

Last night at dinner, he'd expounded at length about the nearby cenote—a freshwater sinkhole created by the runoff undermining the limestone strata that made up the Yucatán. His description—"It's like an outdoor aquarium"—made her drool with longing.

"Oh, Matt," Eve exclaimed, barely able to keep from giving him a big hug. "I can't wait."

She held up the wet suit. A little big but not bad. At least it would help camouflage her thinness. "Where'd you get this?"

"The dive shop down the road. You'll need a mask and snorkel, too, but you have to choose those yourself."

He lounged in the doorway, waiting. But Eve didn't want him to see her skinny body. "I'll be down in a minute, Matt. I need to braid my hair," she told him.

He frowned—he still watched her like a hawk on the stairs, but turned and started to leave. "Don't bother with sunscreen," he said. "It's not good for the ecosystem and the area is pretty shady at this time of day."

He took a step then added over his shoulder, "If you're not too tired, I thought we might eat at Casa Cenote afterward. It's right across the road."

Eve's heart lifted and fell. A date. Of sorts. "Great. I've been resting all day and I feel strong."

"Good," he said. His brown eyes were too far away to read, but his smile looked cautious.

"Don't worry," she said, impatient to get going. "I won't overdo. I'll be good."

"Terrific. I'll hold you to that."

Eve knew how she'd like him to hold her…and it had nothing to do with her being good.

MATT WAS GRATEFUL for the water temperature—a notch above chilly. Being this close to Eve could fry even the strongest man's good intentions, he thought, snugging the rubber strap of her fin tight to her small, shapely heel. "How's that?"

"Perfect. Let's go."

Her impatience made him smile. He'd had his doubts about this outing, but her enthusiasm was infectious.

"Okay," he said, putting out his arms to help guide her into the water. The rocky edge was concave and he couldn't find purchase with his feet, so all he could do was tread water and get out of the way as she slid downward, her flippers splashing noisily.

"Ooo, it's cool," she said.

"Too cold?"

Her eyes—magnified by the lens of her mask— were alight with joy. "No, it's great."

The bottom half of her mask began filling with water, but before Matt could react, Eve tilted her chin and made the adjustment.

"You've done this before, haven't you?"

"I used to dive, but it's been a long time," she said, steadying herself with a hand to his shoulder.

"Can we go all the way to the headwaters? Like the lady at the rental place suggested."

"We can try. But you have to promise to tell me if you start to get tired. Okay?"

Eve placed the mouthpiece between her lips, then put her face downward in the water. A second later she looked up. Through the oval glass of the mask he saw her eyes alight with wonder and awe. She slowly nodded.

With a silent sigh, Matt adjusted his mask and put his snorkel into his mouth, then motioned for her to follow. He'd visited a different cenote on his first trip to the Yucatán and had been amazed by the variety of fish and plant life in the self-contained world created by water, rock and mangrove roots.

Eve stayed right beside him, close enough that he could hear her occasional exclamation conducted through the water.

Suddenly she grabbed his hand. *Look at the colors of that fish!* her grip said as a small fish adorned in brilliant yellow, orange and blue threaded in and out of the tangled roots. He squeezed back.

When she tugged hard, he stopped and looked where she was pointing. A large grayish creature moved languidly around the rock formations at the bottom of the pool. Matt squinted. Although the water was crystal clear, the sun cast long shadows across the water. He spat out his mouthpiece and said softly, "Manatee."

Eve looked at him, her expression so alive and excited, he might have kissed her if they weren't both wearing masks. Eve put her head in the water. Matt did, too, but he forgot his mouthpiece.

He held his breath until the beast disappeared into the gloom of an adjoining tributary. Eve started to swim in that direction, but Matt stopped her. Before putting his mouthpiece into his mouth, he said, "If we reach the headwaters, the current will carry us back."

Matt knew he would never forget this magical interlude. Eve's obvious wonder and joy filled him with satisfaction.

He let go of her hand once to swim down to investigate something glittering on a gnarled root. A bracelet with a broken clasp.

"Do you want it?" he asked.

Treading water, she reached to unzip her wet suit. Matt stopped breathing. The zipper stuck, and Eve looked at him questioningly. He moved to help her. As the tops of his fingers brushed against her skin, he felt the sensation pass through his hand straight to his groin.

He dropped the golden links inside. She wiggled to accommodate it, and Matt experienced a second piercing jab. He rezipped and backpedaled a safe distance.

"This is where the underground river comes in," he said, pointing to a wall of rock. "We should start back."

Eve didn't argue. He sensed her fatigue even though she tried to hide it. His need to care for her outweighed his libido, so he pulled her close and demonstrated how to let the underwater river work for them.

"Kick your feet out in front of you," he said, pulling her into the space between his open legs. "We'll do it in tandem."

Although she seemed startled, she quickly settled

in place, her elbows resting on his thighs. She relaxed with a sigh, but for Matt, the only comfort would be when they were safely out of the water and Eve was fully clothed.

EVE AWOKE SUDDENLY. It took two blinks to realize that what she was seeing wasn't a dream—a beautiful, picture-postcard dream. After they returned her wet suit and snorkel, Eve had suggested they have something to drink at Casa Cenote, the little open-air restaurant he'd mentioned. He'd agreed after making her promise not to move from the white plastic chaise on the beach in front of the thatched-roof *palapa*.

She glanced at the large glass globe on the table beside her. The ice had melted, leaving a reddish-pink soup—her very tasty virgin cranberry margarita—barely an inch from the rim. Matt's chair was empty, as was the lone beer bottle beside her glass.

Drawing herself up, Eve retucked her beach towel above her breast and looked around. The sun was just about out of sight; the evening breeze feathered her hair off her face.

"Hey, Sleeping Beauty," Matt hailed, walking toward her.

He was dressed in belted shorts she hadn't seen before and a white, short-sleeve shirt. His black hair was neatly combed although the wind played with it coquettishly.

"You look great," she said once he'd joined her.

"Shower and a change of clothes. You were sleeping so peacefully I decided to run home and change, but Gary, the owner, says you're free to use the shower in the empty *casita*. I brought your clothes."

He held up the string bag he used for groceries. Eve spotted her tropical print dress, once a sexy little number she'd enjoyed wearing. As skinny as she was, it probably looked better on the hanger.

"Does that mean we're staying for dinner?" she asked, slowly getting to her feet.

"Yes. I reserved a table and two lobsters, although you can order something else if you'd rather." He held out his arm. "Let me walk you up there."

Eve started to protest but changed her mind. She wasn't fully recovered yet. She had to accept the fact, galling though it was.

They climbed to the walkway and he directed her to the closest of the little stucco *casitas,* or guest cabins. The door was open.

"Do you want me to wait for you here or at the table?"

Eve took the tote bag from him. This might be her first chance to show him she was well enough to consider...well, maybe she wasn't well enough for that, but she was well enough to kiss.

"Go. I'll be there in a few minutes." He turned to leave. "And, Matt..." When he looked back, she smiled at him and said, "Thanks."

His grin made her insides churn.

"Save it for Atlanta, remember?" he said, brushing the backs of his fingers against her cheek.

MATT ATE A CHIP dipped in fresh, spicy salsa. Mouth tingling, he reached for his beer the same instant he spotted Eve. "Uh-oh," he groaned, watching her stroll toward the open-air dining area. The string bag dangled in one hand, her sandals in the other. She

moved with such grace a song popped into his head—
something about a girl from some unpronounceable
town.

The dress had been a mistake, he saw. He'd
grabbed it because it was the longest. How was he to
know the material would drape so fluidly about her
body? The scoop neckline had looked innocent
enough on the hanger. Where the hell was the bra
he'd packed? Still in the bag by the looks of her nipples highlighted by the cool breeze pressing the soft
fabric to her body.

She spotted him and waved the hand with the sandals. Her smile seemed to light up the night and Matt
sensed men at adjoining tables turning their attention
her way. He scrambled to his feet and hurried toward
her. She could be recognized anywhere—even Mexico.

He was halfway across the concrete platform when
a napkin tripped him up. His knee buckled. Feeling
ungainly and awkward, he grabbed the back of a
chair. The plastic chair might have crumpled beneath
his weight if Eve hadn't reached him at that moment.

She slipped into the crook of his arm as if she'd
been crafted to serve as his crutch. Her shoulder provided the anchor he needed to get his knee realigned.

"That was fun. Can we do it again?" she teased,
resting her hand on his chest.

"Maybe not." Matt could tell from her puzzled
look that his voice had been gruff. "You're not strong
enough to be carrying me around. Let's give it a few
weeks."

Her smile returned. "Okay. But I should warn you,

now that I've discovered your weakness, I will probably have to use it to my advantage. It's my nature.''

Her tone was teasing, but for some reason her words bothered him. He escorted her to the table. His hand went automatically to her lower back. Unfortunately the back of the dress dipped low and his fingers brushed bare skin. She shivered slightly.

''There's a sweater in the bag,'' he said.

''I know. Thanks. You're the most thoughtful man I've ever known. Even Ren wouldn't have been able to go to my closet and put together the right combination of things for me. I'm impressed.''

He sat across from her. After signaling the waiter to bring her a fresh drink, he said, ''It must come from getting dragged into every shopping mall in the country with Ashley. Is shopping genetic? A female sort of hunter-gatherer urge?''

Her light laugh was musical, and it helped him relax. She seemed refreshed and perky from her nap and shower. She might even be up to a walk on the beach after dinner—if Matt dared risk it.

The waiter returned with her big, pink drink.

''Could be,'' she said. ''But I think it's chemical. I know I go through withdrawal when I haven't been shopping in a while.'' Her eyebrows waggled. ''In fact, I should warn you. I haven't been in a store in months. Things could get ugly if you don't take me shopping soon.''

She leaned forward and took the straw in her mouth. Drawing on it, she closed her eyes and sighed. ''Mmm, yummy. Can I have two more?''

Matt shook his head—more to clear his overheated

libido than to nix the idea. "You'll spoil your appetite. And you need to eat."

"You're probably right. In fact, we'll assume you are, but it's *my* choice. Right or wrong." She looked at him over the rim of the glass. "Okay?"

Matt nodded. Fortunately, he didn't have time to stew about her words because the waiter returned with two of the biggest lobsters Matt had ever seen.

"You could feed a family of three for a week on this," Eve exclaimed.

Matt nudged a saucer of drawn butter her way. "Eat hearty. I promised my mother I'd put some meat on your bones."

His remark drew a frown, but the moment passed with her first bite of succulent lobster. The sea breeze made the light from the tiki lamps dance on the water. Music, soft and foreign, emanated from a distant stereo. Although Matt couldn't understand the words, he knew a love song when he heard one. The romantic setting wasn't lost on him, but he was determined to do the right thing, even if the wrong thing sounded a whole lot better.

"This is incredible, Matt. I don't think I've ever felt so alive," she said, toasting him with her glass.

He'd have given anything to be able to reach out and kiss that perfect mouth with a tiny drop of butter glistening in the corner, but he forced himself to look away. *Think business. Client. Job.*

"I know you don't want to hear this, but I can't help it," Eve said softly. "You're my hero, Matt. You saved my life. And I thank you."

He cleared his throat and pushed back his chair. He

had to stop this craziness now, before it got any further out of control.

"If you want to thank someone, Eve, thank Sara. I only did what I was hired to do. " He glanced around and let out a harsh, ironic chuckle that didn't come close to expressing the gut-level frustration he felt. "It's a tough job, but somebody—"

Eve jumped to her feet before he could finish. Her look held reproach and hurt, but she pivoted and walked away with all the grace of a princess. She hopped from the raised dais and disappeared into the night.

Matt swallowed against the sour taste in his throat. He threw down enough pesos to cover the meal and tip, then rose. Before following after her, he tested his knee to make sure it wouldn't trip him up. For once, it felt stronger than the rest of him. But then, it was made of titanium.

I wonder if anyone ever thought of making a titanium heart, he thought, slamming down the last of his beer. *I'd be first in line.*

CHAPTER ELEVEN

DESPITE MATT'S EFFORTS to make amends, both last night and this morning, Eve's ego was still smarting. His crack about "a tough job" was probably just the slap in the face she'd needed to curb her attraction to him. Unfortunately, he seemed so genuinely remorseful—even offering to take her to see one of the Mayan pyramids—she was having a hard time maintaining her haughty distance.

"Eve, would you please slow down? This isn't a race."

She ignored him. She'd had enough of being treated like an invalid and she'd damn well slow down when she was good and ready. She marched ahead, ignoring the quiver of her protesting calves and the perspiration coursing down her neck and arms. Her white eyelet blouse stuck to her like a leech, and her walking shorts chafed her thighs, but she wasn't about to stop.

"Would it help if I apologized? Again," he added under his breath.

"I told you in the car. I don't need an apology. If you're not interested in me beyond a professional—ahem, make that *business*—relationship, that's fine." Eve hated the way her voice caught on the word *fine*.

Matt swore softly and jogged to her side. She knew

his knee was bothering him, but ever since his stiffly polite lecture earlier that morning explaining why it was "professionally important" to maintain a "personal distance," Eve wouldn't have dreamed of asking why his right knee was laced with purplish scars.

"Dammit, Eve," he barked. "Slow down. Are you trying to have a relapse?"

That one word stopped her in her tracks. *No.* She never wanted to return to that brink of nothingness.

Breathing hard, she leaned forward, putting her hands on her knees. Matt sighed. She heard him fiddling with something but didn't look up until a wholly unexpected funnel of cool water broke across her neck. "Oh!" she exclaimed, arching her back.

When she straightened, the water diverted to her chest. The trickles between her breasts brought a shiver when she noticed where Matt's gaze was riveted. Her nipples puckered from something far different than a chill. "That probably wasn't smart," she conceded, taking a deep breath.

Their eyes met. Matt wore a sleeveless gray tank top. Perspiration ringed the neckline where his sunglasses hung. A lightweight backpack was looped carelessly over one shoulder. "No, it wasn't," he said, passing her the water bottle. "Probably not any smarter than coming here today. I thought it would be cooler in the jungle, but without the coastal breeze, it's like an oven."

Eve brushed back wisps of hair sticking to her face then took a drink. She closed her eyes and squirted an extra blast on her face. She shook her head, thankful she'd plaited her hair in a French braid. "It's beautiful, though,'' she said, handing him the plastic bottle. "I'm glad we came."

She arched her back to release some tension in her lower back and legs and looked around. The jungle had surprised her—a living, breathing entity on the prowl, overtaking even the most accomplished of civilizations in time.

"And I apologize for being such a twit. I'm probably living up to every expectation you had of me—just another prima donna celebrity." She was afraid to peek for fear he'd nod yes.

When she finally got up enough nerve to look, his lips were curved in a gentle, *loving* smile. "You aren't anything like I expected. Which, unfortunately, is the problem." Eve's heart started behaving foolishly again.

"I really have been acting like an idiot, Matt. You've been nothing but up-front and honest with me. It's been my experience that most men say yes first then remember all the reasons they should have said no." She tried to shrug off her disappointment. "Let's forget about everything and just enjoy the day. Our last day in paradise. And it's New Year's Eve. That's gotta count for something."

The shadows cast by the thick canopy of jungle made it hard to read his face, but she thought she read disappointment along with resolve. "Okay, but can we do it slowly?"

"Sure," she teased. "Right after you get me to the top of the pyramid."

Matt's head rolled back and he groaned. "Eve, you promised. Ground-level tourism. Period. That's why we're here instead of Tulum. I knew you'd want to climb the pyramids to see the ocean.''

Eve wasn't positive she had enough energy to make it back to the car, let alone climb a pyramid, but she wasn't above teasing Matt a little. She took his hand and tugged him along the path. "Please, Matt. We can do it slowly. I'll stop every two feet and drink water.''

His hand felt big and sweaty, but his strength seemed to replenish her dwindling supply. They rounded a bend in the path. A group of German-speaking tourists met them and enthusiastically pointed in the direction of a small wooden sign bearing the name Nohoch-Mul, Coba's centerpiece attraction. "We're close, Matt. Please.''

Matt grudgingly followed, but Eve could sense his disquiet. He approached the ancient site like a man facing a hangman's noose. Finally, she took pity on him. Time to end the joke. "Wow. That's bigger than it looks in the guidebook.'' She did an abrupt about-face and plopped her bottom on the step. "You were right, Matt. I can't do this.''

His left eyebrow twitched suspiciously. "Really?''

She nodded. "The whole point of this trip was to get away from publicity. Can you picture what would happen if I made it to the top then passed out or something? Do they have *Rescue 911* in Mexico?''

Matt heaved a sigh of obvious relief and sat down beside her. "Smart move. I seriously doubt if I could carry you down.''

But he would have given it a good try. Eve swallowed a bitter taste in her mouth. Maybe she *had* turned into a prima donna. Somewhere along the way, she'd started thinking about herself alone. *Me, me, me.* I *have to get away from Barry's media blitz.* I *want to go swimming.* I *want to go sight-seeing...* I *want to make love to Matt.* He was right to put on the brake. He was just what she needed to keep her grounded.

A smile tugged at her lips. *Me, again.*

"What are you grinning about?" he asked.

She heaved a sigh and leaned back, resting her elbows on the rough stone of the step behind her. "I've decided you were right to give me a little comeuppance last night." He started to protest, but she stopped him with a touch on his shoulder. "I don't know if it comes from being a *celebrity*—" she made little air quotes "—or from being sick, but I was starting to think this was all about me."

She snorted. "Talk about being out of touch with reality. There is a real world out there. And it's spinning around quite nicely without worrying about poor little me. Jeesch."

Before Matt could say anything, a heavyset woman in white walking shorts and a strawberry-colored T-shirt let out a high-pitched squeal and pointed at them. "That's Eve Masterson."

The woman and the cluster of tourists around her suddenly engulfed Eve and Matt. He put his arms around Eve's shoulders protectively and helped her rise. "It is you, isn't it?" the woman asked suspiciously. "My husband said no way, you're too skinny, but I was sure it was you."

All Eve could do was nod. When prepared, Eve could handle curious fans, but this one had caught her off guard.

"See there, Albert," the woman bellowed triumphantly. "I told you so. It is too her."

Matt gently nudged Eve to one side—toward a small opening of escape.

"You don't mind if I take your picture, do you?" the woman asked, lifting her camera without waiting for an answer. "Nobody back in Center City is going to believe this."

"No, ma'am, you may not," Matt said, putting himself between Eve and the camera. "Ms. Masterson is on vacation."

The lady squinted petulantly. "So what? So are we. Who are you? Hey, wait. Didn't I read something about some mystery guy?"

Eve's head started to spin. The heat and noise zapped her energy. She was sure she'd have collapsed without Matt's support. Something about the woman's piercing voice triggered a memory so deeply buried, Eve doubled over in pain. With a low curse, Matt tightened his arms around her and elbowed his way through the now-growing crowd.

"That was rude," the woman complained. "I always knew those celebrity types were stuck-up." Her words followed after them. "You're not as pretty in person, you know."

The words added to the anguish swirling in her head. They mingled with another voice—the voice on her answering machine back home.

When they got to the car, brushing past two concerned gate attendants who seemed convinced Eve had suffered an injury of some kind, Matt guided her into the seat. A minute later, he started the engine and drove out of the parking lot. Once they were on the main highway, he turned up the air-conditioning and let out a sigh. "Well," he muttered. "Are all your fans that charming?"

Eve took a deep breath. She wiped her face with her hands then dug in the backpack by her feet for the water bottle. "You meet all kinds. I usually handle things with more diplomacy. I just wasn't prepared."

"It bothered you what she said, didn't it? Why? Why do you care what she—or anybody else for that matter—thinks?"

His tone was perplexed. Her mother and father never had been able to understand what drove Eve to excel at beauty pageants or why she chose such a high-profile career. Lately, she'd been asking herself the same question. And now she understood. The memory of that voice brought it all back.

"Some of it comes from being adopted," she said simply. "You knew that, right? I was adopted at birth."

He nodded. "It was in your file, but I didn't give it much thought."

You wouldn't because you know where you belong. "You can't understand, but there's a part of me that finds validation in the attention. I know that sounds vain and shallow, but it's true. It's as if I need everyone to love me because at some level I've always felt unlovable. Why else would my mother have given me away?"

Matt reached out and gripped her hand. "I'm sorry, Eve. I shouldn't have asked."

She squeezed back. "No, it's okay. I want to talk

about it. I was thinking of going to a shrink when I get home. I don't feel crazy, but I want to come to grips with these feelings so I don't make any more stupid choices—like Barry.''

"Barry just happened to come along when you needed a change.''

Eve sighed. "I'd like to believe I did it for the right reason. Deeanna West. A young girl, with her whole life ahead of her, chose to end it because she didn't think she'd ever be beautiful enough to be loved.'' Her voice cracked and she looked down.

After a few moments, she lifted her face. "But now I'm afraid maybe it was more about me. About proving to my birth mother that I could do something good, something lasting. Something beyond beauty.''

Matt cranked the steering wheel sharply and pulled to a stop in front of a large, faded orange structure adorned with colorful blankets of unduplicated designs and patterns.

He rolled down the windows and switched off the engine. Turning to her, he used the hem of the towel to wipe away her tears. "I wish I knew how to make you feel better, but I don't. I'm not even sure I understand, but I do know you are beautiful—inside and out.''

Eve took a shaky breath. His touch, more than his words, helped to heal her pain. A loving touch.

He playfully brushed the towel against the tip of her nose. "I think the real problem is shopping withdrawal,'' he teased. "Didn't you say it's been months since you've been in a store?''

"Shopping?'' Eve looked over his shoulder to the wall of dazzling rugs.

"It might not cure you, but it can't hurt," he said, a huskiness in his voice Eve didn't dare think about. "You've got a purseful of pesos and we leave tomorrow, so you'd better go for it."

Eve couldn't repress the sudden lightness that replaced her anguish. Impulsively, she threw her arms around his neck and hugged him. "Thank you, thank you, thank you."

For once, he didn't complain about her gratitude. In fact, for a second, he hugged her back.

MATT TOOK ANOTHER SWIG of lukewarm beer. It stopped halfway down his gullet. Not surprising since he was scrunched like a folded banana in a rope chair suspended beneath the rafters of the warehouse-size building. Eve had wrongly assumed he liked the uncomfortable thing since he'd been hiding out in it the entire time she was shopping. To reward him for his patience, she'd bought him one to take home.

He gave the *present*—a paper-and-string-wrapped parcel by his feet—a nudge with his toe.

"You'll have to hang it a little farther off the ground," she'd told him when she presented it to him—happy as a child on Christmas morn. "You look a little scrunched."

A little scrunched?

Matt closed his eyes. Watching Eve shop was akin to torture. With her fluent use of language, she haggled and teased, praised and pooh-poohed. Her effervescence shimmered despite the heat, and her voice wove into his thoughts like a subliminal messenger reminding him his world would return to its former pumpkin shape in about sixteen hours.

"What about this for Sara?" Eve asked, intruding on his thoughts.

She materialized before him holding a white cotton nightgown with delicately embroidered butterflies scattered across the bodice. "It opens in front so she can use it when she's breast-feeding," Eve told him.

"It's beautiful," he said, his tone gruff. "I'm sure she'll love it."

"You're getting antsy, aren't you? I'll hurry."

"No," he said sharply. Matt cleared his throat. "I'm fine. Take your time."

Shrugging her shoulders, she pivoted and walked away. Matt followed her with his gaze until she switched aisles. Shaking his head, he softly groaned. The sexual tension between them was practically a living entity.

"Look at these booties, Matt!" Eve gushed, sliding to a stop in front of him. "Aren't they precious?"

She held two pairs of embroidered booties, one pink and one blue, to her cheeks. Even in the dim light, Matt could see the joy in her eyes.

"Do Sara and Ren know the sex of the babies?"

Eve frowned, her lips pouting so becomingly he had to cross his legs, not an easy task given his pretzel-like contortions. "Good point. I'll get the red, white and blue ones. They're cute, too." Decision made, she dashed away.

An hour later, Matt loaded her purchases into the car—including an extra suitcase to accommodate everything. As he pulled the car onto the highway, Eve let out a long sigh. "You didn't overdo it, did you?" he asked.

She pivoted in her seat. "I'm pooped, but it's a good pooped."

Matt understood. "Does that mean you're ready to take on Atlanta?"

"Yes." She wiggled back in place and reclined the seat. "But I *am* tired. Mind if I grab a power nap?"

Matt smiled. That was their code name for her periodic snoozes. She'd gone from six a day to one. "Good idea. If you feel up to it, I thought we'd check out La Buena Vida in Akumal tonight."

"I'd love to—on one condition." Her smile seemed innocent enough.

"What?"

"Tell me what happened to your knee."

Matt sighed. There was no reason not to tell her—she could find out the details by calling Ren once they got home. He'd put off telling her because he hated people to feel sorry for him.

"I told you I was a cop. I was working undercover stakeout when the dealer we were watching got spooked. He was a junkie, too, and nobody knows exactly what happened, but he grabbed his three-year-old daughter and bolted. There were other cars in pursuit, but I was closest."

His mouth went dry and he gripped the steering wheel recalling all too vividly the moment the man dropped an object out his window. *A doll. Let it be a doll,* Matt's mind had cried, but he couldn't take the chance and he'd desperately cranked the wheel away from the tiny form on the street.

"He tossed the kid out the window. I totaled my car and my knee. The doctors replaced it. I'm practically bionic now." He tried for levity, but he could tell she didn't buy it. "Unfortunately, I developed an infection that destroyed some of the connecting tissue. The bottom line—desk job."

That's it. Short and not so sweet. He kept his gaze on the road.

"We're alike, aren't we?" Eve said softly.

"How do you figure?"

"We spent our whole lives chasing our *dream* jobs, then lost them."

Was that it? Matt wondered. *Is that why I feel so drawn to her?* He wished it were that simple, but it wasn't. He was falling in love with her, which might be the biggest mistake of his life.

"I'M THINKING ABOUT cutting my hair when we get home," Eve said apropos of nothing.

They'd been sipping their drinks and staring out the wide-open window at the shimmer of nearby lights on the water. Half a dozen sailboats bobbed in the quiet cove. Their table was on the upper floor of the two-story restaurant, which featured a bar with swings for seats.

"Really?" Matt said, wishing he was close enough to touch the silky black locks. "Why?"

She shrugged one bare shoulder. Her dress was an ankle-length black halter style made of a microfiber that inspired wild fantasies when she breathed. Matt had nearly swallowed his breath mint when she'd first come downstairs. An elegant white shawl embellished with Mayan figures gave her a virginal look in direct contradiction to her sexy dress. Angel or temptress? The answer tormented him.

"I've made up my mind about a few things, my

career, my goals and ambitions. I think I need to project a new image—more businesswoman than sexy reporter."

"Well, cut it if you must, but as one of your fans, I'd like to vote for a compromise."

She smiled. "What's that?"

"Maybe clip off a few inches but not the whole thing." He shrugged. "What do I know? I'm a guy."

"Yeah, I noticed," she said with an appreciative hum.

Matt polished off the last of his wine. "Do you want coffee? Or dessert?" He looked around for a waiter, but Eve reached across the table and put her hand on his arm.

"No, thank you," she said, her gaze never leaving his. "But I do want to talk about something."

Her tone was businesslike, but the look in her eyes connected on a level that didn't need words.

"We should probably go. Big day tomorrow."

"Matt."

She took her hand away and faced him squarely—elbows on the table like a power broker deciding the fate of a multinational company. "You can run, but you can't hide from this. I'm not alone in what I'm feeling. Am I?"

Matt could have handled the power look, but that little-girl *Am I?* did him in. "It's not a good idea, Eve. I've never been a one-night-stand kind of guy. I sure as hell don't want to start with you. You're vulnerable and hurt and I'd be as bad as Barry if I took advantage of that."

Her grin rocked him to the core. "It's that honor and sense of duty that drives me wild," she said, her tone teasing. Her expression changed and she traced a pattern across the back of his hand. "I know this may sound selfish, but I need you, Matt. I need you to prove I'm still attractive, desirable."

He choked on a protest. "You don't need me for that, Eve. Look in the mirror. You're as beautiful as ever. Your eyes are alive and excited about life. That's the biggest turn-on of all."

"Then why won't you kiss me?"

"I have. Twice."

"Baby kisses." She shook her head to make her point, and her hair shivered.

In his nightly fantasy, Eve's hair sheltered them from the world—a silken tent. But fantasies weren't a part of his life. He was a responsible adult. He'd given the casual-fling thing a try and it had brought hurt and pain to a woman he'd truly cared about. He wouldn't risk that with Eve. He sighed and rose. "I'll kiss you good-night when I walk you to your door," he said, bowing slightly. "In Atlanta."

Eve pouted. God, he loved her lips. He'd had fantasies about them, too.

"I want more than a kiss, Matt. I want you to make love to me."

The bold statement made Matt's knees buckle. He sat down hard. "No, you don't."

"Yes, I do. I know you and trust you, and I think we'd be good together. When I get home, I'm going to be too busy—and too wary—to let anyone get close. I'll go my way and you'll go home to your daughter. That's the way it needs to be. I understand that, but there won't be anyone there for me, Matt. I'm going to be alone for a long time."

Matt understood her emphatically. He was in the same fix. He had no romantic prospects on the horizon. He had a new business that would take all his attention to get off the ground, and he might be going back to court to fight for Ashley. Her offer was tempting.

"Nobody needs to know, Matt. If you're afraid Bo will think you've compromised your professional integrity or something, I promise not to tell. The bottom line is—we can make it less complicated if we're both up-front about what we want from this."

Matt cocked his head. For some reason, he had to fight off a grin. "What do you want, Eve?" He held up one hand. "Before you answer, I have to be honest. It's been a while for me and I'm a little out of practice. So if you're hoping for fireworks…"

She laughed and shook her head. "I could say the same thing, plus I have this skinny-waif look going, but that's not what I want." Her eyebrows leveled in a serious look he remembered from her television interviews. "I want equal parts passion and compassion. I want you to make me feel alive and worthy of being in the arms of someone as kind and generous as you are."

Matt swallowed. He already knew what his answer would be, had to be, but he asked anyway, "And what do I get out of this? Besides one night of sex—no strings attached?"

"My undying gratitude?"

Although she said the words mockingly, Matt knew she was serious. She needed him, the way he'd once needed Karen, a woman who'd loved him knowing he didn't love her back. The irony of the situation wasn't lost on him as he said, "Okay, but I'm not promising razzle-dazzle. I might be a little rusty."

Her laugh set his blood singing through his veins. "I knew all that snorkeling wasn't a good idea. Should I check for barnacles, too?"

His hoot drew the attention of neighboring diners, so Matt stood up and held out his hand for Eve. She rose to her feet like a dancer and slipped into the curl of his arms as if she'd been cleaved from his body.

Matt leaned down and pressed a kiss atop her shimmering, fragrant hair. This might be all wrong, but it felt all too right.

FOR ALL HER reputed worldliness, Eve was not in the habit of asking men to sleep with her. Her cheeks burned the whole trip back to the beach house, but so did other parts of her at the mere thought of Matt's hands and body touching hers.

"You can change your mind at any time," Matt said softly as the car nosed to a stop outside their door.

He was looking straight ahead. They'd left the outside light on and in profile his features were strong and harsh. His black eyebrows were scrunched, his jaw tense.

Eve's heart jumped—partly in expectation, partly in fear. "I want to do this, Matt, but I think I should apologize in advance in case it's not all that great." Her blush intensified and she was grateful for the darkness.

He leaned over and kissed her. A warm, wine-flavored kiss. Eve was hungry for more. She put her arms around his neck and pulled him closer.

Slanting her mouth to his, she parted her lips and tasted him. "Mmm," she said, closing her eyes to savor the moment.

He deepened the kiss, his tongue exploring her mouth. "You have beautiful teeth," he told her between kisses. "They feel good."

No one other than her dentist had ever complimented Eve on her teeth. "Thank you. No fillings."

"Really? Let me see." He pulled her closer and she opened her mouth.

He ran his tongue around her lips then across her teeth. Eve smiled.

"Stop smiling. I can't reach those molars," he whispered against her lips.

Eve burst out laughing. "You're crazy. I think I love you."

He pulled back abruptly at her words. "Whoops. I didn't mean that," she said quickly. "I *could* love you, but it's too early to know. Right?"

His face was only inches from hers—she hadn't scared him too badly. His dark eyes were serious, his breathing uneven. "I don't know what to tell you, Eve. I want you. I've wanted this almost from the moment we met."

Eve pushed him away. "Don't lie, Matt. I don't need to hear that."

"It's the truth."

"I was half-dead, filthy and delirious."

He took her hand and kissed her knuckles. "Fragile, hurting, sick, but still beautiful and feisty."

His fingers played some kind of music down her arm, raising a trail of gooseflesh in their wake. He leaned down and planted tiny kisses on her bare shoulder. How had she gone from seducer to seduced?

"Is this wrong, Matt? We're adults. No commitments. No one gets hurt. We can have safe sex." Even as she said the words, Eve's heart sank. She'd gotten into the habit of carrying condoms in her travel bag but couldn't remember seeing any. Had she thrown them out? "Can't we?"

His frown didn't look encouraging. "I *think* so. There used to be some condoms in my suitcase. But I can't guarantee how new they are."

While the frank talk took a little of the sizzle away, Eve appreciated his honesty. It made her feel adult and responsible, not like some hormone-crazed teen—even if her hormones had been acting very youthful all week. "Let's go hunting. Surely the sex gods will smile on us," she said, faking optimism she didn't feel. She grabbed his hand and started leading the way to the house.

Oh, please, oh, please. Oh, please let there be one tiny little foil package in my suitcase.

FIFTEEN MINUTES LATER, Matt was having a debate with himself. He had an out—a lack of condoms. None had shown up in Eve's luggage, or his.

All he had to do was say sorry. But he knew that wasn't going to happen. No matter that it was the smart thing to do, the prudent thing. The look of disappointment on her face was more than he could handle. He sank down beside her on the settee and gently massaged her shoulders.

"Eve…"

She turned to face him, her cheeks a deeper hue of

blush. "I didn't want to discuss this. I mean it's bad enough that we're not exactly doing this in the throes of spontaneous passion, but the fact is I haven't had a period since Panama."

Of their own accord, his thumbs plied her tense shoulder muscles. She arched her neck like a cat. He could almost hear her purr. "Isn't that when you got sick? And started feeling run-down?"

"I guess so. I've never been real regular."

He swallowed. "What you're telling me is you don't think we have to worry about you getting pregnant."

She made a funny sound of pain. "What I'm saying is I'm a freak of nature. I mean, what the hell good is it to have all the showy stuff to attract a mate when your ovaries misfire?"

Matt had to bite down on his cheek to keep from laughing. *Showy stuff?* He cleared his throat. "I don't know a lot about the female reproductive system, Eve, but I do have a sister and a mother who's a nurse and I bet you might find that your… ah…cycle comes back online once you let yourself get healthy."

She stilled. "You're not put off by this?"

So strong, yet so fragile. "I'd say it's a lucky break for us."

Her smile nearly unmanned him. "We can make love?"

He gulped. "If you're comfortable with the usual risks lovers face these days, I think I'm brave enough to forgo any contraceptives."

She hugged him fiercely. "Matt, you have my word of honor. If a miracle happened and I were to get pregnant—not that there's any chance in the universe it could—but I wouldn't expect you to—''

He caught her by the shoulders and looked into her eyes. "I'd expect *you* to let me know. Are we clear on that?"

She nodded, the look in her eyes so full of happiness, triumph and some other emotion, Matt's heart staggered.

"So...?"

This was it. His last chance at sanity.

She placed her hand on his chest, and suddenly nothing else mattered. Eve Masterson wanted him. Only a madman or a monk would turn down that kind of opportunity. Matt was neither.

CHAPTER TWELVE

MATT BRUSHED the crumbling white sand from the bottom of the suitcase before stowing the bag in the trunk of the car. Eve's well-worn leather weekender looked subtly glamorous compared to his basic black duffel—a freebie that had come with his running shoes. He slammed the lid and turned around to rest his derriere on the car.

We're too damn different to make it work, he repeated for the twentieth time since waking to find Eve's head on the pillow beside his own. *There's no way this—thing—can be more than great sex.*

And make no mistake, he thought, stalking around the far side of the house, the sex was great. No, it was better than great.

He plowed toward the beach, his bare feet tingling in the hot sand. He'd originally planned on taking Eve into Cancún early to do a little sight-seeing before their flight, but the morning was half gone when they finally woke up—gloriously spent from the night before.

Matt stopped at the water's edge. The cool blue water beckoned, but he'd already turned in his snorkeling gear. Besides, he knew he was putting off the inevitable. He and Eve needed to talk.

"Are you having regrets?" a voice said behind him. "You seem upset."

Matt turned to find her sitting on the fallen log. A beautiful stranger in the same outfit she'd worn a week earlier. Only now the khaki pants fit. The pale blue blouse—open at the neck and with long sleeves rolled up—showed tanned flesh so healthy and vibrant Matt wanted to reach out and touch her. Gone was the wig. Instead, she wore her hair in a twist that poked out at the crown like a whimsical tiara.

He felt choked by his inability to tell her what was in his heart. Despite what his logical mind insisted, the thought of casually dropping her off at her door and saying goodbye was tearing him up inside.

"I'm worried about what's going to happen when you get back to Atlanta," Matt said, keeping his real fear—that he might have fallen in love with her—to himself. "You have a lot on your plate. You're not going to get run-down again, are you?"

"Never again. I learned my lesson. The key is to listen to my body. And my body needs five basic ingredients—nutrition, exercise, iron supplements and rest," she said, ticking each one off on her fingers.

Her lush lips—tinted with a pale shade of coral—smiled so broadly her sunglasses moved on her face. She pulled them off and tucked them into the pocket of her shirt.

Matt's gaze followed. Instead of seeing designer shades and fabric, he pictured her wondrous breasts, which he'd lavished with attention a few hours earlier in the shower. "Five? That's only four," he said, desperately trying to stay focused on the prudent path.

She rose with grace and halved the distance between them. When Matt looked into her eyes, he saw something he wanted but couldn't allow himself to acknowledge—love. "You. You're elemental to my happiness, which is elemental to my health."

Matt took a step back, his heels sinking in the soft, wet sand.

"I know we said we wouldn't do this, but I can't pretend I don't care. Thanks to you, I feel whole," Eve said with feeling. Her eyes narrowed from either sunlight or tears. "Last night healed a part of me I'd forgotten existed. You've given me back my sexuality, Matt, my femininity...my heart."

Matt heard gratitude in her tone. *Am I just a link in the process of her recovery?* He knew the cards were stacked against any long-term relationship. With his heart thudding the way it did before going into a dangerous situation on the job, Matt took her hand and led her back to the log. As he took a seat beside her, her scent filled his nostrils—an exotic blend of spice and floral that made his chest ache. *How am I going to forget her?*

"Eve, we talked about this last night. If you sort things out with Communitex, your life will be in Atlanta, mine is in New York. Long-distance relationships are doomed to failure. We're not going down that road, remember?" he asked, wishing he dared give himself one last moment of holding her.

"I know, Matt," she said testily. "I told you no strings attached and I meant it, but are you absolutely positive you can walk away from this without regret?"

Hell, no. But I can try. For both our sakes.

She rushed on without waiting for his answer. "Why does it have to be all or nothing? Can't we see each other now and then? Talk, date, meet halfway once in a while?" Her tone came off chipper, hopeful. "We've been housemates and lovers, but shouldn't we try being *friends* before we decide we can't see each other anymore?"

Friends. That had never worked for him in the past. And in all honesty, he just couldn't picture himself in her world, or vice versa. "Eve, let's be honest. Last night was incredible. You're incredible. And I'm pretty sure what I'm about to say is one of the hardest things that's ever come out of my mouth, but…we can't work."

She reached for her sunglasses and shoved them back on her nose. Matt understood the defense tactic—he'd used it often. "Why not?"

"We have no common ground," he said bluntly. "You're up here." He lifted his hand above his head. "I'm down here. That's the basic problem, but we can add all the other variables, too, if you like—Communitex, your career, your health, Ashley, my job." He sighed and added, "Not to mention the media. I'm really looking forward to my role as the mystery man in your life."

His facetious tone drew a sniff. Eve turned her head, seemingly lost in the beautiful view, but he could tell she wasn't thinking of the coral reef.

"I understand what you're saying, Matt, but I'm having a hard time accepting that you can walk away from what we've shared here without looking back."

The earnest dismay in her voice made him put his arm around her shoulders and give a gentle squeeze. "Nobody said it was going to be easy. Hell, maybe I'm kidding myself. I might get to New York and have to turn around with my bedroll over one shoulder so I can camp out on your doorstep like the rest of the paparazzi." His teasing earned him a tiny smile.

He kissed her sun-warmed forehead and leaned his cheek against the top of her head. "Maybe we should hold off making any big life decisions until we see what's going on back in Atlanta."

She nodded. "Good point. Even if the press has backed off, I might be in court with Communitex," Eve said, her voice showing a tremor of fear. "If they fire me, I may wind up a pariah in the industry. Legal action doesn't do much for a résumé."

Matt jiggled her shoulder. "Don't even think that. You're Communitex's golden girl. Without you, the company folds. They need your name and face to save them from financial ruin." He cupped her jaw, tilting her chin so the sun highlighted her profile. "Your beautiful face."

She twisted her chin and jumped to her feet. She took two steps then pivoted, hands on hips. "Do you want to know the truth about this face, Matt? It's not mine," she spat. "At least not the one I was born with."

She whipped off her glasses, slinging them to the sand. "These eyebrows take regular visits to the dermatologist. We're trying to kill the damn follicle so it will quit producing new growth that gives me that Karl Malden look."

Her right finger poked the bridge of her nose. "See that tiny scar? When I was eight a boy at school threw a shoe at me and broke my nose. My parents took me to a plastic surgeon who not only fixed the problem but removed an unflattering bump—just in case I ever wanted to be a beauty queen."

Stepping closer, she leaned forward and pointed to her mouth. "These teeth cost my parents six grand in orthodontia. I won't even tell you how much I spend to keep them pearly white."

She threw up her hands in a gesture of pure exasperation. "I could tell you how many personal trainers I've had, how many diets I've been on, about my flirtation with bulimia, my overdose of diet pills when I was sixteen. This face—this body—comes with a price tag, Matt. A very costly price tag. And, frankly, I'm not sure it was worth it." Her shoulders slumped and she added under her breath. "I mean, what the hell do I have to show for it?"

Matt's heart ached for her, but before he could clamber to his feet, she was gone. He watched her run to the house.

"Oh, Eve, I'm so sorry," he whispered. After stopping to pick up her sunglasses, Matt headed for their rose-colored castle. He paused beside one of the thick posts that supported the shaggy palm-frond overhang. Turning, he took one last look at paradise.

FOR THE BULK of the flight Eve kept her nose in a book—a J. A. Jance novel she'd borrowed from the house. She couldn't have given anyone even the most rudimentary outline of the story, but it kept her from making a total fool of herself by hanging all over Matt and begging him not to leave.

On the long drive to the airport, Matt had explained the underlying reason for his decision to walk away. "Ashley's at a pivotal age, Eve. Her life is in enough turmoil without me complicating matters. I know you understand what I'm saying."

She did—more than he could ever know, but that didn't mean she could accept it with aplomb. She wasn't that good an actor.

But maybe, a little voice said, *he is. Maybe he was faking the rupture part. Maybe he's in the wrong profession. Maybe he ought to be in show business.*

"Eve," Matt said, cutting into her thoughts, "there's something I completely forgot about. We haven't talked about your stalker."

A shot of pure adrenaline made her levitate in the airplane's cramped seat. But before she could respond, the person sitting in the window seat—an Hispanic-looking gentleman with gray hair and thick glasses—asked to be excused.

Eve used the diversion to pick up the phone and call Sara.

"Hello," a woman answered.

"Sara?"

There was a sharp intake of breath, then Sara cried, "Eve, is Matt with you?"

"Of course. Is something wrong?"

Sara's news made Eve's reporter instincts kick in. She reached into her purse for a pen and a piece of paper. Matt's look of puzzlement changed to concern, and he lowered the tray to give her a writing surface.

"Tell me what you know," Eve said briskly.

She scribbled—her note-taking illegible to anyone but her. "How long ago? What does Bo think?"

Her pen stalled when Sara gave her Bo's take on the subject. "Here? Really?"

"It makes sense when you think about it," Sara said. "She loves her daddy and she's hurting. Where else would she go?"

"Okay. I'll tell Matt. We'll call you back when we land." She hung up the phone without saying goodbye. She took a deep breath and turned in the seat to face Matt.

"Ashley's run away."

All color left his face. He opened his mouth to ask something, but Eve put her fingertips to his lips. "Let me tell you what we know. Ashley, her mother and stepfather flew home last night. Ashley went straight to her room. She and her mother had had a fight, and when Ashley didn't come out this morning, Sonya assumed she was sulking."

Matt cursed softly.

"Your ex-wife is distraught, Matt. She thought she was giving Ashley some much-needed space, but when she opened Ashley's door around noon, she discovered the bed hadn't been slept in."

The agony in Matt's eyes almost broke her heart. "Do they have any idea where she went? Maybe my sis—"

"They've checked everywhere. Your parents called Bo because he was one of the last to speak with Ashley."

Matt frowned. "What do you mean?"

Eve consulted her shorthand. "Your ex-wife said Ashley called Bo from their cell phone on the way to the airport. She wasn't trying to eavesdrop but she knows your name came up more than once. Sara and Bo think Ashley might be trying to get to Atlanta to find you."

He muttered another low curse.

Eve took his hand and squeezed hard. "Bo thinks he may have given her enough information to find Communitex. He said she asked about my apartment, but he couldn't tell her anything because he doesn't know where I live. He called a friend of his to stake out the bus depot—she didn't have enough money to afford a plane ticket."

"Why would she take off like that?" Matt cried. "She's never done anything like this before."

Eve could only shake her head. "She and her mother had a fight. I can't tell you the number of times I thought about running away from home when I was her age."

"But you never did, did you?"

Eve looked at her lap. Adopted kids didn't turn on their adoptive families. "No. I wasn't that brave."

"*Foolish* is a better word." He turned toward the window. "I can't believe it. Of all the stupid—"

Eve cut him off. "Don't say something you don't mean. You don't know what was in Ashley's mind. There's no way to be sure she's coming here. Maybe she's hiding out at the horse barn or something."

"It's the *something* that's eating me up inside. She could be anywhere, and I'm not there to help. Some kind of father I turned out to be. When my daughter needs me most, I'm living it up in Mexico." His tone was bitter and full of self-reproach.

"It was your job, Matt."

Her gave her a droll look. "You don't believe that any more than I do, and I can guarantee you Ashley won't buy it for a minute."

Eve reached out and took his hand. She tugged on it until he faced her.

"Matt, Ashley's your daughter, and you're the smartest, bravest man I've ever met. She'll be okay because everything she needs to know about taking care of herself she learned from you."

His eyes narrowed and his lips thinned. She read his misgivings. "Have a little faith, Matt. If she's coming here, Bo's friend will make sure she gets to us safely."

Her unconscious use of the word *us* sank in when Matt's eyebrows quirked. Her cheeks heated under his steady appraisal.

The pilot announced their impending arrival, and Matt turned away. Undaunted by the slight rejection, Eve said, "You'll find her, Matt. I know you will. You found me, didn't you?"

ASHLEY ROSS WASN'T liking her impetuous decision to run away too much at the moment. She and her best friend, Bridgett, thought they'd covered every base when they cooked up this scheme last night in their online chat room. But now that Ashley was sitting in Bridgett's brother's rusty Saab in front of an imposing brick apartment house in Atlanta, she could see some flaws.

Jarrod's going back to college tomorrow. Georgia Tech. It's in Atlanta. Is that not like fate or something? He has to pick up his two roommates in Virginia, but there'd still be room for you, Bridgett had written.

The rest was easy.

But it got hard once they arrived in Atlanta and Ashley couldn't tell them where to go. All she had was the street address she'd copied from a Net listing that gave celebrities' addresses and phone numbers. She'd learned about the underground site from a computer droid she met on the flight to California.

"Are you sure this is the place, Ash?" Jarrod asked for the second time. He leaned across her to squint at the older, unpretentious building. "It doesn't look as glamorous as I thought it would."

Ashley scrunched closer to the door. Jarrod had been pretty cool during the trip—he even bought her a Coke and a burger when they stopped for lunch, but his questions were getting a little too big-brotherly.

"This is the number my dad gave my mom. I doubt if he'd make a mistake," she said, trying to make her tone sound confident.

In all honesty, Ashley had expected something a bit fancier herself. *What if this isn't the right place?*

"You wanna double-check?" Jarrod asked, digging between the bucket seats for his cellular phone. "I had a hard time understanding your mother when she called last night."

Ashley felt herself blush. Jarrod had flat out refused to consider his sister's request to give Ashley a lift without talking to Ashley's mother first, so Ashley had had to fake it with a towel over the mouthpiece. She was thankful the Saab's dim interior and weak streetlights hid her blush.

"Mom has pneumonia," Ashley said quickly. "That's why she sent me down here to stay with my dad. She was afraid I'd get it."

"I don't think pneumonia's contagious," one of the other guys—Brad or Brett, Ashley wasn't sure which—said, leaning over the seat. Jarrod's car was no beauty but it held four without too much crowding.

Ashley tried to think fast, but she was tired and more than a little scared. The repercussions of her escape would catch up with her as soon as she saw her father. That would be bad enough without getting these guys involved.

"My grandma's a nurse and she's the one who suggested I go visit my dad until Mom gets better." Ashley made sure her voice carried a thick coating of "who cares what you think." Brad or Brett slunk back to his corner.

"Well, I guess you know what you're doing," Jarrod said with a sigh. "We could hang around for a few minutes, if you wanna check with the doorman."

Ashley shook her head. "Naw. I don't want to keep you. I'll be fine." She opened the door and crawled out of the car. A stiff breeze almost took off her stocking cap.

Brad or Brett passed her backpack over the seat and Ashley leaned down to grab the strap. "Thanks, guys. See ya'."

"Hey, wait," Jarrod called before she could slam the door. "Don't forget about the picture. Your mom

promised to get me an autographed picture of Eve
Masterson if I did this.''

Ashley swallowed. Another lie. "No problem. I'll
get your address from Bridg and mail it to you." Her
life had become nothing but one big lie. And it was
all her mother's fault. "Bye."

She closed the door firmly and stepped back. A
moment later the little black car disappeared into traffic and Ashley was alone. All alone. In a strange city.
With sixty bucks to her name. Her Christmas money.

Christmas. When was that? A million years ago?

Before she could work up enough nerve to plead
her case to the doorman, a white van came to a
screeching halt two parking places away. Three people piled out of it, a woman and two men, one carrying a big camera. Ashley had seen a crew filming
a Woody Allen movie back home so she knew right
away what was happening.

The threesome plowed past her, talking in low, urgent tones that made Ashley nervous. Not a minute
passed before a taxi pulled up to the curb outside
Eve's building. A man got out. *Dad.*

Before Ashley could say anything, he leaned down
to help someone else out of the vehicle. A woman.
Ashley barely caught a snippet of red before the camera crew attacked.

Her pulse hammering, Ashley hurried toward the
fray. Energy crackled; voices rose and Ashley had a
brief glimpse of her father's angry face and tense
shoulders as he tried to make headway past the leech-
like interviewer.

"Miss Masterson, can you tell us where you've

been? What happened to you? Were you in a drug treatment center? Are you better now?'' The questions pierced the air like bullets, but Ashley's dad provided a screen to protect the woman Ashley could barely make out.

The whole group, along with the doorman, who was carrying several oddly wrapped parcels, surged toward the door. To Ashley's horror, her father faltered at the first step. *His knee.* ''Daddy,'' she cried out.

The reporters—and a big black camera—turned on her. Ashley's heart stopped. Her tongue froze like a big wad of gum in her mouth. She couldn't have spoken if her life had depended on it.

''Ashley, thank God,'' her father said, rushing to her side.

She barely noticed. There was something intoxicating about being in front of a camera. She suddenly remembered to smile, and instead of looking at her father, she gave the camera her most practiced smile—the one Bridgett said made Ashley look like Wynona Ryder.

''Ashley.'' Her father's bark caught her attention.

''Hi, Daddy,'' she said, torn between smiling at him and at the camera.

His big hand caught her mittened paw and tugged. Hard. She went flying forward into the hollow of his armpit. A muffled jabbering of questions followed them inside, but Ashley missed them all thanks to her father's protective hug.

Once within the way-too-silent shell of the elevator, Ashley looked around. Her knees were a little wobbly, but she still felt energized by the encounter out front. She knew her father's rigid stance meant she was in big trouble, but she couldn't stifle a grin. She looked at Eve Masterson—every bit as beautiful, although quite a bit shorter than Ashley had pictured. The woman gave her a shy smile.

Ashley took that as an opening. "Wow. That was like the coolest thing in my whole life. I can't wait to tell Bridgett. Do you think I'll be on television?"

Eve's initial smile faded, and when she looked at Ashley's dad, there was a bleak look in her eyes— almost as if she was ready to cry. She whispered something too low for Ashley to catch, but it sounded like "I'm sorry."

AN HOUR LATER, Matt set the coffee mug down with exquisite care, fighting the temptation to slam it. His nerves were cracked—windshield brittle and ready to explode in every direction. His head still throbbed from Ashley's bombshell. "Mom's pregnant," Ashley had wailed when they were safely in Eve's apartment. "Do you know what that means? Everything changes, Daddy. Everything."

He heard Eve in the hallway. She was making sure Ashley had all the necessary toiletries to spend the night. He clenched his jaw so tight his teeth squeaked.

"I think she'll be fine," Eve said, joining him in the kitchen. "She forgot toothpaste but I had an extra tube in the medicine chest. I'm more organized than I thought."

"This was a mistake," Matt said softly. Anger always pushed him to the other extreme. Ashley hated loud fights.

"The toothpaste?"

"Staying here." He nudged the cup out of the range of fire. In the mirror-like reflection of the window he could see Eve standing behind him. She wore her demure "granny" robe, but even with her hair plaited down her back and scruffy slippers, she looked provocative.

Their brief collision with the press had been an eye-opening experience. Navigating under her own power, functioning in a world she knew and understood, Eve was a stranger to him. A beautiful, glamorous stranger.

"It's just for one night, Matt," she said, reaching for the stack of mail he'd left on the counter. "It didn't make any sense to go out and find a motel with those reporters hovering."

"How did they know you were coming home tonight?"

One slim shoulder rose and fell. "We were probably spotted at the airport. Does it matter?"

"To me it matters. I'm not a celebrity. My daughter is not a celebrity. My life doesn't revolve around being seen, and I want to keep it that way."

He heard her shuffle away. Glancing over his shoulder he saw her disappear down the hall. That she wouldn't give him the satisfaction of an argument fueled his anger. One voice cautioned that this wasn't her fault, but Matt couldn't get past the sickening sensation of seeing Ashley preen and flirt with the camera. It had seemed second nature to her, and the idea of his daughter falling into the kind of life that had nearly killed Eve made him nauseous.

He went after her, pausing at the door of the bathroom. The sound of the shower running meant he had time to finish this once and for all. It wasn't what his heart wanted, but it was the smart thing—the right thing to do.

"We're leaving first thing in the morning."

Eve had removed her robe and draped it across an upholstered chair. Her flannel nightshirt was modest, knee-length. Far from sexy, but that didn't keep his body from responding. He glanced around. The room was a mess—her suitcase open, the packages from Mexico in a pile in the corner. Matt's hammock chair rested at an angle against the closet door.

"I'll have that shipped to you if you leave me your address," Eve said, apparently noticing the direction of his gaze.

Matt withdrew his wallet from his hip pocket and took out a business card. He walked to the dresser, which was a jumble of cosmetics, jewelry and whatnot. Eve's fuzzy red beret and mittens were wedged beneath her purse. He placed the card beside them then glanced up.

Her bottom lip quivered, but she didn't speak.

"It wasn't meant to be, Eve. We're from different worlds. Ashley's at an impressionable age and…"

"I'd be a bad influence on her," she finished, her tone hollow.

"Not you, but your lifestyle."

She laughed bitterly. "Look around, Matt. Does this strike you as the lifestyle of the rich and famous? I work for a living, just like you."

Matt shook his head. "No. Not even close. Your work keeps you in the public eye, and you told me yourself you need that kind of adoration. But the thing is, it's an illusion. A dangerous illusion. One wrong move—one Barry—and you become fodder for the next talk show.''

Eve put a hand to her forehead. He was too attuned to her not to sense her fatigue. She'd been a trouper ever since he found out Ashley had run away. When he wanted to blame himself for not being there when his daughter needed him, Eve had shored him up.

Even the scene in front of the building would have been worse if she hadn't promised the vultures a press conference the next morning. He knew she wasn't ready for that kind of dramatic confrontation, but it let Matt and Ashley off the hook because they'd be long gone before it happened.

"You're bushed, Eve. Go to bed. Ashley and I will slip out in the morning so you can sleep in a little.''

Her shoulders stiffened. "Wishful thinking. Tomorrow I pay the piper,'' she said, her voice flat. "With no knight in shining armor to protect me.'' Her lips twitched in a semblance of the woman he'd known and loved in Mexico. "I've grown pretty fond of those shoulders clearing a path for me.''

Matt frowned. "I did promise Bo I'd make sure you were safe. If Ashley weren't here…''

Eve stepped closer. The scent of her shampoo brought a longing so intense he had to clench his fist to keep from reaching out to touch her. "I understand, Matt. I'll be fine. Ren told me I've got one of the best lawyers in town on my side.''

Eve had talked with Ren while Matt and Ashley used the cell phone to make their calls. "Did he give you any idea what will happen?''

"Not really. I'm prepared to do whatever I can to smooth things over. I don't want a legal battle any more than Communitex does. I'm hoping without Barry fueling the fire, we can work something out. Now that I'm feeling better, I'd really like a chance to do what I was hired to do."

Matt respected her sense of integrity and her goals, but he knew he couldn't stay. He had his daughter's needs to consider.

"Don't let them wear you down, Eve," he said, trying to keep any tenderness from his tone. He turned away, but she stopped him with a light touch. "Matt. A kiss goodbye?"

He hesitated. There was yearning in her tone. He wanted to say yes, but he shook his head instead. "It's late. Ashley and I have to get up early. Good night, Eve. Good luck tomorrow."

That should have been it, but halfway to the door his knee buckled. Eve flew to his side, lending the support he needed to keep from falling on his face. With a low groan, he closed his arms around her, picking her up enough that her body fit against him— man parts to woman parts in perfect harmony. He kissed her hard, like a convicted man saying goodbye to freedom.

Lost in her smell, her taste, he almost missed the small gasping sound behind him. A premonition of doom hit him the instant he heard his daughter say, "Daddy?"

CHAPTER THIRTEEN

EVE PULLED BACK in horror. She'd tried so hard to be cool in front of Matt's daughter. She'd made a concentrated effort to play down any sort of relationship between her and Matt in light of Ashley's tearful announcement that the reason she'd run away from home was that her mother was pregnant. Eve knew the girl didn't need anything as threatening as a new woman in her father's life to fuel the fire of her teenage angst.

Thankful for her years of experience in interviewing reluctant subjects, Eve stepped away from Matt and walked to Ashley.

"This might be a good time to talk," she said, taking the girl's elbow. "Matt, would you care to join us?"

Eve was certain the last thing Matt wanted was for Ashley to have more contact with Eve, but she knew from experience that things brushed under the rug could trip you up in later life.

They walked to the living room. Eve sat on the sofa and indicated Ashley should sit beside her. Matt chose the recliner across from them. Eve took a big breath then said, "Ashley, you're almost thirteen, right? You've probably formed some opinions about men and women, love and relationships."

Ashley nodded. Her hair was pulled back in a ponytail and Eve's heart twisted at the girl's rapt look. *God, help me to say the right thing.* "I don't mean to insult you, but a lot of what people—especially teenagers—think about life is influenced by what they see on television and in the movies. But life is much more complicated."

She glanced at Matt and was encouraged by the nod he gave her. "You know from your parents' experience that relationships don't always work out. Just because you love a person doesn't mean you're destined to live happily ever after. Sometimes you figure that out right away, sometimes it takes a while."

Ashley started to fidget, so Eve decided to cut to the chase. "What you need to know about your father and me is that we figured out right away that what we feel for each other isn't that fairy-tale kind of love. He's a wonderful man. He saved my life. And sometimes, when you survive something as scary as what I went through, it's easy to mistake gratitude for something deeper."

Ashley's frown was so like Matt's, Eve almost reached out to touch her face. But she refrained. "So that kiss was...a goodbye kiss," she said, keeping her tone as even as possible. "Tomorrow, you two fly home to New York."

No one said anything for few seconds then Ashley looked at Eve shyly. "I know I shouldn't ask, but do you think I could have a couple of signed pictures? I kinda promised my friend's brother. He's the one who drove me down here."

Matt made an annoyed sound, but Eve jumped to her feet. "Sure. No problem. If I can find them in this mess." She frowned, trying to figure out where her promotional materials might be. Maybe in the box in the guest room. "Follow me."

"She'll be there in a minute," Matt said. His serious tone made Eve gulp as she hurried to the room that she'd once shared with Matt. That night was a far cry from their passion a mere twenty-four hours earlier, but Eve still treasured the memory.

She clamped down on the sadness that swamped her. She'd have time to grieve later—after Matt and Ashley were gone. In the meantime, she would do the right thing. The brave thing. The *Matt* thing.

When the door opened a little while later, Eve looked up from her spot on the floor, where she was surrounded by the clutter that had filled her desk drawers. Ashley's eyes were puffy and her nose was red. Eve's heart went out to her. The teen years were so damn tough—even without all that Ashley was facing.

"Have a seat," Eve said. "I know they're in here somewhere."

Ashley plunked to the ground like a puppet freed of its strings.

"Are you grounded for life?" Eve asked, trying to sound friendly but not flip.

"And then some," Ashley muttered.

"If you could have seen the panic on your dad's face when we heard that you'd run away, you'd understand why he's so upset with you." Eve pictured Matt's anguish. "I can only imagine the fear, the frustration of not being able to do anything when the safety of someone you love is in jeopardy."

For some reason, her mind flashed to the memory

of Deeanna West's grief-stricken mother. "There's a lot of scary stuff out there for parents—gangs, drugs, sexual predators, teen suicides." She shook her head, certain the last thing Ashley wanted was another lecture.

"I'm not stupid," Ashley said, crossing her legs beneath her. "I know the difference between acceptable risk and doing something dumb. I had it handled."

Her belligerence fit her age. Eve could remember feeling the same emotions. She lowered her voice. "In all honesty, I thought your plan was pretty well thought out. But that doesn't mean what you did was very nice. You upset your mother, which is probably not a good thing in her condition."

Ashley made a face. "Her condition sucks."

Eve looked over the girl's shoulder. Would Matt prefer they didn't get too chummy? No doubt, but Eve couldn't resist offering a little counsel. "My brother, Tim, was seven when I...when our parents brought me home from the hospital. I grew up thinking he hated me—even though I adored him. Later I found out he was just disappointed because I was a girl, not a baby brother."

Ashley frowned. "Well, it's not like your folks could help it."

Eve sighed. "Actually, they could have. I was adopted."

"For real?"

Eve nodded. "Tim and I are pretty good friends now. But it was tough when I was too young to understand." Eve felt a prickling sensation in her sinuses. "I guess what I'm saying is I understand how hard it will be for you to welcome a new sister or brother into the picture, but I hope you'll try to remember it's not his or her fault.''

Ashley made a noncommittal grunt. She picked up a cloth-covered scrapbook that Eve had chucked to one side. It was so overstuffed that newspaper clippings, photos and odds and ends stuck out at all angles. ''Is this your scrapbook?''

Eve made a face. ''Oh, no, not the dreaded paper trail! I thought I burned that.''

Her jest brought a smile to Ashley's lips. ''Can I look at it?''

Eve shrugged. She didn't see how it could hurt. It wasn't as if they were building a lasting bond or anything. ''Sure. But be prepared for big buckers.''

Ashley made a face. ''What?''

Eve winked. ''You'll see.''

As Eve continued to sort through manila folders, some holding nothing more important than a monthly credit card statement showing that her business manager had paid it in full, she listened for Ashley's response to the old clippings.

''Ohmygosh,'' the girl exclaimed a few minutes later. ''Is this you?''

Eve laughed. For some reason, Ashley's reaction didn't bother her—even though it pretty much paralleled Barry's mortified, ''My gawd you were a homely duck!''

''Look at those buck teeth,'' Eve said, craning her neck for a glimpse of the skinny little kid with two new front teeth too big for her face. ''My mom kept telling me I'd grow into them, but I didn't believe her.''

"My fourth-grade picture was pretty horrible," Ashley said kindly. "I wanted retakes, but Mom said we couldn't afford them. I think she just didn't want to be bothered."

Eve didn't try to minimize Ashley's bitterness toward her mother. She didn't know the whole story, but at the moment Ashley felt betrayed. Perhaps by both parents.

"Being a parent is a tough job, Ashley. You have to learn as you go and sometimes you make mistakes." Eve shrugged. "It doesn't mean your mom and dad don't love you to pieces."

Ashley flipped through a few more pages. "What's it like to be famous?"

Eve swallowed. "There's no simple answer, kiddo. For a long time, I thought fame was a goal unto itself. And when I believed that, every little news clip and sound bite was great—better than Ben and Jerry's ice cream. But after a while it got old." She snickered softly. "Or maybe I just grew up."

She glanced at the page Ashley was studying. Eve's crowning glory. Her first pageant win. The rush, the triumph and, later, the horror of facing her past. "Looking back, I have my share of regrets," she said, sighing. "But I learned a lot, too. And eventually, I hope to put that knowledge to good use."

"What do you mean?"

Eve twisted to one side and looked at the pretty young girl across from her. Ashley was part of her target audience, the age demographic Eve wanted to reach. Maybe she'd been given this test case to see if she was up to the challenge.

"For a long time now I've been thinking that society in general and the news media and advertising companies in particular are killing our kids. We've created the impossible dream and we sell it to every young person with a television, CD player, video game and computer.''

Ashley looked up.

Eve rose to her knees. "From day one, kids are fed the idea that perfection is not only attainable but desirable. If you look perfect, eat the perfect food, find the perfect job, connect with the perfect mate and raise perfect children, your life will be whole, happy, fulfilled...in short..."

"Perfect," Ashley chimed in on cue.

Eve nodded with enthusiasm. "But the fatal flaw in that thinking is there's no such thing as perfect. I'm living proof of that."

Ashley frowned. "You're pretty close to perfect."

Eve sank back down. "You just see the outer me, Ashley. The me that bought into the perfection theory lock, stock and barrel. Heck, I didn't go out on my first real date until I was seventeen because I spent every weekend on the road at beauty pageants or dance competitions. I had no close friends until college, and even then I was too busy with my career— my looks—to be interested in anyone who didn't fit into my program."

Ashley seemed a bit overwhelmed by Eve's unburdening. She looked down at the bundle in her lap, picked up a loose sheet of paper and studied it a minute. "You were born in Texas?"

A horde of butterflies took flight in Eve's stomach. She recognized the document immediately—a report from the private investigator she'd hired after moving to New York. She hadn't realized she'd stuck it in there.

"Yes. We moved to California when I was two." She put out her hand to reclaim the page.

"Have you ever met your birth mother?"

Eve attributed the blunt question to normal curiosity. Still, it generated painful memories. "Yes. When I was fifteen. And I've heard from her off and on since then."

Ashley gave up the paper with just the slightest frown of inquisitiveness.

Eve put it on top of the pile she'd already sorted and pushed the entire stack to one side. Fatigue was setting in big time. "Ashley, I think I'll have to mail you those photos. I'm feeling pretty pooped."

The sympathy in the young girl's eyes made Eve want to hug her, but she didn't. They both stood up. Momentarily light-headed, Eve wobbled. Ashley touched her arm. "Are you okay?"

"I just stood up too fast. Your dad wouldn't let me do anything much more strenuous than swing in a hammock the whole time we were in Mexico."

Ashley gave her an odd look. Quietly, almost in a whisper, she said, "You love him, don't you?"

Eve's denial stuck in her throat. She swallowed twice before saying, "Yes, I do, but that doesn't change anything. His life is in New York, with you. Mine's here, with my work."

Ashley frowned. "That sucks."

Eve gave in to the urge and hugged her. "You are a wonderful person, Ashley. Truly beautiful."

She shook her head so hard her ponytail batted

Eve's nose. "I'm not beautiful. My teeth are messed up and my butt…"

Eve put a hand to the young girl's cheek. "That's what I want people to know. There are more kinds of beauty than you can imagine. Kindness is beautiful. Happiness, goodness, imagination, inspiration—all of these are overlooked because we're so darned focused on appearance." Eve sighed. "You *are* beautiful, Ashley. Don't ever, ever doubt that."

Ashley's smile started out tremulous then grew. She gave Eve a quick, spontaneous hug that brought tears to her eyes.

She turned away quickly, almost bumping into Matt. Eve had no idea how long he'd been standing there, but she couldn't handle any more emotional scenes. Chin down, she slipped past him. "G'night," she called, then dashed toward her room.

A good night's sleep and a good cry awaited—she'd earned both.

ASHLEY'S HEART sped up uncertainly as she waited for her father to say something. She'd made such a mess of things. Her mom was in bed with cramps. Ashley knew she'd absolutely die if her mother lost the baby. That was never Ashley's intention. Never. And now she'd created problems for her dad and Eve—even if neither of them would admit it.

She braced for another scolding, but all Matt said was, "You'd better get to bed, hon. We have to get up early."

Impetuously, Ashley decided to ask her father the same question she'd asked Eve. "Do you love Eve, Dad?"

His shoulders tightened as if someone had hit him from behind. Ashley had never seen him look quite so sad and tired—even after he and Ashley's mother split up. Ashley had her answer.

With a long sigh, Matt walked to the far side of the room and pulled out the upholstered desk chair. Its little rollers wobbled against the carpet's nap and he gave it a vicious shake.

"Forget I said anything, Dad. You're tired. We can—"

He interrupted. "No. We'll do it now." He sat down, settled his elbows on the armrests of the chair and leaned forward. "I understand why you ran away. You've worried about your mother and Alan moving to California. You're not happy about the new baby. Maybe you think your feelings in all this might get overlooked, but that isn't going to happen. Ever."

Ashley started to speak but closed her mouth when he shot her a dark look. "None of that excuses what you did, and you know what your punishment is once we get back to New York. What worries me most is how we can get through to you that no matter where you live or how many kids your mom has, we both love you, and that will never change."

Ashley blinked back her tears. "I want to stay with you, Daddy. In New York."

"All of that will get discussed when we get home. You, me, your mom, Alan, Grandma and Grandpa. We're a family, Ashley, and we're all in this together. Alone, we're vulnerable. Together, we're strong."

"How can we be together if I live on the other side of the country? Tell them not to move, Dad. Make

Alan stay in New York." She knew she was asking the impossible but a part of her wanted to believe he was superhuman.

He shook his head. "I don't like this situation any better than you do, honey, but it happens when people divorce."

"Then why didn't you stay married? It wasn't that bad, was it?"

He leaned back. "Ashley, do you remember last summer when one of Aunt Deb's kids got sick? It was one of the twins, right?"

Ashley nodded. "Kevin."

He went on, "Grandma told me a doctor ordered a prescription to help him breathe. Good medicine. Then a different doctor ordered something else for his stomachache. Also good medicine. But the two don't work well together. If Grandma hadn't caught it, Kevin might have had a really bad reaction. Maybe even died. Remember?"

Ashley nodded.

"Your mother and I are like that. Alone we're fine, but put us together and we're dangerous."

"Then why'd you get married in the first place?"

His lips moved in a half smile. "Danger is exciting when you're young and in love. Even the fighting was...stimulating. But it just wasn't what either one of us wanted for you." His look was serious, uncompromising. "Your mother and I both love you more than life. We want what's best for you. She and Alan have a chance to do something good here—for themselves and you."

Tears sprang into her eyes. "I don't want to live

in California, Dad. I saw a girl in a bikini on Christmas Day.''

''Face it, Ashley, there's a lot more to the world than New York.''

''Does that mean you might not stay there, either? Would you move here to be with Eve?''

He glanced up. ''I can't tell you what might happen, honey, because I don't know.''

''You didn't answer my question. Do you love her?''

He slowly stood up. Ashley could tell his bad knee was bothering him because he leaned over and rubbed it. She couldn't see his face when he answered her question, but she heard something different in his voice. ''I can't tell you that, either.''

Ashley didn't push it. In a way, she wasn't sure she wanted to know.

MATT AWOKE in increments. First, his nostrils. *Coffee*. Then his ears. *Eve's off-key hum.* The familiar sound made him smile...until he opened his eyes and realized where he was. *Damn.*

Atlanta, not Mexico. And he was on her couch, not stretched out in a big bed with a warm tropical breeze making the curtains dance.

He was tempted to pull the comforter over his head and go back to sleep. At least in his dreams he could be with Eve. Hold her. Kiss her. Make love with her.

His body responded to the subliminal suggestions and he abruptly flung off the quilt and sat up. In the kitchen, Eve let out a small peep.

A moment later there was a soft scuffling sound of

moccasins on tile then he heard, "Good morning. Did I wake you?"

Matt shook his head and rubbed his shoulder. He hadn't slept well. Between worrying about Ashley and trying to make sense of his feelings for Eve, he was a mess.

"Coffee's ready. Let me bring you a cup."

Matt tried to stop her—he wasn't sure he could keep his hands off her if she got too close—but she spun away. He heard a cupboard door open, then another. He'd unpacked several boxes while she was in the hospital, but Eve obviously didn't know where things were. "Ah-ha," he heard her say.

A minute later, she returned with a mug in each hand. She set his on the coffee table then adroitly melted to the floor across from him. The coffee table seemed a safe distance, but it still took every ounce of self-control Matt possessed not to reach out and draw her to him.

"Thanks," he said, picking up the mug.

"No problem."

"What time is it?" *Where's my watch? I meant to set the alarm.*

"Six. You said your flight was early."

Matt hadn't actually made reservations. He'd been too drained last night. He was tempted to rent a car and drive. The time together would be good for him and his daughter.

He took a sip of hot, bitter coffee—just the way he liked it. He and Sonya had engaged in what Matt jokingly called the "coffee wars." Eat-paint-off-a-car versus sissy-mocha-stuff. Finally, their kitchen had sported two pots brewing in respective corners.

"I suppose I should wake up Ashley…"

Eve gave him a look he remembered from seeing her deal with politicians on television. It was a look that said, "The bull stops here."

"What?" he asked.

"Matt, is it possible that the reason you won't consider letting anything develop between us is that you're afraid?"

Matt inhaled so sharply hot coffee scalded the roof of his mouth. "Afraid of what?"

She shrugged. "Besides the things you've already mentioned—opposing lifestyles, money, careers—I think maybe you're afraid of screwing up Ashley—although, personally, I think that's a long shot. Despite that little stunt she pulled, she's the most grounded twelve-year-old I've ever met."

Matt ignored the small tickle of pride her words gave him, but Eve went on before he could respond. "Maybe it comes down to business. If we wanted to be together, one of us would have to move. You wouldn't want to disappoint Bo, and I know you're close to your parents, so it wouldn't be easy to leave your home."

Matt sighed. "All of that is true, but it's not—"

"Maybe you're afraid of becoming 'Mr. Eve Masterson,'"she interrupted. "I wouldn't blame you, you know. I don't know if I could give up my sense of identity for you, either. I just think we should be honest about why we're not even *trying* to work this out."

Her questions drove to the heart of what he'd wanted to avoid thinking about. *Why am I turning my back on something that feels so good?*

He ran a hand through his hair and rolled his shoulders. "I don't fit into your life, Eve. Remember when Liz Taylor married that guy she met at the dry-out clinic…Larry something. The big star and the average Joe. Definitely not a match made in heaven. Even though they claimed to love each other, everyone knew it wouldn't work."

"I'm a nobody compared to Liz Taylor," Eve protested.

"Not compared to me."

Her eyes seemed black, intense yet inscrutable. For some reason, he had a feeling this was one of those pivotal moments that he'd one day look back on with either profound relief or complete regret.

Eve put down her mug and scooted around the table on her knees. She put her hand on his bare knee—he'd slept in boxers and a T-shirt. "Matt, I know my life bothers you. I have a recognizable face and people consider me a celebrity. The media is interested in me. But that's what I do—not who I am. It's taken me a long time to learn the difference. In fact, it took this near-death experience to drive home the point."

Matt covered her hand with his. The sensation of her touch connected at every level. With his left hand he cupped her jaw. "I know that. And I love who you are, but I don't have enough faith in love to think it can magically make things work between us."

She sat back, her face stricken with sadness, but there was hope, too. And Matt knew he wasn't doing her any favor if he let her think there was any chance they might work things out.

"Besides that, Eve, I'm a dad. And at the moment,

my daughter comes first in my life. Her life is messed up enough without me adding to it. The last thing she needs is to be exposed to all the trappings of your lifestyle—the glitz, the glamour, the paparazzi, calls from your stalker..."

She jumped to her feet and turned away. She paced to the fireplace. Her back to him, she said, "There is no stalker, Matt. The voice on the answering machine is my birth mother. She had throat cancer a few years back and she has an artificial voice box."

"Your birth mother? Why didn't you say so?"

Eve slowly turned. Twins trails of tears glistened on her cheeks. "I never wanted anyone to know about her. She doesn't fit my image," she said with a rueful snort. "Which is totally ironic when you stop and think about it. Here I am, Eve Masterson, beauty queen, celebrity, but if the truth were known, I'm really the bastard child of a woman who tried to sell me. Twice."

Matt rose and started toward her, but Eve glided out of reach. "No," she said, shaking her head. "Maybe on second thought you were right not to get involved with me. I have too much baggage. It could go either way today. And if I have to start over, I'll need to channel all my energy into my career."

With her chin high and the grace of a dancer, she walked to the hallway. She paused and looked back one last time. "Give Ashley a big hug for me. She's a terrific kid. Tell her I'm going to dedicate my first show to her...if I ever get the chance." With a tremulous smile that didn't make it to her eyes, she hesitated a heartbeat, then disappeared down the hallway.

"I STILL SAY you should put me on an airplane then go back to be with Eve. She needs you, Daddy," Ashley said for what had to be the tenth time.

"You sound like a broken record. Will you give me a break?" Matt snapped when she opened her mouth again. "I'm doing the right thing for all of us. The responsible thing."

She made a dry sound of disgust. "That's what adults always say, but tell me what's so responsible about abandoning Eve when she needs you? Love sucks, you know that?"

He started to scold her use of language but sighed instead. This wasn't the impression he wanted his daughter to have of relationships. Matt loved being in love. He'd been crazy happy when he and Sonya were first married, and totally delirious over the birth of their daughter. In all honesty, he felt more alive at this moment than he had in months because of the way he felt for Eve.

"You are so *not* right, Dad," Ashley said, only this time her tone was more sad than argumentative.

Matt glanced at his watch. Their flight would begin boarding in fifteen minutes. By his estimate, Eve would be walking into the Communitex boardroom about now. His stomach made an unhappy sound when a spurt of acid hit the French toast he'd shared with Ashley at the airport restaurant.

"You know I'm right, Dad. Love beats paper, stone and scissors."

Matt stifled a sigh. He truly regretted telling Ashley that Eve had to leave without saying goodbye because she was embroiled in a contract dispute. Ashley immediately jumped on his case about "abandoning Eve in her hour of need."

"What does scissors have to do with Eve's job?" he asked, knowing he would probably regret it.

Ashley lifted her chin in a worldly manner. "Eve went into battle naked." Her dramatic delivery made Matt wince. "She's fighting for her dream, but she doesn't have any armor, no backup. Her parents are in Australia. Her friends live on the West Coast. Her real mom's in Florida. And you—the man she loves—is flying away like some kind of chicken."

Matt frowned.

With a sigh, Ashley added, "I would have gone with her, but I'm already in trouble so I didn't figure that would be much help."

Matt fought back a chuckle. "You got that part right."

They were both silent a minute then Matt asked, "What did you say about Eve's real mother?"

Ashley's cheeks changed color. "I…um…last night when we were talking, I ran across a piece of paper that had her birth mother's name and address on it. She lives in Florida."

Florida. The voice on the answering machine lives in Florida. Matt couldn't say why that idea intrigued him, but it did. Maybe because it offered some humanity to a disembodied voice that he'd deemed threatening. He'd assumed the caller was a stalker. He'd been wrong. Was he also wrong to assume Ashley would feel threatened by his feelings for Eve?

He turned his chin to look at his daughter. "Am I hearing this right? You're encouraging me to stay here? To help Eve?"

"Uh-huh, although I think it would be best if I stayed, too."

Her innocence was so obviously feigned Matt burst out laughing. "You'd do anything to avoid facing your mother, wouldn't you?"

Ashley had the grace to shrug sheepishly. "It was worth a try."

Matt snickered softly. Then asked, "Why do you care about what happens to Eve?"

Ashley rolled her eyes. "Daddy. I'm not blind. You love each other. If it weren't for me screwing things up—like usual—you'd—"

Matt pulled her to him. It was awkward given the airport seating, but he comforted her just the same. "You didn't mess up anything, honey. Eve and I did that all on our own. Mostly, it was my fault. I decided Eve's life was too complicated for me. I couldn't picture myself fitting into a celebrity lifestyle. And I sure as heck didn't want you to be influenced by it."

She lifted her head. "You mean like maybe I'd want to be on TV? Jeesch, Dad, that's crazy. I want to train horses or be a veterinarian. Besides, everybody knows what you see on television isn't real."

His daughter's words floored him. He had to sit back a moment to digest them. Then he rose and told her, "Wait here, hon. I need to make a couple of calls. I'll be right back."

Matt knew he could have used his cell phone, but the possibility he wanted to discuss required privacy. He was about to make a quantum leap, and if he fell flat on his face, the fewer witnesses the better.

CHAPTER FOURTEEN

EVE HAD TO DIG deep for the patience to sit through another minute of legalese. She owed Ren big time for her lawyer. In the four and a half hours since she'd walked out of her apartment that morning, everything in her life had changed. Matt and Ashley had left for New York. She'd engaged in battle with the big boys and won—or lost, depending on your point of view. Communitex had agreed to admit that Eve hadn't intentionally reneged on her contract, but the victory was moot given the fact the entire company had been bought out by a Christian network that didn't want Eve or any "name" newscasters working for them.

Tuning out the drone of voices, Eve absently perused the draft of her original contract. It had represented the door to her dream, and now it was being slammed in her face. Financially, she would walk away with enough money to tide her over quite nicely. But that wasn't the same as a job. And Eve was afraid she might have lost her chance to be more than a face. She wanted so much more than that. She wanted it all, including a husband and family.

I wonder if Matt and Ashley arrived home safely?

No sooner had the thought crossed her mind than Dag LaPointer's secretary opened the door of the conference room and hurried to his side. Eve's pulse jumped. *Oh dear, what now?*

The man, an older, more commanding version of Barry, looked at Eve. Throughout the negotiations he'd treated her with respect, even compassion. Now his eyes narrowed.

He gave his secretary softly murmured instructions then said, "I believe we'll use this opportunity to break for lunch. Ms. Masterson's doctor is outside, and he's concerned that given her recent illness she not overdo."

Doctor? Did he say doctor?

Eve looked at her lawyer, who gave her a confident nod. "We'll iron out the severance details after lunch, then." He rose and politely pulled back Eve's chair as she stumbled to her feet.

Certainly the secretary had made a mistake. Regardless, a break was a good idea. Her head felt a little woozy. For a second, she even imagined she heard Matt's voice in the anteroom.

With her lawyer leading the way, Eve hurried through the doorway, hoping to avoid any face-to-face exchange with Barry, who'd spent the entire morning staring daggers at her.

Stealing a glance over her shoulder, Eve bumped into a man wearing a leather flight jacket. Surprise turned to shock when she heard Matt say, "There you are. What did my nurse tell you about eating regular meals and getting plenty of rest?"

"Matt? What are you doing here?" Eve croaked.

"Checking up on you. I can't afford to lose a single patient," he said, his tone teasing.

Eve started to smile, but Barry's voice cut into her

pleasure. "That man's no doctor. He's a private investigator. He's the one who viciously attacked me."

Matt's predatory smile stopped Barry in his tracks. Without a word, he helped Eve into her calf-length leather trench coat then escorted her from the office to the elevator.

"I can't believe this," she exclaimed. "Where's Ashley? What's going on?"

He squeezed her arm. "I'll explain as soon as we get some food in you. You look faint. Did you drink any water?"

"I can't remember."

"I leave you alone for one morning and you're already ignoring nurse's orders," Matt scolded.

The warm, caring quality of his voice took away any hint of criticism. "You're a very strange man. I don't understand—"

"You will," he predicted. "Can we hold the conversation till we get to the restaurant? You know it's hard for a gimp like me to walk and talk at the same time."

Baloney. But she kept her mouth shut. Suddenly, she was ravenous.

A few minutes later, they were seated across from each other in a quiet, family-style Italian restaurant three blocks from the Communitex building.

Matt held out a glass of water for her. "Drink first, then talk."

She obliged, but only because she felt like a parched camel.

"Okay," she said, dabbing her lips with her cloth napkin, "tell me what's going on."

"Simple. Nobody calls me a coward and gets away with it."

Baffled, Eve shook her head. "Did I call you a coward?"

"No, my daughter did. We were at the airport and she said that abandoning you in your hour of need was tantamount to cowardice of the worst order." He grinned. "Not in those exact words, but there were chicken sounds involved."

Eve shook her head. "I don't believe you."

"It's true. It hurt. I wasn't thrilled to realize my daughter could see the holes in my rusty armor quite so clearly. So I did what any smart man would do. I called my ex-wife and told her to meet Ashley's plane, then I came here."

"But what about all that stuff you told me this morning?"

"Excuses. Plain and simple. I've been running away from life ever since my divorce, Eve. The accident was my excuse to feel sorry for myself!"

Eve looked down and focused on the checkered pattern of the tablecloth. "You know how I feel, Matt. One big emotional goodbye is tough enough. You aren't going to make me do that again, are you?"

Matt reached across the table and covered her hand with his. "I hope not. Because I screwed up badly this morning, Eve. Only a fool would walk away from the chance to love you."

Eve's heart crimped in her chest. "But you said—"

"I said we'd never last. But now I realize time doesn't matter. Ten minutes, ten days, ten decades. I'll take whatever I can get."

"I'm not sure I believe this is happening," she said, her throat squeezed with emotion.

He lifted her hand to his lips and nuzzled it softly. "I know the feeling. I left the airport in a daze. Got lost twice on my way here."

"Was Ashley okay about going home alone?"

"She wanted to stay with me, but her mother vetoed that idea in a hurry." He glanced at his watch then dug his cellular phone out of his jacket pocket and set it on the table. "I told Ashley to call the minute she got home."

He sent her home alone. Why? Does this mean he's staying for good? That we have a chance to be together?

Before Eve could ask any of her questions, a waiter arrived to take their order and deliver the two glasses of wine Matt had requested when they sat down. "Pasta primavera," she ordered, not even glancing at the menu. *My life is teetering on a precipice,* she thought. *Who cares about food?*

Matt ordered the special—whatever that was—then picked up his wine goblet and toasted her. "To fame."

Eve blinked. "I beg your pardon?"

Matt gave her a smug grin. "A lady at the airport recognized me. She said, 'Aren't you that gigolo who took off with Eve Masterson?'"

Knowing how much Matt had hated their encounter with a fan in Mexico, Eve shuddered. "I'm sorry."

He shook his head. "Don't be. It was a hoot. I made up this story about being a CIA operative, and you were helping us with a big telecommunications sting operation."

Too baffled by this completely new Matt to know how to respond, she downed a gulp of wine. "I couldn't be more confused. I thought you hated everything about my life—the fame, the fans, the media..."

He nodded and munched down on a bread stick. "That's true. That's what I said, but then I asked myself why that had to be such a big deal. And do you know what I decided?" Eve shook her head, afraid to even breathe wrong and ruin the moment. "I decided that I'm too serious. I don't laugh enough...except when I'm with you. I work too much...unless I'm with you. And I only feel alive inside when I'm with you."

Eve's heart sped up to an uneven beat that made her giddy. "Really?"

He put down his glass and took her hand. "I love you, Eve, and I apologize for letting you think for even one minute that you weren't worth the effort it's going to take to combine our lives. This isn't going to be easy, but we can do it." He drew her hand to his lips. "If you want to."

Want? Like I want *air to breathe.*

Before she could answer, the phone trilled.

Matt would gladly have picked up the phone and dropped it in the nearest glass of water if he weren't a hundred percent certain it was his daughter. He'd threatened her with bodily harm if she didn't call the minute she arrived in New York.

"Sorry," he muttered, snatching up the phone. "Ashley?"

"No, it's me. Bo."

Matt groaned. "Hang up. I'm busy and I'm expecting a call from Ashley."

"Well, ex*cuuu*se me," Bo snarled. "I just called to give you that information you asked for this morning. Jeesch. Do a guy a favor and—"

Matt smacked the heel of his hand to his forehead. "I'm sorry. I forgot. Give it to me then I'll call you back later." He patted his breast pocket looking for a pen.

"Ahem," Eve said, passing both pen and paper his way.

He mouthed, "Thanks," then started scribbling the information Bo read off to him. "Perfect. I owe you, cuz," he said. He started to reach for the end button, but heard Bo add something else. He listened, a smile growing on his lips.

"Yeah, I guess so. Tell Claudie I said hi. She's too good for you, you know." Grinning, he heard Bo reply, "Same goes for Eve!" Matt couldn't argue. *Eve is too good for me, but that doesn't mean I want to live the rest of my life without her.*

Eve was looking at him expectantly. Matt wasn't ready to share all of Bo's information. He carefully tucked the note in his pocket and returned Eve's pen to her. "Bo's asked me to be his best man at their wedding in June. Ren and I are sharing the duties." Before Eve could say anything, their lunch arrived.

Matt was chewing on his first bite when Ashley called. Her bubbling cheer eased his nervousness.

"Can I talk to Eve a minute, Daddy?" Ashley asked.

Matt hesitated. Nothing had been decided. They were still in the early stages of negotiations at this point. "How 'bout we call you later? When we know what's going on?"

"You haven't asked her?" Ashley squealed.

"We're eating, Ashley. And I keep getting phone calls. Now, go home and be a good girl so your mother doesn't keep you grounded until you're forty." Apparently his stern tone didn't hold much authority because she was laughing when she hung up.

Matt turned off the phone and dropped it in his jacket pocket. "There. Now we're alone."

"Excuse me," a voice said. "I truly hate to interrupt. I promise you I never do this, but I have to ask. Are you Eve Masterson? The lady from the morning news?"

Matt stifled a groan and turned to look at a tiny, silver-haired woman in a thick winter coat. She wore a hand-knitted muffler that nearly touched the floor. At her side was a red-faced man Matt's age.

"Yes, I am," Eve said pleasantly after touching her napkin to her lips. "Can I help you?"

"No, dear, you already have, and I just wanted to say thank you. My son says it's gauche to approach famous people when they're eating, but at my age it doesn't pay to wait for anything or anybody."

Eve smiled warmly. "It's not a problem."

The woman gave her son a "so-there" look, then said, "I just wanted to tell you how much that story you did on teen suicide helped our family. It may have saved my granddaughter's life. When you listed those warning signs of teen depression, a bell went off in my head, and I called my daughter-in-law at work and told her she needed to get Amy into counseling right away.''

Eve reached out and clasped the woman's gloved hand. "I'm so glad it helped."

"No, dear, *you* helped. It was plain to see how much that other girl's death affected you. That's what made me stop what I was doing and listen. It was you, as much as your words, that made a difference. I just wanted you to know."

Matt sensed Eve fighting to maintain her composure. She rose and gracefully embraced the woman. "You have no idea how much this has meant to me. Thank you for stopping, for sharing that with me. I hope your granddaughter lives a long, happy life."

When the two departed, Eve returned to her seat with a long, deep sigh. "Life works in amazing ways. An hour ago I was ready to chuck everything. Hide out at my parents' home for a few months licking my wounds, then *maybe*—" she stressed the word "—start looking for a new job."

Matt stopped chewing. "Does that mean Communitex fired you?"

"Not exactly. A Christian network looking for a way into the Internet market bought out Communitex. The building, the equipment, stock, everything. They even agreed to keep all the staff in place—except for a couple of us," she added with a rueful grin.

"According to the new owners, I'm emblematic of what's wrong with broadcasting in general."

Matt sat back in shock. "How do you feel about that?"

"Relieved, I think. I was prepared to live up to my obligations but, in truth, I'm not sure I could handle an eight-to-five day yet. And turning Communitex around would have taken superhuman commitment. My heart just wasn't in it."

"What's going to happen to Barry?"

She frowned. "Other than that his father has threatened to disown him, I haven't a clue." She sighed. "In all honesty, after this morning I think I can see how come Barry's so screwed up. Having a rich, powerful parent doesn't necessarily ensure you're going to be happy and well adjusted.

"Barry was so determined to make his father acknowledge him, he became blind to everything else."

"At your expense," Matt added with feeling.

She shrugged. "I was a problem he didn't count on. A very costly problem, since Communitex is giving me back wages and a substantial severance package." She snickered. "I heard his father tell Barry he's selling the Rolls to pay for it. Poor Barry. He loved that car."

Matt didn't want to talk about Barry. Instead, he said, "I think it's great. About your job. That means you're footloose and fancy free."

She blinked. "Losing my job is a good thing? Are you crazy? You heard that lady—I do good work, Matt. I help people. I'm not just a pretty face."

The last was said with such passion that nearby diners stopped mid-bite to look at them. There was a groundswell of murmuring. Matt thought he heard someone mention Eve's name.

He rose, dropped three twenties on the table and put out his hand to Eve. "Let's walk."

A warm spell had cleared away any trace of winter, but the breeze still held a bite. Matt turned the corner out of the wind, and pulled Eve into his arms. He kissed her, hard and fast—something he'd been dying to do from the moment she walked out of that boardroom. *So much for my honorable intentions.*

"Thanks," he whispered, brushing her bottom lip with his thumb. "I needed that."

She smiled, her eyes slightly out of focus. "No problem. It was the perfect dessert."

"My car's in the Communitex lot. Can we go there and talk?"

Sighing, she checked her watch. "I have to be back in the boardroom in twenty minutes."

When they were settled in the rental car, Matt edged sideways as much as the cramped space would allow and said, "I know this isn't the optimum time or place—there really isn't enough room to grovel properly."

She tilted her head. "What are you talking about?"

"I want to apologize for being a jerk. For abandoning you when you needed me. And for not being brave enough to tell you what's in my heart."

Although outwardly Eve looked perfectly calm and composed, her bottom lip disappeared beneath her smooth white teeth. "Matt, we said all that this morning. We love each other, but love isn't enough to make a relationship work. You said Elizabeth Taylor tried love and—"

Matt raked his fingers through his hair. "Are you going to remember every stupid thing I say for the rest of our lives? I hope not, because there are going to be more. I guarantee it."

"The rest of our lives?" Eve repeated.

Matt closed the gap between them. "I love you,

Eve. I don't have all the answers. Hell, I don't even have all the questions, but I do know that I want to try to figure this out. With you.''

Eve moved back slightly. She looked as surprised as a person can be without actually fainting—although given her paleness, that was a possibility.

"What about Ashley? Your job?"

"Ashley has a lot on her plate, and I'm sure this is going to cause some extra anxiety, but I honestly think she can handle it. She's a smart kid—even if she makes some dumb moves once in a while.''

He turned her shoulders slightly so he could look into her eyes. He felt her nervous tension, her fear. "As for my job, I was sent here to find Eve Masterson, and I can't leave when there's still a part of you missing.''

She drew her hands up defensively and pushed on his chest. "What are you talking about? I'm here. Unemployed, but I have marketable skills. In fact, I have a whole list of calls from when I was sick, and my old agent Marcella has called half a dozen times. I'll find something. Maybe not just what I want, but—''

He cut off her frenetic ramblings with a light kiss. "That's not what I'm talking about and you know it. I faced my fear, Eve. I want to help you face yours. The voice on the phone.''

She intensified her effort to escape and he released her. She put her hand on the door handle but didn't open it. "You don't understand. You don't know anything about her.''

"No, I don't. But I know that my fear—my feelings of inadequacy—almost kept me from being with you.''

Matt could read the conflict in her face. He gently touched her cheek. "Let me help you, Eve.'' He fished in his pocket for the slip of paper from the restaurant. ''The real reason Bo called was to give me your birth mother's current address. Ashley told me she saw the name on an investigation report and I had him trace her. Let's go see her, Eve. Together.''

She shook her head and tried to flee.

"Eve, running away doesn't help. Trust me, the only way to fight your fear is head-on.''

She took a deep breath and seemed to collect herself. Matt didn't have a clue to what she was thinking. ''I have a meeting to finish,'' she said flatly.

Matt nodded.

''Will you wait for me?''

A slight quiver in her voice gave him the spurt of hope he needed. ''Forever, if I have to.''

A tiny smile made her lips flicker. ''It shouldn't take quite that long.''

Matt leaned across the gap and kissed her. Sweet and significant but far too short. She opened the door and got out. Matt did the same.

They walked in silence until Eve said, ''The first time I ever saw my birth mother was at the Miss Teen America pageant. She was drunk, and she had some guy with a video camera with her. She said I was going to be her vehicle to the stars.''

Matt's knee buckled painfully.

''The irony is, she'd already sold me once. For a car—a 1967 Buick.'' Eve looked at him, eyes glittering with tears. ''Get it? Vehicle? Buick?''

Ignoring his throbbing knee, Matt pulled her tight. "Oh, honey, don't you see what this is doing to you? You have to face the past so you can see yourself the way I do. If I'm brave enough to admit my cowardice, then you have to be strong enough to go to Florida with me...tomorrow."

"Tomorrow?" she peeped.

He nodded. "Why not? You don't have a job at the moment, and Bo said not to come home until I finish things down here. As far as I can see, there's only one thing left to do."

A LITTLE OVER THREE HOURS into their journey the next morning Eve remembered something she'd wanted to tell Sara, who'd called just as Eve and Matt were walking out the door.

Sara, ever the optimist, not so subtly suggested that Eve and Matt might consider having a double wedding with Bo and Claudie in June. "They're planning on renting a catamaran at Lake Tahoe. It'll be a big party. Since Matt's going to be there anyway..."

Sara's leading hint was enough to blow Eve's question straight out of her head. She'd meant to ask what Sara thought of Marcella's idea that Eve return to Sacramento. The previous afternoon—after all the forms and papers had been signed at Communitex— Eve had talked with her former agent at length. Marcella seemed to think Eve could wind up with the executive producer's job at her old Sacramento station if she was willing to do some high-profile PR for the company.

For some reason, Eve had kept the possibility to

herself, not mentioning it to Matt when he'd picked her up to go home.

"Are you hungry?" Matt asked. "There's one more doughnut left."

Eve's stomach was far too knotted to tolerate food. She shook her head and rubbed the embossed design on the brass button of her blazer. She'd spent a solid hour trying to decide what to wear, finally settling for navy wool slacks and a scarlet blouse to wear with her dull gold blazer.

They'd shared her bed last night. Their lovemaking had been bittersweet, needy and silent, but somehow more attuned to each other than the all-consuming passion they'd shared in Mexico.

"You know, I just remembered something," Matt said. "Ashley asked to talk to you and I put her off. Would you mind if we called her?"

"Right now? Isn't she in school?"

He fished his cell phone out of the pocket of his jacket lying between them. "She had an orthodontist appointment this morning and I think Sonya usually brings her home afterward instead of driving all the way back to school. Wanna try?"

Eve hesitated. Finally, she took the phone. "I guess I might as well get it over. But what do I say if your ex-wife answers?"

Matt snickered. "Ask to speak to Ashley."

Eve made a face. "You know what I mean."

He gave her a slow, dreamy smile that made her heart do cartwheels. "We'll talk to Sonya together when it comes to that. One step at a time." Nodding at the phone, he said, "Hit zero one and then send."

Eve did as directed, then pushed her hair out of the

way and put the phone to her ear. She cleared her throat. "Ashley? This is Eve…Masterson."

Ashley's delighted laugh unloosened the knot in Eve's chest. She let out the breath she'd been holding and relaxed back in the seat. "Your dad and I are on our way to Florida. He said you wanted to tell me something."

"I want you to know that you're the first woman I've ever met who's good enough for my dad. Even though Grandma was worried about Dad not dating, it never bothered me because I knew it would happen when he met the right person—someone special who could appreciate him." She paused a second then asked, "You do, don't you? Appreciate him?"

"More than I could ever say."

Ashley let out a long sigh. "Cool…I'm so glad you found each other. Really, I am."

Eve's eyes filled with tears. "That's incredibly nice of you to say."

"I mean it," Ashley said with feeling. "You're awesome. It meant a lot to me seeing your scrapbook the other night. I mean, a lot of adults want you to think they were born grown-up—all perfect and everything. You weren't afraid to let me see you with braces. I liked that. I think we can be friends, if you want to be, I mean."

"I'd be honored. Thank you."

"Sure. No problem. Can I talk to my dad a minute?"

She passed the phone blindly and reached in her purse for a tissue. She tried not to listen to Matt's conversation, and didn't look at him until the phone landed in her lap.

"Well...?" he asked. "Is everything okay?"

"She's wonderful. I could love that girl—almost as much as I love her dad."

Matt chuckled, forcing his jaw to relax. "Good. I'm going to hold you to that."

He glanced at the clock on the dashboard and a ripple of nervous tension passed through his body. Not much longer if his estimate was accurate. They'd been in the car since nine, when they took off armed with two steaming mugs of coffee and a box of Krispy Kreme doughnuts.

The address Bo had given Matt matched the one on the report in Eve's guest room. Patricia Benson lived in a small town in the panhandle of Florida, south and east of Tallahassee. According to the investigator Eve had hired, her birth mother was in poor health from throat cancer. Virtually housebound, Patricia lived in a small mobile-home park a few miles away from her daughter, Jill—Eve's half sister.

When Matt spotted the sign he was looking for, he reached out and took Eve's hand. "We're here."

"Already?" Eve sputtered. She gripped his hand. "Why didn't you warn me?"

"Less time to be nervous."

She grabbed her purse and pawed through it, finally producing a tube of lipstick. Her hand was trembling so badly Matt doubted she'd ever get the color on straight.

"Wait," Matt said.

After pulling into a spot marked Visitor, he leaned over and kissed her, hard and swift. When he backed off, she had a slightly dazed look that made him smile. "Now, the lipstick."

She pulled down the visor and stared into the mirror. For the first time since his impulsive decision, Matt questioned the wisdom of this confrontation. Maybe she wasn't ready. She'd only been out of the hospital a little over a week.

"Are you going to be okay?" Matt asked. "If you've changed your mind, I can…"

Eve inhaled deeply. "Could I have a couple of minutes alone?"

"Of course." He opened the door and got out. The heat startled him. He peeled back the sleeves of his shirt, reveling in the eighty-degree temperature. "Wow. No wonder so many New Yorkers migrate south in the winter. This is great."

Ducking back down, he told her, "There's a convenience store right across the road. I'll be right back. I want to pick up a couple of bottles of water."

She nodded. Matt couldn't read her expression. She seemed composed but caught up in a distant memory. Even sadness couldn't diminish her beauty. *How could any parent give away someone like Eve?* Suddenly choking on the bitter taste of chagrin, Matt realized he'd come damn close to making the same mistake himself.

As soon as Matt left, Eve touched up her blush and quickly blotted her lipstick then ran a comb through her hair, which she'd chosen to wear down and unfettered.

Will she look like me? Eve had only the dimmest memory of the woman who crashed into her life when she was fifteen. True, Eve herself had sought out the meeting after finally goading her adoptive mother into helping her find Patricia. But the storybook meeting Eve had envisioned never took place. Instead, a loud, garishly dressed woman in too-tight capri pants and a tube top had descended the steps of the rehearsal hall with a cameraman in tow.

"There's my baby girl," Patricia had exclaimed, pushing Eve's mother out of the way. "That's her. Even Mine."

Eve's parents had interceded before the cameraman could set up, but even her father's broad shoulders couldn't protect Eve from the other woman's loud demands to a "share of the profits" from Eve's future film career.

"You can tell by looking at her she's the next Liz Taylor," the woman had ranted. "She's exotic. Exotic sells."

Eve never had a chance to ask the question burning in her gut, the one that had haunted her all her life. *Why did you give me up?*

Eve's adoptive parents had tried to minimize the damage, but Eve couldn't stop asking questions, and finally the truth of her adoption came out. The Mastersons had been living in Texas at the time of Eve's birth. Howard Masterson owned a used car dealership. He'd sold a car to Eve's mother who later defaulted on payments. When he tried to repossess the vehicle, he found Patricia drunk...and in labor. He'd rushed her to the hospital.

As an interested bystander, he later inquired about the baby and found out the state planned to take the child away as it had the woman's two older children.

Although the Mastersons hadn't planned on adding to their family, Kathleen had always wanted a daughter, and Eve became theirs. Howard later returned the car to Patricia as a gesture of goodwill.

"I have to do this," Eve said under her breath. "It's now or never."

Leaving her purse on the seat, Eve got out of the car. Her feet felt disconnected from her body, her navy flats looked surreal against the crushed pink rock. Hauling in a deep breath of warm moist air, she looked around.

The court looked clean and pleasant. Most places showed pride of ownership. Flower beds were interspersed with ceramic squirrels and pink flamingos. Patricia's home was by far the smallest. A metal overhang was adorned with a faded rebel flag, tattered on the edges. Three lawn chairs sat on the green artificial turf at the far end of the patio; a woman occupied one of the chairs.

Eve's stomach felt queasy, her knees rubbery. She might have dropped to a crouch behind the fender if Matt hadn't materialized at her side. "How 'bout we do this together?"

Gratefully, she clutched his hand. Faking bravado she didn't feel, Eve led him around the car.

Later, she'd recall odd little sounds, like the gravel crunching under her shoes and the birds squabbling in the mossy birdbath, but as each step took her closer to her past all she could focus on was the small, frail-looking woman in the padded metal chair. Her hair was artificially red, her face the same elongated oval as Eve's. Her eyes were more occidental, her skin a paler hue, her lips withered and drawn.

Matt held open a creaky gate of chain-link material. The woman motioned them forward with one pale bony hand. Eve's step might have faltered if it weren't for Matt.

"Even Mine," the woman said in her odd, artificial rasp. "You came."

If Eve lived to be a hundred she doubted she'd ever forget this moment. She felt like a visitor from another planet watching some strange, inexplicable play. The artificial property of her mother's voice sent a chill up her spine, and Eve was grateful she'd selected a jacket that hid her shiver.

"Hello," Eve said softly. "I've come for a visit. This is Matthew Ross."

Matt stepped closer and held out his hand. Patricia's painfully thin hand shook visibly. Although she nodded politely at Matt, she never took her gaze from Eve. "You came," she repeated. "I told Jilly you would."

Jill. My sister. Fearing that her legs might not support her much longer, Eve walked to the closest patio chair and sat down. Matt positioned himself behind her, hands on Eve's shoulders.

In the silence that fell, Eve studied the woman who had given birth to her. Hints of Patricia's former beauty remained like an image in a smoky mirror. A Georgia peach, withered from too many nights in honky-tonk bars, too many cruel men and too many cigarettes.

Eve didn't have the slightest idea how or even where to begin. *What does one talk about with the woman who traded you for a car?*

Matt took the initiative to break the ice. "Could

you tell us about yourself?'' he asked. ''Maybe explain how you came to give Eve up for adoption?''

The words—which had haunted her for so many years—seemed to fall between them like brittle bones. Eve flinched, and Matt patted her shoulders, reassuring her.

Patricia took a wheezy breath. ''Didn't give her up. The State took her. Put her brother and sister in foster homes.'' She grimaced. ''I was in a bad way back then. Booze and drugs. She was so tiny.''

Her rheumy eyes filled with tears as she looked at Eve in supplication. ''The car man—her new daddy—gave me the pink slip of my Buick just to be nice.'' She sniffed. ''Made it easier knowing he was a nice man.''

Matt dropped to one knee beside Eve's chair. ''Are you okay?'' he asked softly.

She wiped tears from her cheeks with a mangled tissue. ''Would you do me a favor and get my purse? I left it on the seat.''

He nodded with obvious reluctance.

When he was gone, Eve sat forward. ''Patricia,'' she said softly. ''I want you to know you did the right thing by giving me up. My parents are wonderful people. All I've accomplished I owe to them, but I owe you my life. I'm sorry I wasn't able to visit you sooner. I've been sick recently. Anemia.''

Patricia winced. ''You got that from me. Our bodies can't make iron fast enough when we run low.''

Eve started. Was that true? It would explain a lot.

Matt returned a moment later. Eve put the purse on her lap. She dug into its depths then extracted a cashier's check. She and Matt had stopped at the bank before leaving town. Sitting forward, she placed it on her birth mother's lap.

"I tried sending you a check once before and my...sister," she said, stumbling over the word, "returned it in pieces. Her letter said you didn't want money. You only wanted to see me." Eve's voice quivered. "Now you've seen me. Now you can take the money."

Patricia's eyes filled with tears and she picked up the check as if to hand it back. "I used to think money would make everything okay. It doesn't."

Eve's fingers closed over her mother's. "Keep it. Buy yourself something nice. Or donate it somewhere. It isn't much—not even the price of a good Buick."

She managed the last with enough dry humor to make Patricia smile, despite her tears.

They stayed for lunch. A simple affair of ham sandwiches and fresh coleslaw. Eve asked for the recipe, which seemed to please Patricia. As they were finishing their dessert, Eve asked the one question that she hadn't been certain she was brave enough to ask. "Who's my father?"

Patricia looked away, but Eve had no trouble reading the look of shame on her face. She shook her head slowly, tears streaming down her withered cheeks. "I never knew for sure. Too many parties. Young soldiers. All handsome. Fun." She wept softly.

The reality of the admission was both better and worse than Eve had imagined. Better because she wouldn't have to go through this ordeal a second time; worse because she would never know the man, his family or his history.

Reaching out, she touched her mother's shoulder. "It's okay. I have a wonderful father. I was just curious."

Matt fetched a glass of water for Patricia. His kindness made Eve's heart swell. He'd been right. She'd put this off too long.

As they rose to leave, Patricia touched Eve's hand. "I made mistakes. Lots of 'em," she said, pointing to the hole in her throat. "You, I got right."

Eve's eyes filled with tears. She put her arms around her mother's frail shoulders and hugged her. "Thank you," she whispered.

"I've always loved you, Even Mine. Always."

Before leaving, Eve took her half sister Jill's phone number and address. Their brother lived in Tennessee. Patricia called him "a loner." Perhaps one day Eve would cross those hurdles as well.

Neither Eve nor Matt spoke until they were back on the highway. "You know, we're not that far from Mexico," he said, obviously striving for humor. "Shall we swim for it?"

His jest had just the opposite effect. Eve suddenly burst into tears. "Oh, honey," he cried, turning into a used car lot. "I'm sorry. What did I say?"

Blubbering through her tears, she tried to make sense of the tumult inside. "I...I...was going to tell you to take me home," she said between sobs. "But I suddenly realized, I don't know where that is."

Matt patted her back. "Oh, sweetheart."

"Matt, I mean it. I don't have a job. I haven't been unemployed since I was sixteen."

He interrupted her. "All that will sort itself out,

Eve. You don't have to decide anything right this
minute. Well, maybe one thing.''
   "What?''
   "Will you marry me?''

CHAPTER FIFTEEN

MATT HADN'T INTENDED to blurt out his proposal quite so unromantically, but somehow the words just popped out of his mouth. Eve's look of disbelief almost made him take them back until he saw the smile that followed. A brilliant, joyful smile.

"Do you mean that?" she asked. "Truly? You love me enough to marry me?"

A knock on the window made them both jump. Matt hit the button in the door panel to lower the window. A swarthy young man in shirtsleeves and a tie squatted beside the car.

"Hi, folks. I'd guess this is a rental and you're in the market for a car. You've come to the right place. My name is Josh." He put out his hand, which Matt felt compelled to shake. Before Matt could explain about their presence, the fellow leaned inward to do the same with Eve.

Matt sensed the instant Josh recognized her.

"Oh, my Lord," he exclaimed, still holding on to her hand. "You're Eve Masterson."

Matt's stomach rolled. How had he forgotten this small annoying detail? Eve was now and probably always would be a celebrity.

Eve disentangled her fingers from Josh's grip with a small wiggle of her wrist. She smiled and said, "It's

DEBRA SALONEN 285

nice to meet you, Josh, and we're sorry to have interrupted your business, but we're lost. Could you direct us to the highway?''

The ploy worked. Josh nearly killed himself trying to give the most succinct directions. Matt had to bite down on a smile. Now, this was a fan he could like. They left a few minutes later with a free map and Josh's business card.

A few miles down the road, Eve asked softly, ''Do you want to take back your question? Obviously, I have baggage that will follow me—follow us—wherever we are.''

Matt sighed. ''Let's find a park. Somewhere we can talk.''

He blessed small towns everywhere when they discovered a tiny, mostly empty park a few miles down the road. They got out of the car and walked to a wooden bench beneath a huge tree Matt couldn't identify. Its peeling bark littered the grass beneath it; gray moss hung from its branches like an old man's beard.

''Let's be honest, Eve. You know I'm not crazy about all the trappings that come with your fame. There's no denying you have a very recognizable face, but I wouldn't change a single feature.'' He kissed her left eyebrow, then her cheekbone and chin, for emphasis.

''I guess that's a little problem I'll have to deal with,'' he said, smiling to show how very little it was. ''It's not as if I'm perfect, you know.'' He waggled his right leg to make his point.

Eve placed her hand atop his knee. ''Battle scars,

my love," she said softly. "You don't give that wound the honor it deserves."

Matt closed his eyes against the rush of emotion that came from her look of pride and respect.

She turned slightly and looked toward the distant swing set where a mother pushed her young child. "There's something I haven't told you—mainly because I didn't know how I felt about it. I talked to Marcella yesterday. My old station in Sacramento contacted her about the possibility of my coming back to work for them—in management."

Matt flinched. He hadn't seen that coming. Before he could think of a reply, she added, "At first it felt like a step backward, but now I'm wondering if it isn't the break I need, if I'm serious about changing the way television covers stories." She frowned. "It won't be as wide-sweeping as Communitex, but it's a start."

"Sacramento," Matt murmured. Bo needed him in New York.

"Or," Eve said, putting on a falsely bright smile, "I could go back to the city with you and start job hunting."

"But you don't want another on-camera job, and the traveling isn't good for you. That's the last place I want you, but I promised Bo I'd give this P.I. business a shot for at least a year."

Eve closed her eyes and took a deep breath. When she opened them, she said, "I think this is a test, Matt."

"A test?"

"Pass/fail. Do we pick love over possible job opportunities and family obligations? Or do we go back to business as usual?''

Matt swallowed against the tightness in his throat. He hated tests.

''Fortunately, I've always been very good at tests,'' she said blithely. ''I understand them. Sometimes a tricky question is actually very simple—we just make it harder than it is by overthinking the possibilities.''

He noticed the mischievous twinkle in her eye.

''Shall we cheat? Compare answers?'' Her smile made Matt's heartbeat speed up. ''I'll go first.''

She squared her shoulders and said, ''I want to marry you. And if that means I miss some window of opportunity because I'm not at the right place at the right time, then…oh, well. At least I'll be with the man who found me when everyone else quit looking.''

Matt pulled her close. He kissed her as thoroughly as he dared in public. The only spectators seemed to be an old woman and her dog, but he didn't want to share this moment with anyone.

''You stole my answer,'' he said with mock severity.

She laughed. ''How could I? You found me.'' She tapped her chest to make the point.

He cupped her cheek. ''Only because you slowed down enough for me to catch up. I've loved you since the first moment I saw you on TV, but I figured every man in America felt the same way so what chance did I have? Now I know they only saw an image. I see *you*. I love *you*. And I always will.''

She wrapped her arms around him and hugged him

tight. "I love you, too. Thank you for finding me," she cried tearfully.

Blinking against tears of his own, he whispered, "Let's go home."

She dropped her arms and sat back. Bottom lip quivering, she said, "We still haven't figured that out, Matt. Where is home?"

"Right here," he said, placing her hand over his heart. He did the same to her. This, he suddenly understood with perfect clarity, was the true answer. "Home is two hearts together. Everything else is just real estate. Now, let's go celebrate. It isn't every day we pass a test *and* get engaged."

He paused. "You are going to marry me, aren't you?"

Eve's smile was pure joy. "As Ashley would say, 'Oh, yeah.'" Her grin faltered. "Speaking of Ashley, will she be okay with this?"

It was Matt's turn to tease. "In a way, it was her idea. She said that since her life was already totally screwed up thanks to her mother and Alan, I might as well just marry you and get it over with."

Eve made a face. "That doesn't sound very encouraging."

Matt rose and pulled her up, too. "Don't worry. I think she'll appreciate the logic when she realizes that the two most important people in the world to me are both moving to California," he said, kissing the tip of her nose. "She knows me well enough to figure out I won't be far behind."

"What about Bo? Your job?"

Matt shrugged. "He's in love. He'll understand."

Eve gave him an impish grin. "And if he doesn't, Claudie and Sara will explain it to him."

Matt laughed. His poor cousin didn't stand a chance. Besides, in the long run, he knew Bo wouldn't mind losing a business partner if it meant gaining a neighbor.

FIVE MONTHS, three weeks and six days later, Eve adjusted the strap of her mint-green sundress, then turned to scrutinize her profile in the mirror. The built-in bra of the simple linen sheath was a bit tighter than she'd have preferred, but at least the lack of a waistband made her recent weight gain less obvious. *No one will notice,* she decided. *Besides, they'll all be looking at the bride.*

She walked to the window of her tenth-floor suite and stared at the startling blue lake surrounded by pine-covered mountains. She'd arrived in Tahoe the day before after charging up the I-80 with a multitude of other Friday-afternoon refugees from Sacramento and the Bay Area. Her new Infiniti had been filled with the last-minute wedding necessities she'd been asked to deliver.

Matt had flown directly to Reno from New York two days earlier to help Bo finalize the on-site logistics. The wedding was scheduled to take place in less than two hours aboard the *Woodwind II* catamaran. The guest list included Matt's and Bo's parents as well as Claudie's siblings and several residents of One Wish House. The wedding party occupied three adjoining suites, with the other guests scattered about the hotel and nearby casinos.

With all the chaos, Eve felt as though she'd barely

had a minute alone with Matt since she arrived. *You had enough time to tell him,* a little voice said. *You made love twice. You ate breakfast together.*

True, her conscience argued, but a part of her wanted to hold off breaking the news until after Bo and Claudie said "I do." Since moving to Sacramento four months earlier, Eve had come to know and like Claudie. In some ways, Claudie was a closer friend than Sara, who'd been totally absorbed in motherhood since the birth of the twins in April.

Sighing, Eve rested her forehead against the glass—the beauty of the panoramic scene lost on her. Even though she and Matt spoke on the phone daily and professed to love each other and *planned* to marry, the fact remained that Matt hadn't even set a date to move, let alone put a ring on her finger.

Eve intended to rectify that problem in the following week. Matt had ten days of vacation. He and Eve would spend two additional days alone in Tahoe then drive to Santa Barbara to visit Ashley, who hadn't been able to attend the wedding because of a dressage competition. Apparently her new horse—Cypher—was a born winner.

When Sonya and Alan moved to Santa Barbara in early February, Ashley had opted to stay with Matt's parents until school let out. Eve understood how hard it was for Ashley to choose between her parents, and give up her horse, as well. Although Alan had offered to purchase Jester, his owner felt the cross-country trip would have been too hard on the animal and had refused to sell. The new horse seemed to have offset any jealousy Ashley might have had about Kyle Alan Greensburg, her new baby brother.

Eve was anxious to see Ashley, but she was nervous, too. Since their initial meeting in January, Eve and Ashley had seen each other several times, and they'd become e-friends. *What if my news jeopardizes our friendship?*

Eve would never forget how much Ashley's kindness had meant to her when Eve talked to her about Patricia. Since then Eve had returned to Florida twice. She'd met both of her half siblings—Jillian, who had three kids and a trucker husband, and Todd, a mechanic with a drinking problem.

When her parents returned from Australia in early March, Eve flew to New York to introduce them to Matt. The weekend had been a huge success despite Matt's head cold and her father's sprained knee. The two men had hit it off by comparing infirmities.

Eve had flown to New York on two other occasions. Easter provided a chance to meet Deborah's family and spend some time with Matt's parents and Ashley. She returned in May with Bo and Claudie when Matt's uncle Robert, Bo's father, was released from the hospital where he'd been recuperating from a head injury. Eve and Claudie had used the time to shop since the men were closeted in Matt's office, availing themselves of Robert B. Lester's still-sharp business acumen.

Their most romantic weekend came in April when Matt flew to Sacramento to attend the christening of Sara and Ren's twins, Joley and Kara. After the ceremony, they'd driven to the wine country where Matt had to spend half his time comforting Eve, who lamented the fact that her biological clock was gonging loudly.

Eve pressed a hand to her belly. She hadn't had a chance to see a doctor, but her body—and an at-home pregnancy test—told her the same thing.

A wolf whistle cut into her thoughts. "Zowie! Are you sure you're not the bride? You're beautiful enough to be one," Matt said, entering the room from the adjoining men's suite.

Dressed in an ivory linen suit with a sage-green silk T-shirt and topsiders, he was so handsome Eve almost forgot to breathe. He strode purposefully across the room and swept her into a passionate kiss. Giggling, Eve threw herself into the spirit of the moment, kissing him with equal abandon.

"Now, that's more like it," Matt said with relish. "You were a little subdued last night. I was afraid you were waiting to break the bad news to me until after the wedding."

"What bad news?" Eve asked, her heart missing a beat.

"That you don't love me anymore or you found someone else."

She cupped his handsome jaw with her hand. *Now. Tell him now.* "Don't be silly. I could never love anyone as much as I love you. It wouldn't be fair to our baby."

His expression didn't change for a full second, then he tilted his head; his eyebrows drew together. "We have a baby?"

"Not yet. But we will in seven and a half months," she said, catching her bottom lip in her teeth.

His spontaneous smile brought tears to her eyes. "Oh my God," he exclaimed, his voice echoing off the walls.

The adjoining door slammed open. "What's wrong now?" Bo asked, charging in. His suit—white with a black silk T-shirt—was so *Miami Vice* Eve had to smile, but it fit Bo's style.

Claudie—a picture-perfect bride in a knee-length gown of champagne-yellow organza and satin—exited from the bathroom, clutching her veil. She and Matt had switched rooms this morning for propriety's sake. "What's going on?"

"Anything but the cake," Bo groaned, pretending to shade his eyes so as not to see his bride-to-be. "Don't tell me it's the cake."

Matt's gaze never left Eve's. She read the question in his eyes and knew he wouldn't share the news with the others without her permission. His reassuring smile gave her the courage to nod.

"Eve's pregnant," Matt said, grinning with such unabashed joy Eve nearly cried.

"Someone's pregnant?" Sara Bishop asked, entering through the main door. With a child in her arms, she ditched her key and diaper bag on the table then hurried toward the others. A pink receiving blanket draped over one shoulder partly obscured her sleeveless Hawaiian-print dress. She hefted the baby into burping position as she eyed the bride suspiciously. "Why didn't you tell me?"

"Not me," Claudie said huffily. "Eve."

At that moment, Ren Bishop walked in carrying a matching bundle cradled in his arms. On his heels followed a second bridesmaid in the same island-print sarong—Sherry, Claudie's seventeen-year-old sister. The willowy blonde was holding three-and-a-half-year-old Brady's hand.

"What'd I miss? What's wrong with Eve?" Ren asked.

"Nothing's *wrong* with me," she said. Despite her many years on camera, Eve felt herself blush. "Everything's great. I'm pregnant."

Ren exchanged a look with his wife, who was wearing a smug smile. "That's awesome. Shall I go ask the captain about a double ceremony?"

"Good grief, no," Eve blurted out. "This is Claudie and Bo's special day. Besides, we can't get married without Ashley and my parents." Not to mention her new family and the many business friends who'd welcomed her back to Sacramento with open arms and given her a chance to fulfill her dreams. Her teen-targeted talk show, called *Beyond Beauty,* was rated number one in its time slot.

"Yeah," Matt added. "At least give me a chance to get down on one knee and make it official."

"No time like the present," Bo said. He dropped his hand and looked at his soon-to-be-wife. "Public proposals are very popular right now, aren't they, honey?"

Claudie snickered. "It certainly worked for you. Everyone knows the only reason I said yes was to save your cute little tushie."

Bo sputtered indignantly, but before he could reply, Matt marched to the luggage rack in the corner of the room and dug into the side pocket of his suitcase. He palmed a small black velvet box that made Eve's heart miss a beat.

Shaking his head, he returned to stand in front of Eve, then slowly lowered himself to his good knee.

Eve reached out and cupped his smooth jaw and smiled. "You don't have to do this."

Matt tilted his head to her touch. "I was planning something a bit more romantic. Just the two of us." He shot a blustery scowl over his shoulder that Eve was sure fooled no one.

Clearing his throat, he took Eve's left hand in his and said, "You are the other half of my soul, Eve Masterson, and I want us to be together. Forever. Will you marry me?"

Eve's throat was almost too tight with emotion to speak, but she somehow managed a tiny "Yes."

She clutched the small, elegant box to her chest a moment, then with shaky fingers pried it open. Resting on a bed of white satin was a square aquamarine stone set in a slim band of white gold. It was lovely. Delicate.

Before she could say anything, Matt leaned forward with concern then let out a harsh cry. "Damn. Wrong box. Ashley's gonna kill me. That's *her* engagement ring. She wanted to propose, too. That's supposed to symbolize your connection to her life. It's her birthstone."

The women in the room gave a collective "Oh."

Matt started to rise, but his bad knee buckled. Sara, who was closest, dashed to the suitcase and fetched a second black box. "Here," she said softly. "And if it's any consolation, I think this is the most romantic proposal I've ever heard."

Eve heard Ren grumble something to his wife when she returned to his side, but she didn't pay any attention because Matt—after surreptitiously checking the contents of the second box—held it out to her. "Can we try this again?"

Eve opened it slowly. The light from the window made the emerald-cut diamond glitter like a small sun. Her gasp of wonder and delight seemed to be just the release their friends needed, because suddenly everyone crowded forward, chattering and laughing.

Matt coughed loudly. "Excuse me, but aren't we forgetting something." Everyone froze. "Eve's answer," he said pointedly.

Eve slipped the ring on her finger—a perfect fit, and held her hand up to admire the beautiful ring. She'd never been happier and she knew there was no way to adequately express that feeling in front of an audience. "Yes, I'll marry you. The sooner the better. And we can live on the moon as far as I'm concerned, as long as we're together."

Everyone clapped and cheered so loudly the commotion woke up the babies.

Claudie—barefoot with veil in hand—hopped up on the bed once the children were rescued by their doting parents, and hollered, "That will be wedding number two, wedding number one is due to begin in forty-seven minutes, folks."

Her announcement created a momentary panic, which took some of the focus off Matt and Eve, who were locked in each other's arms.

"Sorry about that." Matt whispered, nuzzling Eve's neck.

"Don't be. I'm a public figure, I deserve a public proposal. But," she said, teasing him with a kiss on the nose, "promise me we won't have this big an audience when I give birth."

Matt's booming laugh coincided with a knock on the outer door. Sherry, who was the closest, opened it. A waiter pushing a table topped with two ice buckets and an array of crystal flutes entered. He handed an envelope to the young girl, who carried it to her sister.

Claudie extracted a card and read the note aloud, "'Dearest Claudie and Bo, I'm so very sorry to be missing your wonderful day. But at my age, one doesn't dare pass up a chance to cruise around the South Pacific with a dashing escort. Please know that my best wishes are with you. As my son and wonderful daughter-in-law have proven—love is the most powerful cohesive of all. I am proud of you both, and I wish you every happiness, Babe Bishop.'"

Sara placed her now-quieted pink bundle on the bed beside the twin Ren had been comforting, then poured rounds of champagne and sparkling cider. When everyone had been served, she asked, "A toast, husband dear?"

Ren lifted his glass. "To Claudie and Bo...*and* to Eve and Matt." He put his arm around his wife's shoulders and squeezed her tight. "May you know as much happiness in your lives together as Sara and I have. And may your futures be rich with the laughter of children and the love of good friends. Salud."

Eve looked at Matt. Her heart couldn't begin to express the joy she felt. They were at a beginning, and she couldn't wait to see how their story would unfold.

HARLEQUIN *Super*ROMANCE

Welcome to Montana

BIG SKY COUNTRY

Home of the Rocky Mountains, Yellowstone National Park, slow-moving glaciers and the spectacular Going to the Sun Highway.

Set against this unforgettable background, Harlequin Superromance introduces the **Maxwells of Montana**—a family that's lived and ranched here for generations.

You won't want to miss this brand-new trilogy— three exciting romances by three of your favorite authors.

MARRIED IN MONTANA
by Lynnette Kent on sale August 2001

A MONTANA FAMILY
by Roxanne Rustand on sale September 2001

MY MONTANA HOME
by Ellen James on sale October 2001

Available wherever Harlequin books are sold.

HARLEQUIN®
Makes any time special ®

COMING SOON...

AN EXCITING
OPPORTUNITY TO SAVE
ON THE PURCHASE OF
HARLEQUIN AND
SILHOUETTE BOOKS!

*DETAILS TO FOLLOW
IN OCTOBER 2001!*

YOU WON'T WANT TO MISS IT!

PHQ401

HARLEQUIN WALK DOWN THE AISLE TO MAUI CONTEST 1197
OFFICIAL RULES
NO PURCHASE NECESSARY TO ENTER

1. To enter, follow directions published in the offer to which you are responding. Contest begins April 2, 2001, and ends on October 1, 2001. Method of entry may vary. Mailed entries must be postmarked by October 1, 2001, and received by October 8, 2001.

2. Contest entry may be, at times, presented via the Internet, but will be restricted solely to residents of certain geographic areas that are disclosed on the Web site. To enter via the Internet, if permissible, access the Harlequin Web site (www.eHarlequin.com) and follow the directions displayed online. Online entries must be received by 11:59 p.m. E.S.T. on October 1, 2001.

   In lieu of submitting an entry online, enter by mail by hand-printing (or typing) on an 8½" x 11" plain piece of paper, your name, address (including zip code), Contest number/name and in 250 words or fewer, why winning a Harlequin wedding dress would make your wedding day special. Mail via first-class mail to: Harlequin Walk Down the Aisle Contest 1197, (in the U.S.) P.O. Box 9076, 3010 Walden Avenue, Buffalo, NY 14269-9076, (in Canada) P.O. Box 637, Fort Erie, Ontario L2A 5X3, Canada.

   Limit one entry per person, household address and e-mail address. Online and/or mailed entries received from persons residing in geographic areas in which Internet entry is not permissible will be disqualified.

3. Contests will be judged by a panel of members of the Harlequin editorial, marketing and public relations staff based on the following criteria:

   - Originality and Creativity—50%
   - Emotionally Compelling—25%
   - Sincerity—25%

   In the event of a tie, duplicate prizes will be awarded. Decisions of the judges are final.

4. All entries become the property of Torstar Corp. and will not be returned. No responsibility is assumed for lost, late, illegible, incomplete, inaccurate, nondelivered or misdirected mail or misdirected e-mail, for technical, hardware or software failures of any kind, lost or unavailable network connections, or failed, incomplete, garbled or delayed computer transmission or any human error which may occur in the receipt or processing of the entries in this Contest.

5. Contest open only to residents of the U.S. (except Puerto Rico) and Canada, who are 18 years of age or older, and is void wherever prohibited by law; all applicable laws and regulations apply. Any litigation within the Province of Quebec respecting the conduct or organization of a publicity contest may be submitted to the Régie des alcools, des courses et des jeux for a ruling. Any litigation respecting the awarding of a prize may be submitted to the Régie des alcools, des courses et des jeux only for the purpose of helping the parties reach a settlement. Employees and immediate family members of Torstar Corp. and D. L. Blair, Inc., their affiliates, subsidiaries and all other agencies, entities and persons connected with the use, marketing or conduct of this Contest are not eligible to enter. Taxes on prizes are the sole responsibility of winners. Acceptance of any prize offered constitutes permission to use winner's name, photograph or other likeness for the purposes of advertising, trade and promotion on behalf of Torstar Corp., its affiliates and subsidiaries without further compensation to the winner, unless prohibited by law.

6. Winners will be determined no later than November 15, 2001, and will be notified by mail. Winners will be required to sign and return an Affidavit of Eligibility form within 15 days after winner notification. Noncompliance within that time period may result in disqualification and an alternative winner may be selected. Winners of trip must execute a Release of Liability prior to ticketing and must possess required travel documents (e.g. passport, photo ID) where applicable. Trip must be completed by November 2002. No substitution of prize permitted by winner. Torstar Corp. and D. L. Blair, Inc., their parents, affiliates, and subsidiaries are not responsible for errors in printing or electronic presentation of Contest, entries and/or game pieces. In the event of printing or other errors which may result in unintended prize values or duplication of prizes, all affected game pieces or entries shall be null and void. If for any reason the Internet portion of the Contest is not capable of running as planned, including infection by computer virus, bugs, tampering, unauthorized intervention, fraud, technical failures, or any other causes beyond the control of Torstar Corp. which corrupt or affect the administration, secrecy, fairness, integrity or proper conduct of the Contest, Torstar Corp. reserves the right, at its sole discretion, to disqualify any individual who tampers with the entry process and to cancel, terminate, modify or suspend the Contest or the Internet portion thereof. In the event of a dispute regarding an online entry, the entry will be deemed submitted by the authorized holder of the e-mail account submitted at the time of entry. Authorized account holder is defined as the natural person who is assigned to an e-mail address by an Internet access provider, online service provider or other organization that is responsible for arranging e-mail address for the domain associated with the submitted e-mail address. **Purchase or acceptance of a product offer does not improve your chances of winning.**

7. Prizes: (1) Grand Prize—A Harlequin wedding dress (approximate retail value: $3,500) and a 5-night/6-day honeymoon trip to Maui, HI, including round-trip air transportation provided by Maui Visitors Bureau from Los Angeles International Airport (winner is responsible for transportation to and from Los Angeles International Airport) and a Harlequin Romance Package, including hotel accomodations (double occupancy) at the Hyatt Regency Maui Resort and Spa, dinner for (2) two at Swan Court, a sunset sail on Kiele V and a spa treatment for the winner (approximate retail value: $4,000); (5) Five runner-up prizes of a $1000 gift certificate to selected retail outlets to be determined by Sponsor (retail value $1000 ea.). Prizes consist only of those items listed as part of the prize. Limit one prize per person. All prizes are valued in U.S. currency.

8. For a list of winners (available after December 17, 2001) send a self-addressed, stamped envelope to: Harlequin Walk Down the Aisle Contest 1197 Winners, P.O. Box 4200 Blair, NE 68009-4200 or you may access the www.eHarlequin.com Web site through January 15, 2002.

Contest sponsored by Torstar Corp., P.O. Box 9042, Buffalo, NY 14269-9042, U.S.A.

PHWDACONT2

In August 2001

New York Times bestselling author

HEATHER GRAHAM

joins

DALLAS SCHULZE

&

Elda Minger

in

TAKE5

Volume 3

These five heartwarming love stories are quick reads, great escapes and guarantee five times the joy.

Plus

With $5.00 worth of coupons inside, this is one *delightful* deal!

HARLEQUIN®
*M*akes any time special®

HARLEQUIN Super ROMANCE

CREATURE COMFORT

A heartwarming new series by
Carolyn McSparren

**Creature Comfort, the largest veterinary
clinic in Tennessee, treats animals of all
sizes—horses and cattle as well as family
pets. Meet the patients—and their owners.
And share the laughter and the tears with
the men and women who love and care
for all creatures great and small.**

#996 THE MONEY MAN
(July 2001)

#1011 THE PAYBACK MAN
(September 2001)

*Look for these Harlequin Superromance titles
coming soon to your favorite retail outlet.*

HARLEQUIN®
Makes any time special ®